FRANC
THE THREE

C000182043

Francis Vivian was born Arthur Ernest Ashley in 1906 at East Retford, Nottinghamshire. He was the younger brother of noted photographer Hallam Ashley. Vivian laboured for a decade as a painter and decorator before becoming an author of popular fiction in 1932. In 1940 he married schoolteacher Dorothy Wallwork, and the couple had a daughter.

After the Second World War he became assistant editor at the Nottinghamshire Free Press and circuit lecturer on many subjects, ranging from crime to bee-keeping (the latter forming a major theme in the Inspector Knollis mystery *The Singing Masons*). A founding member of the Nottingham Writers' Club, Vivian once awarded first prize in a writing competition to a young Alan Sillitoe, the future bestselling author.

The ten Inspector Knollis mysteries were published between 1941 and 1956. In the novels, ingenious plotting and fair play are paramount. A colleague recalled that 'the reader could always arrive at a correct solution from the given data. Inspector Knollis never picked up an undisclosed clue which, it was later revealed, held the solution to the mystery all along.'

Francis Vivian died on April 2, 1979 at the age of 73.

THE INSPECTOR KNOLLIS MYSTERIES
Available from Dean Street Press

FRANCIS VIVIAN

THE THREEFOLD CORD

With an introduction by Curtis Evans

DEAN STREET PRESS

INTRODUCTION

SHORTLY BEFORE his death in 1951, American agriculturalist and scholar Everett Franklin Phillips, then Professor Emeritus of Apiculture (beekeeping) at Cornell University, wrote British newspaperman Arthur Ernest Ashley (1906-1979), author of detective novels under the pseudonym Francis Vivian, requesting a copy of his beekeeping mystery *The Singing Masons*, the sixth Inspector Gordon Knollis investigation, which had been published the previous year in the United Kingdom. The eminent professor wanted the book for Cornell's Everett F. Phillips Beekeeping Collection, "one of the largest and most complete apiculture libraries in the world" (currently in the process of digitization at Cornell's The Hive and the Honeybee website). Sixteen years later Ernest Ashely, or Francis Vivian as I shall henceforward name him, to an American fan requesting an autograph ("Why anyone in the United States, where I am not known," he self-deprecatingly observed, "should want my autograph I cannot imagine, but I am flattered by your request and return your card, duly signed.") declared that fulfilling Professor Phillip's donation request was his "greatest satisfaction as a writer." With ghoulish relish he added, "I believe there was some objection by the Librarian, but the good doctor insisted, and so in it went! It was probably destroyed after Dr. Phillips died. Stung to death."

After investigation I have found no indication that the August 1951 death of Professor Phillips, who was 73 years old at the time, was due to anything other than natural causes. One assumes that what would have been the painfully ironic demise of the American nation's most distinguished apiculturist from bee stings would have merited some mention in his death notices. Yet Francis Vivian's fabulistic claim otherwise provides us with a glimpse of that mordant sense of humor and storytelling relish which glint throughout the eighteen mystery novels Vivian published between 1937 and 1959.

Ten of these mysteries were tales of the ingenious sleuthing exploits of series detective Inspector Gordon Knollis, head of the Burnham C.I.D. in the first novel in the series and a Scotland Yard detective in the rest. (Knollis returns to Burnham in later novels.) The debut Inspector Knollis mystery, *The Death of Mr. Lomas*, which was published in 1941, is actually the seventh Francis Vivian detective novel. However, after the Second World War, when the author belatedly returned to his vocation of mystery writing, all of the remaining detective novels he published, with two exceptions, chronicle the criminal cases of the keen and clever Knollis. These other Inspector Knollis tales are: *Sable Messenger* (1947), *The Threefold Cord* (1947), *The Ninth Enemy* (1948), *The Laughing Dog* (1949), *The Singing Masons* (1950), *The Elusive Bowman* (1951), *The Sleeping Island* (1951), *The Ladies of Locksley* (1953) and *Darkling Death* (1956). (Inspector Knollis also is passingly mentioned in Francis Vivian's final mystery, published in 1959, *Dead Opposite the Church*.) By the late Forties and early Fifties, when Hodder & Stoughton, one of England's most important purveyors of crime and mystery fiction, was publishing the Francis Vivian novels, the Inspector Knollis mysteries had achieved wide popularity in the UK, where "according to the booksellers and librarians," the author's newspaper colleague John Hall later recalled in the *Guardian* (possibly with some exaggeration), "Francis Vivian was neck and neck with Ngaio Marsh in second place after Agatha Christie." (Hardcover sales and penny library rentals must be meant here, as with one exception--a paperback original--Francis Vivian, in great contrast with Crime Queens Marsh and Christie, both mainstays of Penguin Books in the UK, was never published in softcover.)

John Hall asserted that in Francis Vivian's native coal and iron county of Nottinghamshire, where Vivian from the 1940s through the 1960s was an assistant editor and "colour man" (writer of local color stories) on the Nottingham, or Notts, *Free Press*, the detective novelist "through a large stretch of the coalfield is reckoned the best local author after Byron and D. H. Lawrence." Hall added that "People who wouldn't know Alan

Sillitoe from George Eliot will stop Ernest in the street and tell him they solved his last detective story." Somewhat ironically, given this assertion, Vivian in his capacity as a founding member of the Nottingham Writers Club awarded first prize in a 1950 Nottingham writing competition to no other than 22-year-old local aspirant Alan Sillitoe, future "angry young man" author of *Saturday Night and Sunday Morning* (1958) and *The Loneliness of the Long Distance Runner* (1959). In his 1995 autobiography Sillitoe recollected that Vivian, "a crime novelist who earned his living by writing . . . gave [my story] first prize, telling me it was so well written and original that nothing further need be done, and that I should try to get it published." This was "The General's Dilemma," which Sillitoe later expanded into his second novel, *The General* (1960).

While never himself an angry young man (he was, rather, a "ragged-trousered" philosopher), Francis Vivian came from fairly humble origins in life and well knew how to wield both the hammer and the pen. Born on March 23, 1906, Vivian was one of two children of Arthur Ernest Ashley, Sr., a photographer and picture framer in East Retford, Nottinghamshire, and Elizabeth Hallam. His elder brother, Hallam Ashley (1900-1987), moved to Norwich and became a freelance photographer. Today he is known for his photographs, taken from the 1940s through the 1960s, chronicling rural labor in East Anglia (many of which were collected in the 2010 book *Traditional Crafts and Industries in East Anglia: The Photographs of Hallam Ashley*). For his part, Francis Vivian started working at age 15 as a gas meter emptier, then labored for 11 years as a housepainter and decorator before successfully establishing himself in 1932 as a writer of short fiction for newspapers and general magazines. In 1937, he published his first detective novel, *Death at the Salutation*. Three years later, he wed schoolteacher Dorothy Wallwork, with whom he had one daughter.

After the Second World War Francis Vivian's work with the Notts *Free Press* consumed much of his time, yet he was still able for the next half-dozen years to publish annually a detective novel (or two), as well as to give popular lectures on a plethora of intriguing subjects, including, naturally enough, crime, but also fiction writing (he published two guidebooks on that subject), psychic forces (he believed himself to be psychic), black magic, Greek civilization, drama, psychology and beekeeping. The latter occupation he himself took up as a hobby, following in the path of Sherlock Holmes. Vivian's fascination with such esoterica invariably found its way into his detective novels, much to the delight of his loyal readership.

As a detective novelist, John Hall recalled, Francis Vivian "took great pride in the fact that the reader could always arrive at a correct solution from the given data. His Inspector never picked up an undisclosed clue which, it was later revealed, held the solution to the mystery all along." Vivian died on April 2, 1979, at the respectable if not quite venerable age of 73, just like Professor Everett Franklin Phillips. To my knowledge the late mystery writer had not been stung to death by bees.

Curtis Evans

CHAPTER I
THE MYSTERY AT BOWLAND

FOUR MILES from the city of Trentingham lies the village of Bowland. Its seven hundred inhabitants are variously happy, unhappy, or merely insentient, living their lives in accordance with laws of which most of them are unaware, puzzling over effects without reaching back to the causes—unless it should be some unusual and startling manifestation rare to their general experience. Such an event was the violent death of Mr. Frederick David Manchester, who was found half-decapitated in the grounds of his own house, and following as it did on two other peculiar events in the same house it set tongues wagging freely in the Social Service Institute and the bar-parlour of the Anchor Inn. It was these first two events which brought Inspector Gordon Knollis from New Scotland Yard to Bowland.

"Go down to Trentingham," said Superintendent Hatch, "and report to Colonel Mowbray. He is the Chief Constable in case you don't know. Something screwy has been happening in a potty little village in his diocese, and although he gives no clue as to its nature, I'm willing to bet that it amounts to no more than the chalking of rude words on a garden gate. You see, I know old Mowbray. He's a member of the old school, and possesses a very rigid mind. A crime to him is not necessarily an offence to be found in the statutes, but some offence against his own code. However, let me have a report as soon as you can, because I'm not wasting you down there if I can help it. I don't want to send you at all, but Mowbray has influence in the right quarters, and, in diplomatic language, it is politic to acquiesce. Oh, and be nice to him, no matter how you may feel—there's a Chief Inspectorship going begging in case you are interested."

So Gordon Knollis collected his luggage and his Sergeant Ellis, and set forth to St. Pancras. Later that same day they were shown into the Chief Constable's office in the Guildhall at Trentingham, where the three gentlemen took stock of each other as they mouthed the conventional introductions and greetings.

Colonel Mowbray saw before him a lean man with a long nose and steady grey eyes which peered keenly through slits in his sharp features. He may have been capable of smiling, but there was no proof of it at the moment. If ever a man looked like a detective, this was he. A child of twelve could not have made a wrong guess at his probable profession. There was an attitude of reserve about him, and he had the bearing of a gentleman; looking intelligent without being highbrow, inquisitive without being vulgarly curious, and firm without any of the pugnacity of a bully. Above all, he gave the impression of being efficient.

Beside him was a stocky little fellow with pleasing features which bore traces of the quizzical humour of the Cockney. There were creases at the corners of his eyes, and lurking humour in his lips. He had heavy black eyebrows, a thick and bristly moustache, and thick curly hair which was well-oiled and still refused to take its brushing lying down. He held himself respectfully, and yet there was no servility in his attitude. Here was the British workman in essence; he knew his job, knew that he knew it, and would defer to no one who could not surpass him in skill.

Knollis, for his part, saw a tall and aristocratic man in check tweeds who wore a monocle in his right eye, a man whose chin was clean-shaven and held just a trifle too high; a man whose gaze wandered over him almost impertinently; a man whose military moustaches were those of a martinet of the old school; a man who obviously took upon himself the role of the centurion of old and would not brook either argument or disobeyal of his orders. He took the monocle from his eye and screwed it back again—it appeared to have a clockwise thread. He then grunted, herrummed, and glanced again at Knollis's card.

"Inspector Gordon Knollis. Pleased to meet, you, Inspector. First trip to Trentingham?"

"I've been through the city on several occasions, sir," Knollis replied, "but I cannot say that I know it very well."

Colonel Mowbray grunted. "Pretty fine place, Trentingham. Hope you like it—if you get time to see any of it."

"I liked what little I saw as we came from the station," said Knollis.

The Chief Constable's chin went a shade higher. He twiddled with his monocle and looked out through the window. "No mean city, Inspector."

"You have a job for me, sir?" asked Knollis, anxious to steer the conversation into less unbusinesslike channels.

The Chief Constable opened his mouth, stared at the opposite wall, and spoke a few seconds later. "Ah-h, yes. Infernal nuisance, but Fred Manchester has influence and I dare not turn down his request for an investigation—especially as he asked the Lord-Lieutenant at the same time!"

Knollis raised an eyebrow. The name struck a chord.

"Fred Manchester, sir? The furniture magnate?"

The Chief Constable nodded despondently. "The same. You know of him, Inspector?"

Knollis nodded grimly. "In my early years, while still pounding a beat in Burnham, my wife and I bought a suite from him. Ever since I have hoped to meet him and express my opinions about the sideboard, the back panels of which bear the Oriental legend: *Orange Pekoe*.

"That is Manchester all over," sympathised the Chief Constable. "Thus far, you are prepared. I'll tell you the rest about him—assuming and hoping that you never fell foul of his fouler methods. He started in Trentingham some twenty-five years ago, as a journeyman furniture-maker with Ponsonby. Ten years later he found financial backing and opened up on his own account. Five years later he had four shops in the city, and to-day—"

"Manchester is everywhere!" quoted Knollis.

"You can't get away from his damned advertising, can you?" said the Chief Constable. "Three hundred branches in England alone. In all truth, Manchester *is* everywhere. He has made a fortune, and it was only the legislation with regard to hire purchase that prevented him from making two or three more fortunes."

Knollis raised his eyebrows in silent enquiry.

"Oh, nobody likes the fellow," said the Chief Constable. "He is endured because he has money, and can be milked of it providing he thinks he is creating an impression. He pushed the Lord-Lieutenant into pushing me into pushing the Yard to send you down. That is Manchester all over; a pusher, with cash instead of steam for the motive power."

He inched the cigarette box across the table and indicated that Knollis and Ellis were to help themselves.

"Yes, he's a dirty dog all right. His old method of making money was to sell a complete home to a working family for about fifteen bob to a quid a week. Came bad times, and hire payments fell into arrears. There was no mercy from Manchester! Oh dear, no! His van called at the house, and collected the whole home. The account was closed. The furniture was tickled-up and repolished, and resold on the same terms, as new stuff."

"And now?" Knollis murmured politely, as if he was totally ignorant of the laws which he helped to uphold.

"He has to leave behind such of the furniture as squares with the amounts paid by the purchaser, hiree, or what have you. He is, thank God, tied down!"

"And his present trouble, sir?"

The Chief Constable coughed. "I—er—hate to tell you, Inspector."

"I take it that it is a very trivial matter?"

The Chief Constable made a rude noise not at all consonant with the dignity of his position.

"May I ask why the Trentingham C.I.D. is not dealing with the matter, sir?"

The Chief Constable sniffed. "You may, and I must answer the question. Manchester said, in so many words, that my staff were not competent. He was the great I-Am. He could pay for the best, and he was goin' to have the best. Well, he's getting it, and he's going to pay for it. Regard that as a compliment," he added, throwing the line away.

Knollis permitted himself the trace of a smile. "He is one of the new aristocracy, sir?"

The Chief Constable gazed on him with affection. "Ah, I see you are a man of discrimination, Inspector!"

"We must discriminate in our profession, sir. The human race is made up of all kinds of people."

"True enough," the Chief Constable said regretfully. "Anyway, I've booked two rooms for you at the Crown. I chose it because it has a good table and a most excellent bar. You'll find me there most evenings. Your luggage will be sent round to you."

"But the job, the assignment?" persisted Knollis. The Chief Constable glanced up in a guilty manner, and twined the telephone flex round his fingers. "Ah yes, the job."

Knollis waited with all the patience for which he was noted among his colleagues.

The Chief Constable hemmed behind his hand. "Well, it—er—started with the budgerigar, and then there was the cat!"

Knollis jerked into startled attention. "Wha-at?"

"Yes, I'm afraid that is it, Inspector. You see, Mrs. Manchester found her pet budgie lying in the boudoir with its neck broken—that was on Sunday morning. It had a silken cord tied loosely round its neck. Yesterday noon she found her cat in the cactus house in similar circumstances. . . ."

"Mm!" muttered Knollis.

The Chief Constable shuffled in his chair, and pushed the cigarette box still nearer to Knollis. "Have a smoke, Inspector! Do have one! And you, Sergeant!" Knollis and Ellis took cigarettes, lit them, and waited. Colonel Mowbray played with his monocle.

"The name of the bird was—er—Sweetums, and the cat was Boofuls. . . ."

He pushed back his chair, stamped across the room, returned to the chair, and sat down. "Oh, this is too bloody for words! I'm sorry, Inspector! So help me heaven, I'm sorry! I think it's a darned shame to drag you down from London. Oh lor', what a mess!"

Knollis cast a long and sorrowful look at Ellis. Ellis leaned back in his chair and began to chuckle quietly. "Sweetums and Boofuls!"

"What's so darned funny?" demanded Knollis.

"Wait until Fleet Street get hold of this!" exclaimed Ellis. "*The case of Sweetums and Boofuls, or Death Stalks the Vil-*

lage! Can't you see the banner across the front page of the *Daily Distress*? Oh, my Gawd!"

"Oh, shut up!" said Knollis, and immediately said "Sorry!" for he was not by nature a crude man.

"He's right, you know," said the Chief Constable. "It's going to make a laughing-stock of the whole Force. And this is what comes of money without breeding behind it. Damn all social revolutions!"

"Why does he insist on an investigation, sir?" Knollis asked curiously.

"Showing off, for one thing—and he got a scare out of it. I don't agree with him, of course, but I can see how his limited intelligence has reached what appears to be a logical conclusion. Mind you, it wouldn't scare an educated man! His wife is the cause of it all. She's constantly saying that her life would be empty but for her budgie, her cat, and Freddy—in reverse order, I imagine. So Manchester reasons that these two deaths are warnings that his own is to follow, which is damned rot!"

Knollis sat quietly for a couple of minutes or so, and then looked up. "When can I interview him, sir?"

The Chief Constable blinked to mental attention. "You don't mean to say that you are getting interested in the silly affair?"

Knollis's eyes vanished into the secrecy of his keen features. "*Were* the animals strangled with the cords?"

"Eh? No, as a matter of fact, they weren't! Manchester fetched a vet to both bodies, and he reported that the cervical vertebrae had been dislocated in each case—just as you'd wring a fowl."

"Interesting," murmured Knollis. "I would like to see Manchester as soon as possible, sir."

"But, man, it's dam silly!" protested the Chief Constable. Then he stopped, and looked hard at Knollis. "Or is it?"

Knollis replied slowly and cautiously. "If the bird and the cat had been strangled with the cords, I would be inclined to say that it was nothing but spite, possibly directed against Mrs. Manchester, but as the two pets were killed by manual pressure, and the cords placed round their necks afterwards . . . "

"Yes, Inspector?"

"Well, the cords may have a significance!"

"Mm, ye-es," the Chief Constable admitted grudgingly.

"The bird was found on Sunday morning?"

"Shortly after breakfast."

"And the cat yesterday—which was Monday—at noon?"

"Yes, that is right."

"So that, if Manchester's scare-idea is correct, he should be killed at tea-time to-day?"

The Chief Constable opened his eyes so wide that his monocle fell to the length of its retaining cord. "Good God! You've an imagination like a fiction writer?"

"Thanks for the compliment, sir."

The Chief Constable waved an impatient hand. "It's bosh! Only the good die young, and at that rate Manchester will reach the ripe old age of a hundred and fifty. Go and get settled in at the Crown! Have your tea, a smoke, a drink, a bath, and I'll send a car for you about six o'clock. If he's pacing up and down his cage, let him pace. It will work off some of his energy."

"Well, as you wish, sir," Knollis said reluctantly.

"That's giving you an hour and a half in which to prepare yourself to meet him. It's—yes—half-past four now."

He broke off irritably as one of the half-dozen telephones on his desk broke into song. "Yes, speaking. Who? All right. Show him up."

He replaced the handset, and grimaced. "Prepare to meet a fate worse than death in the lions' den. Manchester is on his way up!"

CHAPTER II
THE SUSPICIONS OF MANCHESTER

KNOLLIS EYED the furniture magnate closely as he entered the room and plodded across the deep carpet to the Chief Constable's desk. He was of medium height, and carried so much fat, in so many rolls, that it was impossible to guess at the shape

Nature had intended him to be. His face was a pink bladder, from which piggish eyes peered by permission of necessity. His neck consisted of three pink tyres, beneath the lower of which showed the bottom edge of a blue-striped collar, with which he was wearing a vivid blue tie. He was dressed in a suit of bluish Harris tweed, and across the vest was festooned a gold watch-chain decorated with two football medals, a Devonshire pixie, a massive red seal, and a watch key. His feet, shod in black patent leather, were so small that it seemed impossible that his bulk could balance on them.

He extended a podgy paw to the Chief Constable, who took it reluctantly and did not disguise his distaste.

"Thought I'd better run down and see what was what," said Manchester. "I like to see things getting done—never was one for hanging about. You said you was going to let me know when the tecs arrived." Knollis and Ellis winced, and the Chief Constable passed them a sympathetic glance.

He forced a smile. "The detectives arrived but a few minutes ago, Mr. Manchester. Allow me to present Inspector Knollis and Sergeant Ellis, both of New Scotland Yard."

Manchester nestled his lower chin in his hand, and looked them over as if he was buying them. "So you fellows are the tecs! Well, I hope as you are good, because I want my money's worth. I got it to pay with, see. That's Fred Manchester!"

"I think I understand," Knollis replied quietly.

The Chief Constable grimaced.

Manchester turned on him, rather than to him. "Told 'em anything yet?"

"The bare details only," said the Chief Constable. "I was acquainting them with the matter when you arrived."

"Happen I'd better tell him myself, and in my own words," remarked Manchester. "I won't take as much time as you. Now, Inspector, it's like this. My wife has always reckoned as she'd have nothing to live for if it weren't for me, and the cat, and the budgie. Sweetums and Boofuls, she calls them, and she calls me Humpty—when we're private-like. Daft, but that's a woman all over, even the best of 'em, and I've got the best. Anyway, the little woman's all upset, and thinks as it might be me next. Now I can look after myself, and don't need no watchdog, but the little woman must be set at ease. I'm a successful man, you see, Inspector, and successful men have enemies—mainly them what's jealous. That's the way of the world—jealous of them what's got on because they haven't been scared to force the pace."

"Have you any suspicions with regard to the identity of the perpetrator of these two outrages?" asked Knollis, anxious to stem the flood of self-praise from Manchester.

The furniture magnate blew out his fleshy cheeks, and then scratched his ear. "Yes and no. There's a good few as doesn't like me—mainly because of what I was just saying about me being—"

"Quite! Quite!" Knollis interrupted.

"Yes, well, there's Tanroy for one!"

"Sir Giles Tanroy!" exclaimed the Chief Constable. "Nonsense, Manchester!"

"Nonsense my foot," retorted Manchester. "Doesn't he reckon as I worked him into a tight corner so as he'd have to sell Baxmanhurst to me?"

"He has said as much," the Chief Constable replied quietly.

"Did I hell as like!" Manchester bawled. "Tanroy's like the rest of his sort—no businessman. If he's mug enough to buy shares in a duff company he can't blame anybody except himself for what happens."

"You—er—did advise him to buy them, I believe?" queried the Chief Constable.

Manchester sniggered. "I can advise you to jump in the river, but you ain't mug enough to do it if you can't swim. I could have made a packet out of them shares. Tanroy hadn't the sense."

The Chief Constable glanced at Knollis and shook his head sadly.

"Tanroy would give me a knock if he got half a chance!" Manchester said defiantly.

The Chief Constable leaned across the desk, his features expressing his outraged feelings. "You are surely not suggesting that Sir Giles Tanroy forced his way into your house, and into your wife's boudoir, in order to commit so petty an act as wringing a bird's neck?"

Manchester clenched his fists and took a step forward. "That's it! Side up with him! He's one of your own set. That's why I wanted a tec from the Yard. They are im—impartial. Aren't you?" he suddenly demanded of Knollis.

"I hope so," Knollis replied, shocked by the outburst.

"So do I! By God, I'll stand for no incompetence or shilly-shallying!"

"You know," the Chief Constable pointed out quietly, "you may just as well accuse the rest of the world of being against you. You are letting your imagination run away with you, Manchester."

"And why not?" shouted Manchester. "Isn't the world against me? Hasn't it tried to stamp me down ever since I started trying to get on? There's Temple—my own gardener— for one. He reckons as I did him for two hundred quid a few years back. And for why, you asks? Here's me, trying to help the working man, and what happens? He can't pay, and I have to fetch the stuff back because I'm in business for a living. And I get abused! Abused, mind you! What the hell do they think I am? A charitable institution?"

The Chief Constable shook his head, silently.

"There you are, then," continued Manchester.

"Temple'd do me in if he got half a chance. I wanted to help him, but I wouldn't have kept him for a week if he hadn't been a good gardener. I pays for the best, and I want it."

"I am going to be frank," said the Chief Constable, leaning across his desk. "You took him on, as you call it, because you created such a bad impression in court when you sued him for arrears. You knew that the case was going to damage your business, and so you acted the part of a man who, having been robbed of his cloak, was willing to give his tunic. You know that I am speaking the truth!"

"Do I get protection and justice, or don't I?" Manchester protested. "Or is it kept for your own sort," he added sneeringly.

Colonel Mowbray polished his monocle and screwed it back into his eye. "The law of the land protects the persons and properties of everybody, Mr. Manchester. Myself, the policeman on his beat, and these gentlemen from London are only concerned with our duty, and we do not question the ethics and morality of our work, satisfied as we are that those above us who make the laws are capable of doing so. You get protection and justice if you ask for it."

Manchester spread his hands in a dramatic gesture, appealing to Knollis and Ellis; the latter was busy with notebook and pencil.

"There you are then. Protection and justice are what I'm asking for. I'm asking for protection against them as hate me—and that's me that don't hate nobody! I don't hold no grudges against nobody. Inspector Kollis—"

"Knollis," the Chief Constable interposed.

"Inspector Knollis," went on Manchester, "I'd even forgot, in my own mind as Temple'd tried to do me for the furniture, and employed him because I was sorry for him, and what does he do?"

"What does he do?" Knollis asked simply.

Manchester took a deep breath. "Give me patience! Two pints inside him at the local, and he's breathing mutiny and calling me everything from a pig to a swine!"

"Definitely a case for the R.S.P.C.A.," chuckled the Chief Constable, "but anyway, Manchester, are there any other people you suspect?"

Manchester fingered his nose in an ungentlemanly manner. "I ain't so sure about Dana if it comes to that. No, I ain't at all sure!"

"Who is Dana?" Knollis asked in the manner of the learned judge.

"Dana? She's Dana Vaughan, the actress woman. I wouldn't have her in the house for five minutes if it wasn't for Milly—that's the wife. Been pals for years, they have. She was playing in that thing in London what's run for three and a half years. Hm! I can't think of its name now!"

"*The Hempen Rope?*" suggested the Chief Constable.

"That's the one!"

"Oh yes, I remember seeing her in it," said Knollis. "What are your objections to this lady's presence in your house, Mr. Manchester?"

Manchester opened his great toad-like mouth and sought for words, meanwhile inelegantly scratching the back of his neck. "We-ell, she's a fine actor and all that, Inspector, and I do give her that, but she don't like me."

"May I ask why, Mr. Manchester?" ventured Knollis.

Manchester shuffled his feet. "It's this way, Inspector. I mean, you do understand human nature, don't you?"

"To some extent," Knollis replied. "The study of human nature is part of my profession."

"Well, that'll help you to see my point," Manchester said bluntly. "Some years ago, at a dance, I got a bit lit up and made love to her—or so she said next morning. She took me all wrong, and thought as I'd meant something as I didn't say. You get me?"

"I—er—get you," said Knollis.

"Well then, I was engaged to Milly, and Dana threatened to tell her. I managed to quieten her down, but I always have a sort of feeling as she's never forgot. It's the way she looks at me sometimes. . . ."

He glanced round the room, and then back at Knollis.

"She looks as if she'd like to do me in!"

"And she is at present staying with you and your wife, Mr. Manchester?"

"She is, Inspector. Her nerves went bust with murdering the same fellow on the stage every night, and she had to leave the show. Milly asked her down to re—re—"

"Recuperate?" suggested the Chief Constable.

Manchester grated his teeth together. "I knew the blasted word all right. I just couldn't get it out. Anyway, as I was saying, Inspector, she's been here for two months, and I'll be glad when she packs off again."

"And you consider that any of these three people may be capable of strangling a pet bird and cat? I do understand you correctly, Mr. Manchester?" said Knollis.

Manchester stared at Knollis with something akin to admiration showing in his eyes. "You got it all right. Yes, I reckon as I've got the right men to work this thing out for me."

"Sir Giles Tanroy, Temple, and Dana Vaughan—bird and cat slaughterers," the Chief Constable murmured. He twisted his monocle round in his eye and stared through the window. "How are the mighty fallen! Tell it not in Gath! Publish it not in the streets of Askelon!"

He suddenly turned on Manchester. "Pardon my manners, Manchester, but you are a darned fool!"

Manchester thumped the table with his fist, and the Chief Constable swore as the ink jumped from the well.

"I know one of them three done 'em in, and they'll do me!" Manchester shouted. "I know it, I tell you!"

The Chief Constable sighed. "Well, you may be right, and consequently we must investigate the matter." Manchester's right eyebrow lifted. "Now you're talking sense, Colonel! I wouldn't be a bit surprised if one of 'em wasn't out to do me in, same as Milly says. There's *something* in the wind—I can sniff it!"

"There seems to be a little bad odour somewhere," the Chief Constable admitted.

"Inspector, I'm relying on you," Manchester said grandly. "I know a good man when I see one!"

"Thank you," said Knollis. He gave a slight bow in order to hide the smile that was creeping to his lips.

"That's all right," Manchester said magnanimously. "Now then; when are you coming to Baxmanhurst?" Knollis looked at his watch. It showed a few minutes to five o'clock. "Seven o'clock? Will that be convenient?"

"I could do with you a lot earlier."

"The Inspector needs food, and a wash and a rest, after his journey from London," the Chief Constable pointed out.

"Well, seven o'clock then, and don't forget!" said Manchester.

He turned to Colonel Mowbray. "I've got Tanroy calling at my place at five o'clock. It'll do him good to hang around a bit. I think I'll have it out with him when I do see him!"

"Just a moment, Mr. Manchester," interrupted Knollis. "I would prefer that you do not discuss this matter with anyone. I also suggest that you keep to the house until we arrive, and make sure that you are in the presence of at least one other person."

Manchester's eyes widened. "So you really think as somebody is laying for me!"

Knollis shook his head. "I merely mean that I don't wish you to take any risks, either physically or verbally."

Manchester turned to the Chief Constable. "He means . . . ?"

The Chief Constable smiled, the first genuine smile he had exhibited since Manchester walked into the room.

"The Inspector is too polite to say so, but he wants you to stay indoors and keep your mouth shut."

Manchester nodded. "Put that way, I see what he means. Yes, I see!"

He ambled towards the door. "Seven o'clock then! So long, all!"

As the door closed behind him, the Chief Constable flicked a switch and spoke into the blower. "I want this room disinfected while I am at tea."

"And that is that," said Ellis, closing his notebook and returning it to his pocket. "Some gentleman!"

"Passed unanimously, Sergeant," said the Chief Constable. "I must tell you both how sorry I am about this case. Really, I am!"

"Please don't apologise, sir," said Knollis. "I understand now why you advised me to rest before going out to Bowland. I'll need a good meal to bolster up my stomach before I have a second dose of Manchester. Well, Ellis, let's away to the hotel."

"A minute, please, Inspector," said Colonel Mowbray. "You really think there is something behind these two apparently minor events?"

"Yes-es, I think so, sir," Knollis replied cautiously. "I can't tell you why I think so. It is just an intuition, and intuitions are so unscientific, aren't they? And yet it may not be an intuition, but something that has reached the back of my mind during the interview with Manchester. Something that you have told me, or something that Manchester has said, that has soaked away into my mind and stirred a chord. I'll look through Ellis's note later; they may give me the clue."

The Colonel rose and stretched himself. "Well, we'll see you after tea, and then try to find out whether we are on a wild-goose chase or not. On the face of it, we are, but I can't ignore your judgment."

An hour later the Chief Constable strode into the dining-room at the Crown Hotel. Knollis looked up in surprise. "You are early, sir! You gave me an hour and a half!"

Colonel Mowbray nodded grimly. "They didn't give Manchester as long as that!"

Knollis started from his seat. "You mean that—"

"I always said he'd get it in the neck, and by God, he has! Somebody has chopped him with an axe or some similar weapon. Nearly fetched his head from his shoulders. They found him dead in the grounds just over twenty minutes ago."

"You'll want the Yard to take the case, sir?"

"Most assuredly. I'll fix the authority later. Let's get moving." Knollis looked at Ellis. "The murder bag, Ellis!"

CHAPTER III
THE EVIDENCE OF SMITH

BOWLAND, like most English villages, grew up around the church. The magical processes of time mellowed the stone cottages, and brought to full maturity the elms, ashes, and chestnuts that lined the roads and dotted the meadows. In some mysterious way, the red rash that afflicted the countryside in the thirties ignored the environs of the village, leaving it slumbrous and content, a haven of rusticity in an industrial area.

The Elizabethan manor-house has long been a ruin, and the children play in it and tear the stones down as if eager to destroy all vestiges of a more glorious England. In its place, during the

Regency, the Tanroy family built two large square houses, one opposite the church and on the edge of the hurst from which it took its name, and the other on the north-eastern boundary of the village. Tall, three-storey buildings they are, of plum-red brick, with stone sills and doorways. Of the fifteen windows in each wall, seven are imitations painted on wood; relics of the Window Tax, and proof of the Englishman's love of quiet display and dislike of taxes in any shape or form.

Baxmanhurst has long been the centre of the life of the village. The Squire Tanroys of many generations have given out advice, largesse, and orders with equal readiness and impartiality. If Widow Martin was ill, a large basket of provisions was sent round from The House. If her son failed to deliver the load of logs at the stipulated time, then he was sent for and dressed down. When he needed advice over his mother's will, then the Tanroys sent him to Lawyer Willis, paid the score, and bade him give ear to wisdom and experience.

Times changed. Cash became scarce in the Tanroy family, and the present squire, young Sir Giles, sold out and went to live in the other Tanroy house, Knightswood, with the remains of a cadet branch of the family. Fred Manchester moved in. He took over the house, the grounds, and the hurst. He hoped to take over the manorial rights and privileges as well, but although the villagers had moved with the times to some degree, tradition still held them in thrall, and they continued to regard young Sir Giles—he was twenty-eight—and no one else, as the titular head of the community. To them, Manchester was "him that's in Baxy," an interloper with whom they did not even care to drink in the Anchor Inn lest it place them under an obligation. And now he was lying dead in the Green Alley, at the north-eastern corner of his rural palace.

"A nasty mess!" Knollis commented as he stared over the shoulders of the local doctor and the Trentingham police surgeon.

"He never saw it coming, and that's a certainty," said the police surgeon. "A good square blow! The guillotine couldn't have done a better job—except that it would have completed the decapitation."

"Looks as if it was done with a cleaver or some similar implement," remarked the local doctor. "Severed his spine as neat as can be."

"How long has he been dead?" asked Knollis, while Ellis stood by with his notebook.

"Well under the hour," replied the police· surgeon.

He turned to his colleague. "You agree with that, Denstone? You were the first on the scene."

Dr. Denstone nodded. "Yes, I agree. According to Smith, the chauffeur, I arrived quarter of an hour after his discovery of the body. The slight temperature drop was consistent with his statement."

"Can we remove him yet?" asked the police surgeon.

"A few more photographs, and he is all yours," Knollis replied. "Now, Ellis, let's review the scene. A square building with a modern annexe on the north side; one storey only. It almost comes up to the boundary wall, which is quite sixteen feet high. Can anyone tell me what the annexe is?"

Dr. Denstone looked up. "Staff bathroom, Inspector. Manchester had it built shortly after taking over the property. The sanitary arrangements upstairs are poor."

"The door facing us? It is the only entrance from outside the house?"

The doctor nodded.

"Queer, surely, putting an outside door on a bathroom," murmured Knollis.

"Doesn't go directly into the bathroom," said the doctor. "There is a narrow L-shaped passage through the doorway. Enter, turn left, and you are in the passage leading to the kitchen, pantry, and staff sitting-room. There is no exit at all on the west side of the house, and Manchester had this one built to stop the staff crossing the front of the house when leaving the premises, the staff entrance and exit being on the south side of the house. Old Charles Tanroy was too much concerned with windows and not enough with doors when he built Baxy."

Knollis turned and considered the wrought-iron gates at the entrance to the drive. "Is that the only entrance to the grounds?"

Dr. Denstone nodded. "Just the one way in, and the one way out. Of course, if you go across the front of the garage on the south side, you can take the footpath through the hurst, but the entrance gates constitute the only official entrance and exit."

He jerked his head towards the lean-to greenhouse that was built against the high boundary wall. "This is the cactus house, and was Manchester's pride and joy. Looks almost as if he was leaving it when he was smitten down."

Knollis looked wonderingly at the doctor. "You seem to know a great deal about this place, Dr. Denstone!"

The doctor grinned. "This is a village, Inspector. Everyone knows everyone else's business, and Manchester's habits were almost as familiar to me as my own."

"I may ask you to help me later."

"I'll do all I can to assist," the doctor replied.

"Thank you," said Knollis. "Now where do I find the chauffeur?"

"He lives over the garage, but you'll most likely find him in the kitchen. He's courting Freeman, the maid."

"You are very helpful," said Knollis.

"The case doesn't look quite so funny now, does it?" said Ellis as they walked towards the staff door.

Knollis grimaced. "There was a certain grim note in the story even when it seemed farcical. Bodies, bodies, bodies! My life is littered with 'em!"

Rounding the corner of the house they met a pleasant-looking fellow dressed in a blue uniform coat and breeches.

"You Smith by any chance?" asked Knollis.

"Yes, sir. I'm the chauffeur."

Knollis introduced himself. "I would like to ask you a few questions. I understand that it was you who found Mr. Manchester?"

"That is so, sir," Smith replied correctly.

"Tell me about it, please."

"Well, sir, I ran him back from Trentingham about ten-past five. He told me to put my foot down as he had an appointment with Sir Giles Tanroy. I had to get clear of the town traffic before I could really get cracking, but I did the four miles in just under ten minutes. I dropped him at the front door, parked the car, and then went to the kitchen to scuffle my tea down me."

"Why scuffle it? Why the haste?" Knollis asked.

Smith grinned feebly. "I was due to take my girl out at a quarter to six, sir. It was her evening off, and I had finished for the day."

"That would be about twenty-five-past five?" suggested Knollis.

"Er—yes, I suppose it would, sir. Yes, it would, because after bolting my tea I came back to my room to change into my flannels—I live over the garage—and my clock was telling twenty-five to six. It didn't take me many minutes to change, and then I went back to the kitchen."

"You have since changed back into uniform," Knollis pointed out.

The chauffeur nodded. "Yes, sir, I could see that I might be wanted."

"Carry on, please."

"Well, Freeman—that's my girl—said she would be a few more minutes, so I took a walk round to the cactus house. Mr. Manchester has some queerish-looking plants in there, and they always fascinate me. I went through the passage on the north side, and saw him lying there—well, like you've seen, sir."

"So it was roughly a quarter to six when you found him? You agree on that?"

"Within a minute either way, sir."

"And next?" prompted Knollis.

Smith grimaced. "I took one look at him and I knew it was Upton—"

"Upton?" Knollis murmured, raising an eyebrow.

"Slang for all up, or finished," Smith explained with a faint smile. "I ran back to the kitchen, told the women on no account to go into the Green Alley—that's the stretch of green between the annexe door and the main drive—and got busy on the telephone. I 'phoned the police, and then Dr. Denstone. It was just on six when he arrived. Price, the village constable, was on his heels."

"And Mrs. Manchester?" said Knollis.

"I went in and told her that Mr. Manchester had met with a nasty accident, and that she mustn't go out to him."

"How did she take it, Smith?"

Smith pushed back his peaked cap and scratched his head. "Remarkably well, sir, but then I've noticed before that women of breeding always do take bad news like that. She said 'Oh!' and then asked exactly what had happened. I told her I was afraid that someone had killed him. She said 'Oh' again, and went on with what she was doing—for all the world as if she hadn't taken in what I'd been saying to her."

"What was she doing?" asked Knollis quietly.

"Darning Freddy's socks—pardon, sir. We used to call him Freddy between ourselves. No disrespect, sir."

"That's quite all right," said Knollis; "it is quite a normal practice. Now can you tell me who was the next person to see Mrs. Manchester?"

"Well," said Smith, "I stood there, and she looked up after a minute and told me to inform Mr. Brailsford, if I could find him."

"And who is Mr. Brailsford?"

"A friend of Mr. Manchester's who is staying here."

"Miss Vaughan was also in the house?"

"Yes, sir."

"Did you find Mr. Brailsford?"

"He was in his room, sir, reading a novel. I told him what had happened, and after a few seconds he said he would come down with me. We got as far as the annexe door, which I'd left open, and he took one look and said we'd better not disturb the body or the police would complain."

"Quite right, too," said Knollis. "Tell me, Smith; have you seen much of violent death?"

"I was a volunteer in the Spanish Civil War, sir."

"Then you have," said Knollis with an emphatic nod. "From your own experience, would you say that Mr. Manchester had been dead very long?"

"He couldn't have been dead many minutes when I found him, sir. His body was still twitching. In fact my own opinion is that I must have been right on the heels of whoever did it."

"And you saw no one about?"

"No one, sir."

"I think that will be all for now," said Knollis. "Perhaps you would be good enough to go round there now; they may require help to lift him into the ambulance."

Smith went without any show of reluctance, and Knollis touched Ellis on the arm and led the way into the kitchen. A stout motherly woman faced them as they pushed open the door.

"May I come in?" called Knollis. "I'm from Scotland Yard—name of Knollis. Shocking affair, isn't it?"

"It's terrible bad, sir," she sighed. "Can I offer you a cup of tea? I've just made a pot, 'cause I felt I needed it."

"We'll accept gratefully," said Knollis. "Our own tea was disturbed by the news."

Her bosom rose and fell as she emitted another deep sigh. "It was a chance in a thousand that Smithy found him. Usually, you can't get him near the bogey-house."

"Bogey-house?" murmured Knollis.

"That's what we call the cactus house with all them queer-shaped things in it, sir. Some of them aren't decent, I'm sure, and Smithy always says that if he had his way he'd burn the lot."

Knollis and Ellis exchanged glances.

"Ah yes, the cactus house," said Knollis. "Smith was waiting for his girl, was he not?"

The lady shook her head. "I don't know what they were trapesing about at. First Smithy comes in for his tea—him getting it late with having to take the Master to town. He gobbles it down him and says he is going across to change. Then Freeman squitters downstairs and chases after him, and then she came back. Smithy followed her in and wanted to know how long she was going to be. She said she'd be a few minutes yet, and Smithy said he'd have a walk to the bogey-house and look round."

"Interesting," said Knollis. "By the way, I don't think I know your name, do I?"

"Mrs. Martha Redson, sir. A widow these ten years. I'm the cook here. Yes, Smithy was waiting for Freeman. You know what modern girls are with their paint and powder and all this titivating up and so on. She told him to hang on, and he went through to the alley because he said he was looking for something he'd mislaid."

"Oh!" Knollis said quietly.

"So if he hadn't gone through the Master might have been there yet and nobody to look after his poor dead body!" she added.

"Quite so," agreed Knollis. "Was Mr. Manchester a good employer?"

She held out two cups of tea. "A very good master, sir. He paid well, and he wasn't afraid of telling you when he'd enjoyed a meal. He always said he could pay for the best, and he expected the best. Well, he always got my best. I wouldn't have reigned long if he hadn't, so that's a reference on its own."

"Tell me," said Knollis; "what happened after Smith reported his discovery?"

"Well, I just sat and flopped. I went weak all over. Freeman, who'd just come downstairs again, ran through to Madame."

"How many have you on your staff, Mrs. Redson?"

"Just the three of us, sir—Freeman, Smithy, and me. Domestic labour's a bit hard to find. I have a day-woman from the village every day to do the rough cleaning, and she finishes at four and has tea before she leaves."

"And how many people are in the household?"

"Master and Madame, and two visitors just now, them being Mr. Brailsford and Miss Dana."

"Mm!" murmured Knollis. "Miss Vaughan is a friend of Mrs. Manchester's, is she not?"

"A very old friend, I believe, sir."

"And Mr. Brailsford?"

"A friend of the Master's, sir. He's been here before. Miss Dana used to come down about twice a year, apart from short week-ends."

"I see," said Knollis. "Where is Freeman? Is it possible for me to speak with her?"

"Nothing easier," replied the cook. "I'll ring for her. She'll be in her room."

She pulled on an old-fashioned bell-pull, and Knollis could imagine a handbell jangling in some remote corner of this wilderness of a house.

Two minutes later a tear-stained girl of about twenty years entered the kitchen. "You wanted—"she began, and stopped abruptly as she caught sight of Knollis and Ellis.

"This gentleman from Scotland Yard wants to speak to you," said the cook. "Here, there's a cup of tea for you, love. That'll put you to rights in no time."

The girl, who was probably pretty when not tearful, edged timorously into the room and accepted the cup and saucer.

"Do take a seat," Knollis invited. "You have no cause for nervousness. I only want to ask if you can tell me where various people were round about the time that your master met his death. Mr. Brailsford, for instance? Where was he?"

Freeman lowered herself nervously to the edge of a hardwood chair, and opened her mouth to speak, but no words emerged.

"Come on, girl!" snapped Mrs. Redson. "The gentleman is not wanting to eat you or arrest you!"

"He—he passed me on the stairs," she stammered.

"Going up or down?" Knollis prompted as gently as he could.

"I was coming down, sir, and he was going up. I thought he would say something because I wasn't using the back stairs, but he didn't. He seemed to be thinking of something."

"And Miss Vaughan?"

"She was in her room, sir, because I heard her moving about while I was downstairs."

"Mrs. Manchester?"

"In the sitting-room, sir, darning socks. I wanted to do them, but she said it was my evening off, and I must not keep Smithy waiting. I'm—I'm walking out with Smithy, sir. He's the chauffeur."

One of Knollis's rare smiles appeared. "He looks a solid type of fellow. Quiet and reliable."

"Oh, he is, sir! He's—he's very good to me," she said slowly, and there was something in her tone that caused Knollis to give her a long and curious glance.

"So he should be to a pretty girl like you," he said. "He probably knows when he's lucky!"

Freeman stared at the toes of her tan shoes. "He is—very good—to me. Oh dear!"

"You are happy working in this house, Miss Freeman?"

She looked up and tried to smile. "Very happy, sir. Both Mr. and Mrs. Manchester have always been very nice to me."

"Tell me," said Knollis; "what was the first you heard about this—occurrence?"

She had just taken the spoon in her hand to stir the tea. At Knollis's question it slipped from her fingers and tinkled across the stone-flagged kitchen floor.

"The—the first thing?"

"Yes," Knollis repeated patiently. "Who was the first person to tell you about it?"

She appeared to have difficulty in framing her words. "Why, it was Smithy! Of course it was. Yes, it was Smithy!" she said slowly and jerkily.

"Of course," said Knollis in a cheerful tone. "Who else could it be? Smithy found him—didn't he?" Freeman looked anxiously about her, as if for a means of escape. "He—he found him, sir! Yes, sir, who else could it be?"

"And you went straight through to minister to your mistress? That is right?"

"Yes! Oh yes, that is right, sir," she replied, and appeared to snatch at the explanation rather than to agree with him.

"How often do you go to the bogey-house?" Knollis next asked.

"Oh, you know our name for it, sir? I go in every day—although it's funny you should ask."

"Why do you go in every day, Miss Freeman?"

"Well, those funny little plants. They are—funny! I like to watch them. I think they are quaint, but I can't make Smithy see it. He thinks they should all be burned out of the way."

Knollis was silent for a minute, and Ellis scribbled on in the corner.

"Have you any idea what it was that took Smithy through the annexe door to the cactus house if he had such a horror of cacti, Miss Freeman?" Knollis asked at last.

Freeman stared. Her eyes seemed to grow larger and larger. At any minute now she was going to descend into hysterics. Knollis hurriedly turned to the cook, leaving the question to go unanswered.

"Mrs. Redson, I wonder if you can tell me whether anyone heard any unusual noise about the time that Mr. Manchester was killed?"

The cook shook her head. "I don't know of anything like that, sir. I never heard anything myself, and nobody else said anything."

"No crying out, nor doors closing?"

"This house doesn't have echoes, sir. It's like in a book I once read where it said that all the echoes died at birth. Everything is thick-carpeted, and there's a lot of heavy old furniture in it. No, sir, even if the Master had cried out it wouldn't have been heard from the house."

"Hm!" grunted Knollis. "That is quite an idea! The road is beyond the boundary wall?"

"Yes, sir, and higher than the garden by a good many feet— but you can't see over the wall into the garden from the road. It's about seven feet high on the road side of it."

"You think you would hear a cry if you were on the main road? You do agree with that?"

The cook nodded. "I should think so, sir, but you know more than I do about such things."

Knollis looked at Freeman. She had pushed her cup of tea on the table and was now sitting with her face in her hands, quietly weeping.

"Thank you both," he said as he rose. "I must see if it is convenient to have a talk with Mrs. Manchester." As he and Ellis left by the south door they were approached by Colonel Mowbray, the Chief Constable.

"I've been looking for you, Inspector. Wondered where you'd got to, y'know!"

"Oh, I decided to have a chat with the staff," Knollis replied airily.

"Good lor', man!" the Chief Constable exclaimed. "Surely it was more important to see the dead man's wife!"

Knollis smiled enigmatically. "At the moment, the staff hold the information I need."

The Chief Constable blinked. "They do? Why? What have you unearthed?"

"Up to now," replied Knollis, "I've unearthed one whacking big lie, and a little girl who daren't tell what she knows. But she will! Oh yes, she will!"

CHAPTER IV
THE LADY OF BAXMANHURST

MRS. MILDRED MANCHESTER received Knollis in the sitting-room, a room with an Adams ceiling, an Adams fireplace, and neo-Manchester furniture. Knollis was no aesthete, but the room clashed on his senses. Manchester was everywhere, and it was impossible to escape him even now that he was dead.

The Lady of Baxmanhurst was tall. She was thin. Her neck rose from a dove-grey dress in a gentle curve. Her whole attitude reminded Knollis of a swan which had recently scented danger and was now settling down again. She was like a tense spring that was in the process of relaxing. He was puzzled by her, for her eyes, pale blue ones, had the pained expression of a bitch which had just been thrashed—the bitch of the canine race being notoriously more sensitive than the dog. Her hands, long-fingered and yellowish, chafed against each other restlessly as if they were alive with irritation. Her general attitude, her eyes, and her hands were all contradictory, while her low, soft-modulated voice as she said "Well, Inspector?" all added to the mystery that was confusing him.

Knollis gave a light bow. "I am sorry to disturb you at such a time as this, Mrs. Manchester, but you will of course realise the necessity."

"That is quite all right, Inspector," she replied. She removed a pile of magazines from a chair and silently invited him to be seated. "You have something to say to me?"

"At the moment I have not. I wish to ask you several questions. Have you anything to tell me which might prove useful?"

"I am bewildered and puzzled," she replied. "I know that many people disliked my husband, but I had no idea that anyone hated him—and hated him so much!"

Knollis leaned forward. "I want you to go back three days, Mrs. Manchester, and tell me about the budgerigar."

"My poor little bird," she murmured. "I went to my boudoir shortly after breakfast, and found his little body on my dressing-table. His neck was broken, and a short blue cord was tied loosely round his neck."

"You have it?" asked Knollis.

"It is in my boudoir, Inspector."

"Perhaps I could see your boudoir?" suggested Knollis.

Mrs. Manchester rose. "If you will follow me, Inspector. . . ."

In the boudoir she pointed to a gilded cage on a tall stand. "That was Sweetum's little home. I am certain that the door was closed when I went down to breakfast, and then—"

"Pardon the interruption," said Knollis, "but were all the members of the household at breakfast?"

Mrs. Manchester considered, a finger to her lower lip. "Well, Miss Vaughan came down late, and Fred was fetched to the telephone during the meal, but neither of them would have—that is obvious, surely!"

"Quite," said Knollis. "Now the cord; may I see it, please?"

She opened the dressing-table drawer and handed him two lengths of blue silk cord; one just over six inches long, and the other a full foot.

"It is embroidery silk," she said, "taken from my workbox. The shorter one was tied to Sweetums."

"And the longer one to the cat, of course."

She lowered her head in answer.

"Tell me about the cat," said Knollis.

"I found Boofuls in the cactus house at noon yesterday, lying amongst Fred's plants with his neck broken, and that longer cord tied round him."

"Are you in the habit of visiting the cactus house at, say, regular hours?"

"I go in most days, usually before lunch."

"So that," said Knollis, "whoever was responsible would know that you were the most likely person to find the cat. You can agree there?"

She stared vacantly at him. "Whoever was responsible would know that either myself or my husband would find Boofuls, Inspector. Temple does no work in there, it being my husband's especial hobby and charge."

"Temple? Oh yes, he is the gardener," Knollis said quietly.

He looked at the cords as they lay in his hands. "This evening, Mrs. Manchester; you saw your husband on his return from Trentingham?"

"Oh yes! He came into the sitting-room and asked if Sir Giles Tanroy had called. He had an appointment with him for five o'clock. Sir Giles had arrived earlier, and Fred was later than he had expected being. He chatted with me for some minutes about the changes which Fred had made round the place, and he seemed annoyed because Fred had chopped down the vines in what is now the cactus house. He said that the old orders were changing with a vengeance, and he wasn't at all sure that he liked it. I told him that things were perhaps not as bad as he imagined them, and that he might change his mind if he took a walk to the cactus house and viewed it with an open mind. He replied that he liked to be fair, and so he would take a look round, with my permission, and I told him that he was always as free of the estate as when it had belonged to him."

"Your husband went to look for him when he returned from Trentingham?"

Mrs. Manchester nodded. "Yes, Inspector. That was the last I saw of him."

"Then you have no idea whether he saw Sir Giles or not? Sir Giles did not return to the house?"

"I have no idea, Inspector—but I do hope you are not connecting Sir Giles with my husband's death. Sir Giles is a gentleman, with all a gentleman's instincts, and I am sure that—well, it was murder, wasn't it? I am sure that such violence is entirely foreign to his nature."

"At the moment," Knollis replied quietly, "I am not in a position to connect anyone with the murder. Now I am sure that you will forgive this question, Mrs. Manchester, but I must ask it, as a formality. Were you happy with your husband?"

Her features assumed an expression of quiet rapture. "I was very happy, Inspector. Fred was a good man and a kind husband. I was the centre of his life, and he never ceased to tell me that I was his wife, sweetheart, and mother in one person."

She paused, and regarded Knollis earnestly.

"I know what you are thinking, Inspector! Fred was badly abused on account of his business methods, and he was sneered at by the County set because of his lack of culture—but is culture everything? Did not the poet say that kind hearts were more than coronets, and simple faith than Norman blood? Fred was a man of the people, a man of simple faith. His code may not have coincided with that of the people with whom he tried to mix, but he had a code, and he lived according to his lights. He was a good husband, a firm friend, and would have been a wonderful father if circumstances had not made it impossible for me to bear them for him. If he had a fault—and yes, he had one!—it was his yearning to mix outside his class. He could not see that his happiness lay at hand, and not in the Mountains of the Moon."

She gave a dry, harsh laugh. "Oh yes, Inspector, I knew him! I had the advantages of an education, and I know that Fred felt his social inferiority very keenly. Well, I wonder what the County will say about him now!"

Knollis coughed. "Tell me, Mrs. Manchester; whom do you suspect of being responsible for his death?"

"How can I suspect anyone, Inspector?" she asked, gesturing with her hands. "I never even suspected that anyone hated him so much as to bring him to his death in such a horrible manner."

"Quite! Quite!" Knollis murmured sympathetically. "Well, thank you for your assistance, Mrs. Manchester. I will be around the house for some days, but I will not disturb you more than is absolutely necessary."

She bowed her head. "I appreciate your thoughtfulness, Inspector Knollis. Is there anything else I can do for you?"

Knollis considered. "I would be grateful if you could place a small room on the ground floor at my disposal. I shall need a temporary office, some place in which I can interview your servants, and, I'm afraid, your guests."

"I quite understand," she replied. "You shall have Fred's study. I will tell Freeman to show you to it, and to get you anything you may require."

On the way downstairs, Knollis rah into a plumpish man who was about to ascend, but who stood aside to allow him to pass. He was a peculiar-looking fellow with a face as full as the moon. His features were so queerly distorted that he looked rather like the man-in-the-moon, his left eye being higher than his right one by a good half-inch, and his mouth twisted across his face so that he had a permanent sardonic grin. He touched Knollis on the arm as he reached the floor of the hall. "You will be the detective from the Yard," he said in a high-pitched voice.

"Yes. I am Inspector Knollis."

"I am Desmond Brailsford, Manchester's best friend. If there is anything I can do . . ."

"There is," Knollis replied. "I am at a loss for certain details regarding Manchester's life. I would like a chat with you in the study in about half an hour's time. Can you make it convenient?"

Brailsford patted his arm, and leered. "I'll be there."

Knollis went out into the grounds and sought Ellis in the darkness, to find him looking round the cactus house with the aid of a torch.

"Any joy?" he asked.

"Not in here, sir," Ellis replied, "but I found this crammed into Manchester's outside breast-pocket."

It was a third cord of the same embroidery silk, about two feet long. Knollis produced the other two and laid them on his hand. "All the same stuff, my Ellis. It came from Mrs. Manchester's workbox. Even a blind man can see that there is a significance attached to them, but what is it? I cannot see it at the moment. Three cords, and three deaths. Good headline stuff for Fleet Street, but a most damnable riddle for us."

"Do you think the colour holds any significance?" asked Ellis.

"Your guess is as good as mine," Knollis replied. "Anyway, you can't do much good out here, so I want you to come indoors and take statements. Mrs. M. couldn't tell me much except that she was head over heels in love with her husband, that no such man ever lived before, and that he liked to be mothered."

"She told you all that?" Ellis asked quickly.

"Not deliberately," Knollis explained. "I gathered so much from what she did say. It has given me an idea. By the way, where is our Colonel?"

Ellis grunted his disgust. "Gone back to town on urgent personal business. I suspect that he was missing his dinner."

They walked from the cactus house, and were turning into the house by the main door when a small sports car whipped down the drive and came to a sliding halt beside them. A good-looking man of about twenty-eight leaped out, adjusting a coloured silk scarf. He peered through the gloom, which was only relieved by his own headlights and the lamp over the doorway. "I say!" he called. "Are you the police? I've got to talk to someone immediately."

Knollis turned back and introduced himself, adding: "Thank heavens that someone wants to talk. I take it that you are Sir Giles Tanroy?"

"Tanroy it is. Look, Inspector, where can we talk?"

"I am using the study. We can go there."

He led the way indoors, and then hesitated, realising that he did not know which was the room. Tanroy said "Excuse me!" and pushed past him, to indicate a door on the right. "This is it."

He stood aside for Knollis and Ellis to enter, then followed them and closed the door. The light was switched on, and a new sheet of blotting-paper lay on the writing-table.

"I didn't know about Manchester's death until a few minutes ago," Sir Giles explained. "I was in the bath when Jackson shouted through the door, but I put a jerk in it and dashed down. He was found outside the cactus house, wasn't he?"

"That is correct," said Knollis, casting a professional eye over the young squire, and noting his frank features and clear blue eyes.

"With his neck severed?"

"That is also correct," replied Knollis. "News travels fast, doesn't it?"

"This is a village," said Sir Giles, echoing the doctor's words. "Anyway, have you found the weapon?"

Knollis's chin jerked upwards. "The weapon? No, we have not. Why do you ask that, Sir Giles?"

Sir Giles shrugged his shoulders. "That is why I hurried down. I think I know what it was done with. You do know that I was here shortly before the killing?"

"Yes," said Knollis. "Mrs. Manchester informed me that you had been here."

Sir Giles took a turn about the room, talking as he patrolled the carpet. "I was supposed to meet Manchester here at five o'clock over a spot of business. I was somewhat early, and after a chat with Milly I went out to the cactus house to see what sort of a mess Manchester had made of it. I got impatient after about ten minutes, cut round the garage, and went for a walk in the hurst, eventually making my way home by way of the meadows. You know the lay-out of this house? You have seen the door leading into the annexe?"

"Yes, I have noticed it," Knollis understated.

"When I went through to the Green Alley there was an axe leaning against the wall—one of those fireman's things with an insulated handle. You know the type!"

"Yes, I know the type," Knollis replied. "And it was leaning against the wall? Interesting!"

"Yes, beside the door. It occurred to me as I was climbing out of the bath that it would be a handy spot in which to leave the thing if you had intentions regarding Manchester's life."

Knollis nodded. "It would indeed! But why do you tell me this?"

Sir Giles ceased his peregrination, fiddled with his scarf, and gave Knollis a frank and direct stare. "I dunno, I'm sure. If it comes to that, why shouldn't I? I mean, I really did see the thing!"

"You haven't realised your position, have you?" Knollis asked with equal frankness.

"My position?" Sir Giles murmured vaguely. "Have I got one, Inspector?"

"A very awkward one on the face of it, Sir Giles. You came here to meet Manchester on business, and went to the cactus house to wait for him. *You* say that you got fed up with waiting, and went for a walk in the hurst. *You* say that you saw an axe leaning against the wall. *You* say that it would be a handy spot for it if anyone considered the killing of Manchester. *You* say that you left the premises shortly before Manchester was killed. Now do you see what I am driving at? All circumstantial evidence, admitted, but distinctly awkward for you."

"Good lo-ord!" exclaimed Sir Giles. "You mean that I am a potential—heck, Inspector! Have some sense. Do I look like a killer? I ask you!"

Knollis relaxed his features, and even allowed a smile to tinge them. "Tell me, Sir Giles; what does a killer look like?"

Sir Giles pondered the question, and then nodded glumly. "I see the point. A killer can look like anybody else, can't he? You mean that he isn't a type—Lombroso and all that. You mean that me, and you, and your sergeant are all potential killers. Mm! I suppose you are right. And that makes it damned awkward for me, doesn't it?" he added cheerfully.

"You've read Lombroso?" asked Knollis.

"Oh heck, yes! His theory went flop several decades ago, didn't it? It's all finger-prints, and *modus operandi*, and black museums, and all that nowadays, isn't it?"

He suddenly broke off, put a hand to his mouth, and said: "Glory be!"

"Why so?" asked Knollis anxiously.

"Finger-prints," said Sir Giles. "If you find that axe you'll find mine all over it. I picked it up and sort of swung it. As a matter of fact I was mentally connecting Manchester with the edge of the blade."

"You didn't like him?"

Sir Giles bit his lower lip, and shook his head. "Couldn't stand him. He was a nasty piece of work. I never understood what Milly saw in him—but then she's a good woman and can't see evil· in anybody. A hell of a life she'd have had with him if she'd been capable of seeing straight. He was such an exacting— but we must not be abusive about the dead, eh?"

"You know," said Knollis, "I'm not so sure that I shouldn't give you the usual caution. Everything tends to incriminate."

Sir Giles laughed. "Judges' rules, and all that? Oh, you needn't bother, Inspector. I'm as innocent as the proverbial new-born lamb."

"You've read a fair amount of criminology. Am I correct?" asked Knollis.

"Crime and aircraft are my only two interests," Sir Giles replied. "You must run up to Knightswood and have a look round. I've built a miniature landing-ground behind the house and fly my own Austerchild from it. Then gliding, of course! I go into Derbyshire almost every week-end. No, Inspector; sorry and all that, but I haven't time for doin' murders and being hanged for 'em."

"An awkward question for you," Knollis murmured. "Have you an occupation, or are you a gentleman of leisure and independent means?"

"Me?" Sir Giles laughed. "I'm the busiest man in the district with one thing and another. Among other pursuits I'm trying to form a flying club on a site at the other side of town. That is why I came to see Manchester—"

"I thought the reason would emerge in due course." Knollis smiled.

"Well, you could have had that for the asking!" Sir Giles protested. "I was trying to get him to invest in it."

"Am I correct in suggesting that Manchester let you down pretty badly some time ago?"

"That's true enough," he replied glumly. "He egged me on to sink some money in what proved to be a phoney company. The shares ebbed badly, and I thought I was stranded. Manchester came to the rescue—his own words—and offered to buy Baxmanhurst from me. I had to sell, damn his hide! A month later he made me an offer for the dud shares, and like a fool I sold. Two months afterwards they rose to forty-two shillings. Freddy, in short, had wangled me. I knew nothing whatsoever about markets, and I must have been easy game."

"And yet you were prepared to play with him again?" Knollis asked incredulously.

There was a certain *naiveté* in Sir Giles's reply.

"I figured it out this way, Inspector. He had done me for several thousand pounds, and I didn't see why he shouldn't help me to get back on my feet. Law of compensation and all that. I do know my aviation, and I could have kept a check on him."

"And now that he is dead?"

Sir Giles shrugged his shoulders. "I'll have to find someone else with money. There are no two ways about it, are there?"

Knollis was silently thoughtful for a minute, and then he lifted his head and looked slowly at Sir Giles.

"Who do you think killed Fred Manchester?"

"Damned if I know," he replied. "I haven't the foggiest idea, but good luck to him or her. Sorry for Milly and all that, but I've no personal regrets over Freddy. Of course, it's rotten having a murder in the village, and especially in what was once my own house, but I'm not sorry that he's gone. Further to the point, and I'm being really frank here, I've done a spot of thinking on the way down, and I think Milly may be prepared to sell Baxmanhurst back to me. I'll have to arrange a whopping mortgage, but I've been tormented by the ghosts of ten generations of Tanroys since I sold."

"So that you can benefit by Manchester's death?" Knollis said accusingly.

"Mm—yes! If you put it that way, I can. Indirectly, of course. Does that make it look blacker still for me?"

"It doesn't improve matters," Knollis admitted gloomily, "but I shall be disappointed if it does turn out to be you."

Sir Giles nodded. "So shall I! Makes my neck ache to even think of it."

Knollis toyed with a paper-clip that he found lying on the writing-table. "Look, Sir Giles; you needn't answer this question if you don't feel inclined, but suppose—and I do say suppose— that you had killed Manchester with the axe, and wanted to hide it; where would you have put it?"

Sir Giles took out his cigarette case, and opened it. His hand remained poised over a cigarette as he thought about the question, and it did not tremble.

"Oh well," he said at last, "that is comparatively simple, me knowing the place. At the east end of the cactus house, behind a pile of bushes and shrubs, is a water-butt. I think I should have chucked it in there."

"A water-butt?" exclaimed Knollis. "I certainly never noticed it." He turned his head. "Ellis!"

Ellis left the study, and the two men faced each other in silence. Then Sir Giles shuffled uncomfortably. "I suppose it does look pretty grim for me, but I do assure you that I didn't knock him off. I mean, such things simply aren't done. I'd plenty against him, but I don't bear malice, and I was going to let him stew in his own juice, and settle it with his own conscience— time having its own revenges and all that."

Ellis returned, shaking his head. "It's not there, sir, but I think it has been. It looks to me as if something or other has been rinsed in the water-butt, because there are splashes down the side—and it hasn't rained for several days."

Knollis turned to Sir Giles. "Can you give me any information on the source of the axe?"

Sir Giles shook his head. "Looked like one of those A.R.P. axes to me. This place was used as the local warden post until the official one was built. Temple was in charge of the equipment."

"Temple?" mused Knollis. "He seems to keep bobbing in and out of this affair, and I haven't seen him yet. Well, Sir Giles, I must thank you for volunteering your information."

When he had left, Knollis tapped his pencil on the table in a thoughtful manner. "Ellis, I think you should get the Trentingham fellows organised on a weapon hunt."

CHAPTER V
THE EVASION OF DANA VAUGHAN

DESMOND BRAILSFORD was knocking on the study door almost before Sir Giles Tanroy was out of the house, and asking, in his peculiarly high-pitched voice, for permission to enter. "I want to go into town in half an hour or so, Inspector," he said, "so I thought I'd better call on you now."

"The interview will be pointless," Knollis said subtly, "unless you have anything to tell me about the causes of Manchester's death."

Brailsford further distorted his features as he registered intense thought. "I don't really think there is anything I can tell you—except that somebody was talking under my window about the time that Fred was killed. Perhaps I should say just before he was killed."

"Which is your room?" Knollis enquired keenly.

"First floor; the room on the north-east corner. There are two windows; one facing east, and one to the north. The voices were under the north window, of course."

"Interesting information," commented Knollis. "Did you recognise either of the voices—or both?"

"Well," Brailsford said slowly, and it almost seemed reluctantly, "one was definitely Fred's. The other sounded like a woman's voice. I wasn't really listening, because I wasn't interested. I didn't know that anything untoward was happening. We never do, do we?"

"We do not," Knollis agreed. "That is one of the great difficulties we encounter when interviewing witnesses. Tell me, Mr. Brailsford; how long have you known Manchester?"

"Oh, for years, on and off," he replied casually, "but it was only during the past two years that we became friends as distinct from acquaintances."

"Your business interests brought you together, I presume?" Knollis suggested.

Brailsford shook his head, and his lips achieved even more of a leer than usual. "No! It was a mutual interest in beer drinking more than anything else. I used to drop across him in London, in a pub in Wardour Street, at odd times, and we sort of gravitated together."

Knollis leaned back in his chair and played with his pencil. "Do you mind telling me the nature of your occupation, Mr. Brailsford?"

Brailsford laughed, and his left eye stared at the ceiling while his right one winked at Knollis. "I have an interest in a small publishing firm."

"Was Manchester in any way connected with the firm?"

"Yes and no," Brailsford replied. "He had an idea for writing a book on cactuses—or should I say cacti? Anyway, he seemed to realise that he had no literary ability, and I was going to arrange a ghost for him whenever he settled down to write it. I think he must have been reading adverts in the papers, because he wanted to be an author in one easy lesson. All you need is pen, ink, and paper. Y'know the stuff!"

"And in return?" Knollis asked simply.

Brailsford grinned. "You're nobody's fool, are you, Inspector?"

"I hope not," Knollis replied. "Not often, that is!"

Brailsford considered the remark for a half-minute, and then stuck his hands into his jacket pockets. "This being a murder investigation, I suppose I'd better be perfectly frank with you, because if you know your job you'll find out what I don't tell you."

"Thanks for the compliment," said Knollis.

"A compliment, when sincere, is merely an expression of the truth, Inspector. I was hoping to get Fred to sink a couple of thou. in the firm. I'd like to branch out a bit more. Our scope is too restricted for my liking."

"You often come to Baxmanhurst?" Knollis asked.

"Three or four week-ends a year, and I occasionally drop in mid-week for a few days. Just depends what there is on in town."

Knollis grunted. "I may take it that you knew Manchester pretty well?"

"Ye-es, quite well, I think!"

"What kind of a man was he—to you?"

Brailsford wrinkled his nose in what may or may not have been an unconscious gesture of disgust. "Hail-fellow-well-met on the surface, and as shrewd as a rat under it. He liked a drink, and a game of cards, and he wasn't below taking an interest in a pretty woman if it could be done discreetly. Very sharp in business, and very open-handed out of it. Too open-handed, actually. Fred always overdid it."

"In what way?" Knollis ventured.

"Overtipping is a good example," Brailsford replied. "Where you and I would leave ten per cent, and perhaps not as much as that, Fred would leave thirty or forty. Damned silly, actually, because it marked him out as a fellow who wasn't used to money—and that was something he was always trying to make out he was."

"It seems to have been a very marked trait in his character," commented Knollis. "Other people have remarked on the same idiosyncrasy. He was sensitive about his lack of education, and his position in the social scale? You would agree with those criticisms?"

Brailsford cocked his left eye at the lamp-shade, and gave a hearty laugh. "You've soon got a handle on Fred's character, Inspector! I said you were no fool. Fred was as touchy as a frog!"

Knollis affected an air of surprise. "Are frogs touchy, Mr. Brailsford?"

Brailsford gave a sharp laugh which irritated Knollis. "Touch one with the sharp end of a piece of straw and see for yourself. Freddy was like that, only he developed a carapace for himself.

He was all right as long as he could keep up the bluff, but once you'd poked underneath it he'd squirm like the devil."

"You've tried it?" Knollis said softly.

"Oh, just for devilment," Brailsford replied easily. "That was one way of getting your way with him. As long as he was the lord of the manor and cock of the muckheap you could do nothing with him, but if you pricked him and reduced his inflated ego he'd agree with you in order to get back in your good books. That was when Milly used to catch it hot!"

Knollis showed renewed interest, and the distaste faded from his keen features. "You mean . . . ?" Brailsford waved an airy hand. "It's common knowledge in the house that he used to give her hell. He'd use her as a whipping boy, and take it out of her when somebody else had taken it out of him—and then he'd have a fit of contrition and do everything he could to make it up to her. A very elemental type was Fred. But mind you, he'd never apologise openly! Oh dear, no! He'd show his remorse in a dozen ways, but no apologies for Fred!"

He lit a cigar and then twisted his head so that he appeared to be looking at Knollis with his right ear. "You know, Inspector; Milly is a saint. Nobody else would have put up with him."

"You did, apparently," Knollis said softly.

"Ah yes, but that was different. I didn't have to live with him, and as I've said I'd be frank I'll also add that I was hoping to get something out of him. I guess that will shock you, Inspector!" he sniggered.

"I'm a recorder of facts, not a judge of ethics," Knollis said frigidly.

Brailsford's features relaxed. "Anyway, he was a good companion in a man's sense, but I'm darned glad that I wasn't his wife!"

Knollis scribbled idly on the pad as he asked: "Tell me, Mr. Brailsford; what do you know about Miss Vaughan?"

"Dana? Well, not much, Inspector. She's an actress, and a fine lady. I've a great deal of respect for her. She has a warm heart, and a pretty good brain." Knollis eyed his man narrowly as he asked him the next question. "It couldn't have been her voice you heard under your window this evening?"

Brailsford started, and stammered. "I—I hadn't thought of that when I told you, Inspector. Still—no, it couldn't have been."

"And why not?" demanded Knollis. "Have you evidence to the contrary?"

"Well, no," said Brailsford, shuffling a foot on the carpet. "It might have been. Again, it might not. I can't say. Why do you ask? Do you think it likely?"

"I must reserve the right to ask the questions," Knollis replied gravely. "There are only four women in the house. You are well acquainted with the household, and cannot say which of them it might have been. You cannot suggest the presence of a fifth woman, can you?"

"Can't say that I do," said Brailsford. "There's the day-girl, but I believe that she leaves about four o'clock. Besides, this voice was cultured, and the day-girl uses the local dialect."

Knollis rose as an indication that the interview was at an end. "Thanks, Mr. Brailsford. You are not likely to leave Baxmanhurst for a few days?"

"I'll stick around," said Brailsford. "I want to see how the affair ends, and I have no pressing business in London."

Ellis sauntered across to the desk when Brailsford had left the room. "Doesn't seem to be much there, sir!"

"I'm not sure," Knollis replied slowly. "I'm interested in the fellow. That is, I'm interested in his deformity."

"Rather a mess, certainly," Ellis agreed.

Knollis gave a grim smile. "I don't mean his facial deformity, Ellis, but the corresponding mental twist. He is a sadist. I don't suggest that he was responsible for Manchester's decease, but I'm interested in the relationship between them. You took full notes of the conversation."

"Verbatim." Ellis nodded.

"Good. Now I wonder if you can find Miss Vaughan for me. A short interview with her, and we can close shop for to-night. Leave your notes. I'll have a look through them. See," he added with a grin, "I can read your shorthand, can't I?"

"You should," Ellis replied happily. "I'm one of the most legible shorthand writers in the Yard."

"And so modest!" returned Knollis. "Hop it, Watson; I'm getting hungry."

Ellis came back a few minutes later, grinning broadly. "I called in the kitchen. Mrs. Redson is sending in three cups of tea. Miss Vaughan is coming down shortly."

"As usual," Knollis remarked absently, "your organising is of the highest order. I'll remember this when I get my promotion."

"What promotion?" Ellis blinked.

Knollis toyed with his pencil. "Well, there is a rumour . . ."

"Chief Inspector Knollis," murmured Ellis. "Sounds good to me. Does that mean that I'll lose you?"

"Not necessarily, my lad. Anyway, it's no more than a rumour at present."

"Where there's smoke there's fire," said Ellis. He broke off to open the door as a light knock sounded on it.

Dana Vaughan did not enter the room. She made an entrance, and there is all the difference in the world between the two. She made a dignified entrance, but all her art could not conceal the fact that she had been weeping.

Knollis went forward to meet her and conduct her to a chair. "I regret having to disturb you," he said, using his favourite opening, "but I will detain you no longer than I can help."

"At a time like this, one must expect to be disturbed," she replied in a level voice.

Knollis ran his mental tape-measure over her. She was not as tall as Mildred Manchester, but rather more buxom and considerably younger, probably twenty-nine or thirty. Her hair was brown. Her eyes were dark grey, large, and solemn. The white blouse and grey-flannel costume suited her figure admirably, and she carried herself as gracefully as a queen. The only item, to Knollis, that spoiled the effect was a gold-tipped cigarette that hung from the ringless fingers of her left hand.

Knollis quickly catalogued her in his mind, and gave an embarrassed laugh. "This is a terrible question to ask you, Miss Vaughan, and I do not wish you to read implications into it that are not intended. Whereabouts in this house were you when Fred Manchester was being—er—killed?"

She regarded him with large and solemn eyes. "Dr. Denstone tells me that Fred died about twenty minutes to six. If that is correct, then I was in my room, Inspector. I think that Freeman will be able to substantiate that statement, inasmuch as she was busying herself between Mildred's room and mine. Mrs. Manchester, you know!"

"Thank you," Knollis said quietly. "You are taking a holiday here, I believe?"

She nodded. "Convalescing, Inspector. I suppose you know that I am an actress?" She asked the question proudly, as if there could be no doubt.

"I have had the pleasure of seeing *The Hempen Rope* three times, Miss Vaughan."

She bowed her head. "The compliment is implied, and no less pleasurable to me for that."

"I understand that the part you played affected your nerves to the extent that you had to leave the cast?"

"That is right, Inspector. You have complimented me on my performance, and so you will probably understand me when I explain that to get such a part over to an audience it is necessary to get right into the skin of the character?"

"Yes," said Knollis, "I think I can appreciate that point, Miss Vaughan."

She gave a wry smile. "I did it too well. My subconscious mind accepted the characterisation, and I began to relive the part in my sleep. A great deal happened in the ensuing months, but the final result was a nervous breakdown. I am now taking an enforced rest for six months."

"Disastrous," Knollis said earnestly.

"Very," she replied dryly. "Still, this can have no bearing on Fred's death, Inspector. Is there any way in which I can help you?"

"I have met Mr. Brailsford for the first time this evening," said Knollis. "He seems an unusual fellow. Can you tell me anything about him?"

Dana Vaughan was about to reply when a knock sounded at the door, and Mrs. Redson entered with a tray.

"Had to bring it myself," she explained volubly. "Can't make out what's wrong with Freeman. She's gone to her room, and she's sobbing her eyes out. Shouldn't have thought as the Master's death would have upset her like that, 'cause he wasn't any too gentlemanly to her once or twice. Still—"

"Mrs. Redson!" snapped Dana Vaughan. "You forget your place!"

"Sorry, I'm sure," the cook replied, unabashed, "but it's the truth, and that never hurt nobody!"

"You should remember your place," said the actress.

"Pardon me!" Knollis interrupted. "I happen to be chairman of this meeting, and I'm interested in what you were saying, Mrs. Redson. Suppose you finish it?"

The cook cast a glance at the actress, and then her chin went up. "These folk don't like the truth, Inspector, 'cause it lets the side down, they say. The Master was a good payer, but he was no gentleman, and that's the truth of it. Freeman has nothing to be ashamed of, and if it hadn't been for Smithy being here she'd have left months ago. Always stopping her on the landing and trying to kiss her and that—mainly that nasty, dirty old man he was where a young girl was concerned!"

"This—this is awful!" exclaimed Dana Vaughan. "I refuse to sit here and listen to such stuff!"

She whisked out of her chair and left the study.

Knollis gave a dry smile. "You can talk now, Mrs. Redson. Look, why not sit down and join us in a cup of tea? Miss Vaughan won't need hers now."

The cook bobbed in a half-curtsy. "Thank you, I'm sure, sir. It's a good cup o' tea, although I say it myself. Yes, sir, I'm glad to get it off my chest. Freeman used to tell me about him, but she always made me promise as I wouldn't say anything about it—especially to Smithy, because he'd have created a row as sure as anything."

Knollis nodded understandingly. "So he liked kissing maids on landings, eh? You know this household very well, don't you, Mrs. Redson?"

"I should do, sir."

"Quite so. Would you describe it as a happy household, or otherwise?"

The cook sipped at her tea and considered the question. "No," she said finally, "it isn't. I've watched, and I've seen, and I've kept my mouth shut—as a good servant should until the proper time comes to open it. Her that's just gone out, for instance! I don't know what she's here for, but it isn't for friendship, and I says that as a woman. There's things happening in this house, sir. Things that you can *feel*. Perhaps you don't know what I mean, sir?"

"I think I do," Knollis assured her.

"The Master now; he was good enough to me, as I told you when you first asked me about him, but he used to watch Madame like a cat watches a mouse. Do you know as she's only been out of the house twice in six months? Out of the grounds, that is."

"I didn't know," Knollis murmured. "It is an incredible state of affairs."

"Exactly my own words, sir! She went down to Trentham—as we call it—on the bus, and when the Master found out when he came home at night he played her up no end. Said that she wasn't to go out like that, and that she knew why. Oh, and a lot more like it, sir! It was more than flesh and blood could bear. If Smithy hadn't held me down in my chair I'd have gone right in and told him he ought to be ashamed of himself."

Knollis slowly drank his tea, pondering on what he was hearing.

"And that Mr. Brailsford, sir," the cook continued. "He isn't here for anybody's benefit but his own. I never did like him, with his twisted ways. Moves about the house as if he was scared of being seen and heard. You walk down a passage and find he's on your heels all the way. Gives you a proper turn!"

"I can well imagine that," said Knollis. "Now tell me about Temple. What kind of a man is he?"

The cook planted her empty cup in the saucer and put them on the tray. "Ah, now you are on to something, sir! Temple agrees with me as the Master was no gentleman. He had some sort of trouble with him years ago. The Master put him in court for some money as he owed him, and then offered him the job as gardener. Temple was out of work and couldn't do any less than take it. The Master gave him the cottage across the way—Gates Cottage—but he has to pay five shillings a week rent for it. He always says the same as me, that he wouldn't stop here if it wasn't for the money. The Master certainly did pay well! Temple gets a pound a week more than he'd get anywhere else."

"Does he still—er—harp on the trouble he had with Mr. Manchester?" Knollis asked.

"He's quiet enough about it when he's sober, but when he's drunk he carries on no end. I've been a bit frightened of him one time or another—although I don't think he'd do anything desperate."

"Has he had any disputes with Mr. Manchester since he came here as gardener?"

"Well," the cook replied slowly, "you can hardly call them disputes, because the Master used to pitch into him and he'd stand there and take it. Later, when he'd been round to the Anchor, he'd come into my kitchen and say what he was going to do to him one day, but he'd fall asleep as a general rule, and that would be the end of it. The Master told him off this morning because the hedges hadn't been trimmed for a week. He said it was bad enough at ordinary times, but worse when he had friends staying in the house. Knowing Temple, I reckon that his wife has put him to bed and he's sleeping it off again."

"He went out to drown his sorrows as usual?" Knollis asked urgently, and yet striving to conceal his impatience.

Mrs. Redson nodded. "He called in just after lunch and said he was going round for a quick one, and I haven't seen him since—" She broke off, and alarm showed in her eyes. "You don't think, sir . . . ?"

Knollis smiled to reassure her. "It doesn't sound like Temple to me," he said. "I wouldn't worry. Well, I think we must be getting back to town now. Thanks very much for the way in which you have sketched the household for me, Mrs. Redson. Oh yes, and thank you for the cup of tea. It was most enjoyable."

"I'm glad you liked it, sir," she said, rising. "Thank you, sir!"

She collected the tray, and left them. Ellis grinned at his chief. "Nice people, with nice manners."

Knollis looked grim. "Come on, Ellis. Let's look for Mr. Temple! I would like to interview him."

They left the house and walked up the gloomy drive to the main road and thence to the door of the lighted cottage facing them. Knollis's knock was answered by a roly-poly little woman with bright eyes and glowing cheeks.

"Is Mr. Temple at home?" Knollis asked.

"I'm afraid he isn't, sir. Is there any message I can take for him?"

"I'm afraid not," Knollis replied. "I am the detective in charge of the enquiry into Mr. Manchester's death, and I wanted to ask your husband a few questions about his employer. To-morrow will do just as well as to-night. I don't suppose you can tell me where I can find him?"

She hesitated. "Well, he went down to the Anchor Inn just after dinner, sir, and later I saw him going back down to Baxy, but he hasn't been home since, so I think he must have gone back to the inn—he often does that." She added apologetically: "He gets these fits now and again, sir."

"We all have fits and moods at times," Knollis replied soothingly. "I'll see him in the morning. Perhaps you will tell him that I have called?"

"Oh certainly, sir! What name shall I say?"

"Inspector Knollis, ma'am."

"I'll remember, sir," she said, and closed the door.

"Get the car from Baxmanhurst, Ellis," Knollis said briskly. "I think we should look into the local. I'll wait here."

He glanced at his watch. "A quarter to ten! Lord, how the night has flown!"

Ellis returned with the car, and Knollis got in beside him. "Now where is this pub?"

"I think I can find it," said Ellis. "I noticed it on the way here. It lies a few yards farther up the main road." He smacked his lips. "I know a good home for a pint of mixed!"

Knollis laughed. "I think I can help you. The evening has been so interesting that I'd nearly forgotten about the important business of victualling."

Ellis turned to glance at him. "You sound quite happy, sir! Think you are on to anything?"

"Don't I usually sound happy?" Knollis enquired in a surprised voice.

Ellis chuckled. "No!"

"Oh well, I'm not really miserable even when I'm not demonstrative. I'm interested in my job, Ellis." Ellis refrained from comment, and stared under the railway bridge that spanned the main road. A hundred yards farther on he drew in beside the inn. It was well lighted, and a subdued murmur came from it, a murmur that grew into a mild hubbub as they opened the door and entered the saloon bar. Knollis ordered two tankards.

"Make mine a pint, please," said Ellis. "It's nearly closing time."

The landlord eyed them with rural curiosity. "You'll be the gentlemen from Scotland Yard?" he said hopefully.

Knollis lowered an eyelid. "Keep it quiet, if you don't mind."

The landlord laughed. "You've a hope, sir! The whole village knows you and your personal history by now. They have been talking you over all night in here."

"Too bad!" Knollis replied. "By the way, I think you can help me. Which is Temple, the Baxmanhurst gardener?"

"He isn't in, sir. He hasn't been in to-night."

"Oh!" exclaimed Knollis. "He was here earlier in the day?"

"Well, yes, as a matter of fact, he was. Came in about one-ish, and went with the rest of them when I closed at three."

"Er—was he sober?"

The landlord registered deep reflection. "We-ell, to be quite fair, sir, it doesn't take much to get Matt wuzzy, and he was a bit under the weather when he left here, but nothing out of the ordinary."

"Is he troublesome when he gets wuzzy?"

"No-o, not really. He talks a lot after the first two pints, and then he goes very silent, and just keeps on drinking. Occasionally he falls asleep over the table."

"And then what do you do with him? Get someone to take him home?" Knollis asked.

"I have done that," the landlord answered. "On odd occasions I've just let him stay where he is. He sleeps through until we open again, and then staggers home."

"Was he making any threats against his employer this afternoon?"

The landlord's mouth opened, and he planted his hands flat on the counter and stared. "So that's the way of it, sir!"

"No, it isn't!" Knollis replied sharply. "Please don't jump to conclusions. I want Temple because I think he may be in a position to give me information about a caller at Baxmanhurst. I think you'd better refill these," he said, pushing the pint jar and the tankard forward. "Perhaps you will join us?"

"Well, a glass, thank you, sir."

As the landlord gathered the receptacles and put them under the pumps he said: "Sorry if I said anything out of place, sir. It—well, it just looked as if that was the drift of your talk. Matt Temple's all right, sir. He wouldn't harm a fly."

"But he was making threats?" Knollis persisted, returning to the attack.

"He was, sir. He always does—for the first two pints, and then he gets maudlin."

"He has a good character in the district?"

The landlord nodded. "Very good, sir, and he's one of the best gardeners there is."

He glanced at the wall-clock. "Well, sir, I'll have to call time. We've run over a bit to-night with talking. Time, gentlemen, please!"

Knollis put his mouth to Ellis's ear. "So Temple is missing, eh? Drink up, Watson. There is work to be done."

CHAPTER VI
THE COGITATIONS OF KNOLLIS

THE CHIEF CONSTABLE was champing his bit when Knollis and Ellis reported to the Guildhall at nine the next morning. "Ah-h!" he exclaimed with deep satisfaction. "You're here!"

"Good morning, sir," Knollis greeted him. "Any news come in during the night?"

"Have you any news yourself?" the Chief Constable retorted.

"Very little at the moment, sir. I left orders last night for your men to hunt for the murder weapon, and for Matthew Temple. You will have read my report, sir?"

The Chief Constable rubbed his hands together, and smiled broadly. "Yes, I read your reports, and also the typed statements of the Baxmanhurst people. So Manchester thought we were incompetent, did he?" he chuckled.

Knollis raised an enquiring eyebrow.

"We are not so dim as a candle, nor yet so bright as a searchlight," the Chief Constable paraphrased, "but we suffice. You wanted Temple, and the axe—we've found them! The axe was in Temple's dustbin, wrapped in yesterday's *Trentingham Advertiser and Courier*, and Temple was in the woodshed at Baxmanhurst, as soused as the proverbial herring."

"Good work!" Knollis commented. "At what time was he found, sir? He left the inn at three o'clock, and the landlord said that he was no worse than usual—whatever that may mean."

The Chief Constable glanced at the reports lying on his desk, and then threw them across to Knollis. "Five minutes to midnight, and he was still flat out."

"Very strange, surely!" Knollis muttered under his breath. His eyes became mere slits as he stared blankly at the opposite wall. "Did a doctor see him?"

"Oh yes! The sergeant sent for Clitheroe! We wouldn't omit such a simple item of procedure."

"I'd like to talk to Clitheroe, sir, and as soon as possible."

The Chief Constable nodded. "You shall, Inspector. Meanwhile, here is another interesting piece of information. Clitheroe and Denstone made a more thorough examination of Manchester when they got him to the mortuary, and they report that they found a nasty-looking bruise over his left ear."

"Oh!" said Knollis. He began a piece of pantomime which momentarily startled both the Chief Constable and Sergeant Ellis. He raised his hat above his head with his right hand, and stepped forward, at the same time bringing his arm down across his body from right to left. The Chief Constable flinched.

"What the devil—?" he exclaimed.

Knollis ignored him. He stared thoughtfully at his hat. "It couldn't have been Dana Vaughan."

Ellis blinked, while the Chief Constable removed his monocle, and rescrewed it into his eye.

"You see," Knollis explained slowly, "Dana Vaughan is left-handed. Manchester's back must have been towards the killer—that much is obvious. A left-handed person could not have wielded the blow. It would entail bringing the arm into the body instead of across it. That lets out Miss Vaughan. I'm willing to wager that the end of the wound nearest to the right ear is deeper than that nearest to the left ear. Obviously so, for the lower point of the blade would meet the flesh first."

He shook himself, and seemed to return to normality. "The axe proved to be an A.R.P. one, sir?"

"Uh?" grunted the Chief Constable. "Oh yes! Black insulated handle. Spike on one side and blade on the other. According to this report—oh, you've got it there! Well, according to the report, it looks as if it has been rinsed, but not thoroughly washed. The paper containing it was sodden."

"Your water-butt, Ellis," Knollis remarked.

"There are traces of blood on it, Inspector. It's in the dabs room if you want to see it."

"I do, sir," said Knollis. "Well, that is a little more towards the eventual solution. By the way, sir, what are the terms of Manchester's will?"

"I've contacted the solicitor," the Chief Constable replied. "He leaves Mrs. Manchester an annuity of a thousand a year, and the interest from his holdings in Manchester Furnishings for the period of her lifetime. The capital? On her death the whole estate goes to two young nephews, aged twelve and four-teen respectively. They are the sons of his only brother. There are minor bequests to his friends, but nothing of importance. Now, how do you think you are going?" he asked anxiously.

"Well enough, considering the time," Knollis replied. "I've got the atmosphere of the house, and that is always important. There are undercurrents which need investigating, sir. Nobody seems to love anybody else—apart from the chauffeur-maid affair. Those two are deeply in love with each other, too deeply for my fancy."

"I don't understand you, Inspector," the Chief Constable protested. "Suppose you enlighten me?"

"One of them," said Knollis flatly, "is shielding the other."

"You don't mean that one of them killed Manchester?"

"Good lord, no! I don't mean that. I mean that something other than murder has taken place, and I haven't discovered what it is. And now I'd like to see the axe, sir, so perhaps you will tell Dr. Clitheroe where I am if he arrives?"

"Certainly," said the Chief Constable, "but what is your pro-gramme for to-day?"

Knollis turned at the door, nearly treading on Ellis's toes. "I'll be making my way back to Bowland when I've seen the body, and the axe, and the doctor. By the· way, I suppose Temple was taken to his home?"

"Er—yes, I suppose so."

Knollis and Ellis went to the finger-print department, where a sergeant was working on the axe. "Any luck?" Knollis asked as he joined him at the bench.

"Two very imperfect ones, sir. I doubt if I'll manage to bring them out—to mean anything, that is. I'm sending it along to the pathological section next for the bloodstains. That in order, sir?"

"Oh quite!" replied Knollis. "I suppose you had it photo-graphed before starting work on it?"

"Naturally, sir. They'll be ready any time now."

"Good enough. Now if Dr. Clitheroe should come looking for me, will you please tell him that I'm in the mortuary? Thank you."

They were directed to the mortuary, where they stared silently at the cold slab on which Manchester's remains lay.

"Well, here goes!" said Knollis, grimacing. He drew back the sheet, to expose the body which had once housed the furniture magnate.

"It's some bruise, sir," Ellis commented as they bent over the dead man's left ear.

Knollis straightened his back, and put his hands on his hips. "I hope you realise what this means—if the bruise was made at the same time as the death stroke!"

Ellis nodded gravely. "I was weighing that up, sir. It means that his killer stunned him, and then chopped him while he was laying on the ground. That sounds like a fury of a woman, or a very warped personality."

"Hm! A very warped personality, eh, Ellis? I wonder!" ·

"There's red mist and mad fury in it," Ellis added softly.

"Yes, mad fury. . . . Now I wonder . . . ?"

"Yes?" Ellis enquired in a hopeful tone.

Knollis shrugged his shoulders. "Merely a wild surmise. Help me to roll him over. I want to examine the wound."

"I don't," Ellis said frankly, "but I'll help."

A few minutes later they replaced the body in its original position and drew up the sheet. Knollis turned his back on it, and rested his weight against the edge of the slab. "A right-handed person did that, as I surmised."

Ellis brushed his moustache away from his lips in a manner that indicated that he was clearing the decks for action. "But look," he protested, "a left-handed person could have done it if the body was lying on the ground!"

"Could he?" Knollis asked mildly. "Come, my Watson, use your imagination. Imagine the body lying face down on the ground, and yourself standing beside it ready to take a swipe at the neck. You are right-handed, so which side of the body will you stand on while you chop?"

Ellis performed various manoeuvres which would have convinced a layman that he was not quite in possession of his senses. "Why," he said at last; "on his right—facing the right side of his body, that is!"

"And if you were left-handed?"

Ellis again manoeuvred into position. "The left! That way I'd have all of the body below the neck on my own right."

"Exactly," Knollis said with quiet satisfaction. "Now, as a right-handed man, try to whack him from the left side of the body."

"No can do," replied Ellis. "It's clumsy."

"And it would be equally clumsy for a left-handed man to whack him from the right side. *Ergo*, Dana Vaughan is out."

"You were really suspecting her?" Ellis asked with astonishment paramount in his voice.

"We-ell, yes, along with the others. You know my methods, my dear Watson!"

"Oh," said Ellis. Then he brightened. "Why the bruise over the *left* ear. Why not the right?"

Knollis groaned. "You must have slept too heavily, Ellis. You are not on your usual form this morning. Here, take your hat in your right hand. Now I'll turn my back on you, and you must imagine that you want to lay me out by bashing me over the ear with the flat of the axe."

A chuckle came from Ellis. "You want me to lay you out so that I can chop your cervical vertebra?"

"Of course, man!" Knollis replied sharply. "How are you going to do it?"

Ellis laughed. "I'm going to bash you over the top of the head. It's far easier, and I don't have to wangle into an awkward position."

Knollis turned him slowly, his mouth open a mere fraction of an inch. "Oh!"

"See what I mean?" asked Ellis.

Knollis nodded. "Yes—-blast it! Bang goes a beautiful theory."

"Well, what now?" Ellis enquired.

"I'm the one who has slept too heavily," Knollis replied. "Of course you would hit me over the head. Then that means—"

"That the bruise was caused by his fall?"

"No-o, I don't think it could be that. I admit that the murder took place on grass, but I noticed that there was a fair amount of pink gravel among it, such as might have been swept on to it, or carried by boots. In that case he would have broken the bruise, or at least have grazed it, and there was no gravel evident and no graze. Now how the dickens did he get it?"

Ellis grimaced. "I can see one way. . . ."

"Your imagination coming to life, eh? Well, how was it produced, Watson?"

"If you won't allow a fall, or a swipe with an axe, then there is only one possible way in which it could have been done—if it was caused at the same time as death."

"Go on then," Knollis said impatiently.

Ellis stared at the sheeted figure on the slab.

"It's dirty, but it's possible. His killer kicked him in the face after he had laid him out."

Knollis became as brisk as if a spring had been unleashed within him. He swung round and tore back the sheet from the dead man. He walked round the slab and re-examined the bruise. Then he looked up at Ellis with slit-like eyes. "I wonder if you are right! I almost think that you are, man!"

"I often wonder if I am!" came a deep voice from the doorway.

"Ah, Dr. Clitheroe!" said Knollis. "Just the man we need. Look, this bruise; how was it caused?"

The tall doctor took long strides to Knollis's side. "The bruise. Yes! Denstone and I tried to fathom that last night. Frankly, we reached no decision. Have you a theory?"

"Sergeant Ellis has," replied Knollis, "and it isn't often he goes astray."

The doctor bent over the bruise, turning the head so the left ear was almost parallel with the table. "Mm! The light is better this morning. I don't like artificial light for examinations, and it's worse still for doing a P.M."

"When are you doing the post-mortem?" Knollis asked. "To-day, I presume?"

"This afternoon. Care to be present?"

"Not me! I'm squeamish."

The doctor shook his head. "I'm not keen on them myself. Messy businesses. Somehow, too, it doesn't seem the right way to treat the dead—and that from a doctor, eh? Still, in the interests of science and justice such things have to be done, and somebody has to do it. . . ."

He broke off, and bent lower over the head. "There seems to be a slight indentation, a half-moon-shaped indentation. Does that help your sergeant's theory?"

Knollis looked over the doctor's back, and smiled grimly at Ellis. "Well, Dr. Watson? Are you satisfied?"

"Could—could it have been caused by the toe of a boot?" Ellis asked anxiously.

The doctor unbent his long body and planted his hands on the edge of the slab. "It could; a narrow-pointed boot or shoe?"

"I'm suggesting, sir, that the killer kicked him in the face after he was dead."

The doctor grimaced. "A nice thought that, Sergeant! And yet it is feasible. Ye-es, it is highly probable. I'm inclined to agree with your supposition."

Knollis gave a quiet chuckle. "I told you that he was good."

"He seems to be," commented the doctor. "Have you any further points needing my help, Inspector?"

Knollis went over the angles which he and Ellis had discussed, adding: "As Brailsford says that he heard Manchester talking with a woman, I was naturally interested in the possibility of the one left-handed person in the house being responsible—that person being a woman, of course."

"I'm with you there, Inspector," said Dr. Clitheroe. "I don't think it was committed by a left-handed person, and I am inclined to rule out the possibility of the guilty party being a woman."

"You are?" Knollis exclaimed. "On what grounds?"

"The degree of violence. I cannot bring myself to believe that any woman in that house has the necessary strength to produce such a deep wound. You do realise, Inspector, that the spine has been completely severed?"

"I have the use of my eyes," Knollis replied somewhat testily.

Dr. Clitheroe wagged a didactic finger. "If you have read of executions by decapitation—and I take it that you have?"

"I've read the memoirs of a famous French family of executioners."

"Ignore the guillotine," Dr. Clitheroe lectured on.

"Cast your mind back to the earlier decapitations by the axe. You will realise that a strong man and a long-handled axe were needed to effect a complete severance of the head from the body—a long-handled axe or a long-handled sword."

"But this murderer was intent on causing death, and not complete decapitation!" Knollis protested.

The doctor gave a gesture of despair. "I'm only trying to help you, Inspector, but I still think, as a medical man, that the only limiting factors between partial and total severance of the head are strength and leverage. Degrees of leverage are dependent only on the shortness or length of the handle of the weapon. You have a short-handled axe in this case, indicating that a powerful person was needed to wield it in such a manner as to cause such a wound. And to that you wish to add the minimum of strength—as provided by a woman. I don't agree! I can't agree!"

Knollis flashed a warning glance at Ellis. The doctor must not be further enraged. In a soothing tone he asked: "I wonder what is the length of this axe?"

"I had a look at the sergeant's notes in the dabs room," Ellis interposed. "Fifteen inches overall length, and eight and one-eighth inches from the tip of the spike to the edge of the blade."

"Thanks, Ellis," Knollis said gratefully. "You are most helpful. Fifteen inches."

"And the executioner's axe—or sword—had a handle at least a yard long!" Dr. Clitheroe remarked dryly.

Knollis grunted, much in the same way that Galileo might have done when he agreed with the Inquisition that the sun went round the earth, and not the earth round the sun.

"How about Temple?" he asked in an endeavour to change the subject.

Dr. Clitheroe smiled frostily. "Temple was in a bright state when they found him last night. They sent for me, of course, and I put him to bed. He had certainly taken a load on board!"

"Would you mind describing his general appearance?" asked Knollis. "You see, I wasn't about when they found him."

"Oh, he was just very drunk. Further to the point, the wood-shed in which they found him was very damp, and the fellow was distinctly shivery."

"Any signs of cold sweat?" Knollis asked softly.

"Hm? Cold sweat? Why, yes!"

"Did you happen to notice his eyes?"

Dr. Clitheroe pursed his lips. "Why, yes, they were slightly contracted—what are you getting at, Inspector?"

Knollis smiled. "I was merely pondering on the possibility that chloral hydrate might have been administered in his beer."

"Knock-out drops!" Ellis exclaimed. "I hadn't thought of that!"

The doctor looked from one to the other. "I don't see it. Will you kindly explain?"

"It is no more than an idea in my mind," said Knollis. "Temple was in the local for two hours, from one o'clock until three. He walked out under his own steam, and no worse, apparently, than he usually leaves the place. Nine hours later he is found in a woodshed, practically unconscious. You know, Dr. Clitheroe, I don't think that the modern brands of beer could do that to him. He would have drowned before he got drunk."

The doctor put a thoughtful hand over his mouth. "Mm! Such a possibility had not occurred to me. But with what object would dope have been given to him? Tell me that."

"I needn't insult your intelligence by asking if you know your forensic medicine," said Knollis, "but I will ask you what is the first thing that a murderer tries to do—one of the probables, that is, according to his temperament."

"Well," replied the doctor, using his hands as aids to effect, "he will try to make it look like accidental death, suicide, or death from natural causes."

"He did none of those in this case," said Knollis, "so failing that, Dr. Clitheroe . . . ?"

"Dispose of the body, of course!"

"The body is before your eyes."

"Well, that leaves one line only! He will try to foist the guilt for the commission on to someone else."

"That," said Knollis, "is the answer. Try to foist the guilt on to another person. And that leads us in a straight line—to whom? To someone else who hates him, and that someone must also be someone who is well known as a hater of the one to be killed."

"Fair reasoning," the doctor admitted.

"Simply a matter of thinking in a straight line," Knollis replied. "Now here is the theory, and it is no more than that at the moment. Someone has planned to kill Manchester. He has to provide a scapegoat. Temple is right on hand. He is a man with a grudge against Manchester, and he talks about it when he is not drunk, but just off-sober.

"That morning, Manchester had taken Temple on the carpet and given him a dressing down. Temple goes to the inn breathing fire and revenge against Manchester. Somehow, somebody dopes his beer. Temple leaves the inn. He is missing for nine hours, and is found in what appears to be a drunken stupor. And while he is both stupefied and missing, someone kills Manchester."

"And then?" the doctor asked briefly.

"The murderer says: *Ha-ha! The stupid policeman will think that Temple did it with his axe while fighting drunk, because only a few hours before he was saying that he would do him in.*"

Dr. Clitheroe laughed. "You are certainly not a stupid police-man. Your man has underestimated you."

"I hope so," said Knollis. "I may be stupid, but I am not igno-rant of the ways of killers. That is where the mistake is general-ly made. The average killer is not a professional, and he knows little or nothing about the police, while the police know a lot about the mentality of killers. There is an example of the law of averages in murder records. So many think this way; so many think that way; and a few think in a manner which is entirely individual and against the book."

"Big sticks, little sticks, and medium-sized sticks," suggested the doctor.

"Yes, but I expressed it badly," said Knollis. "Anyway, as I said, this is only a theory, and I would not dare to propound it to Colonel Mowbray. As a general rule I keep my theories strictly to myself, waiting until the evidence justifies the building of one. To be perfectly honest, we haven't yet reached that stage."

"There is a great deal more to be done?" murmured Dr. Clitheroe.

"I hate to think how much!" Knollis replied.

"Every person in that house has an alibi, of sorts. They can't all be true, and so they will have to be torn to pieces. And then we'll have to learn how the axe got from the door of the annexe to Temple's dustbin."

"You mean that the axe was seen previously?"

"By Sir Giles Tanroy. It disappeared after the murder."

The doctor shook his head. "It doesn't look too good for Temple, does it?"

"No—if circumstantial evidence is to be taken as truth. Then we want to know who was the woman heard talking to Man-chester in the Green Alley shortly before his death. And I'm very anxious to learn why Smith told a lie, and why Freeman is still weeping her eyes out. All very mysterious points."

"Think you'll see your way through them, Inspector?"

Knollis's eyes disappeared. "A mystery is only a mystery be-cause the causes of the effects you are witnessing are not immediately apparent. My job is to trace causes. And now I'd like you to come to Bowland with us and re-examine Temple."

CHAPTER VII
THE AXE OF MATTHEW TEMPLE

MATTHEW TEMPLE was lying in his bed when his visitors entered the room. He was a lean, weather-beaten fellow, with a sharp nose, red-veined cheeks, and large ears. He looked straight at Clitheroe, at the same time shielding his eyes from the light. "I've got a hell of a head!" he moaned. "Didn't think the stuff could do it to me."

"How much did you drink?" asked Knollis, easing his way round the doctor.

"Four or five pints, sir. No more, I do know, 'cause I hadn't the money on me for it." He cast an anxious glance at Dr. Clitheroe. "I'll be all right, sir?"

"You'll be all right," he was assured. "I've brought this gentleman to see you. He's from Scotland Yard, and would like to ask a few questions."

Temple screwed up his eyes against the light, and looked wonderingly at Knollis. "Scotland Yard? I don't understand, sir. What have I got to do with Scotland Yard?"

"Has nobody told you?" Knollis said softly.

"Told me what?" Temple demanded querulously.

"About your employer, Mr. Manchester."

Temple wriggled into a sitting position, and regarded Knollis with wide eyes. "Have they really got him at last—the rotten twister? Well, I always reckoned as he'd meet somebody sharper than himself in due time. He's robbed hundreds like me, and—"

"One moment, please," Knollis interrupted. "I don't think you understand. Mr. Manchester is dead." Temple jerked forward, and then clasped his head. "Oh, this head! Dead, did you say, sir? Fred Manchester dead? Then he's got away with it after all. How did it happen? Was it his heart?"

"Why his heart?" Knollis asked with deep interest.

"Them tempers of his," Temple said shortly. "I always reckoned as he'd go off in one of them. Used to swell up and go red in the face—you know."

"I'd like you to tell me," began Knollis, but the doctor interrupted him.

"Excuse me, Inspector, but I want Temple to take these tablets before he does any more talking. They will ease his head. Let me look at your eyes, Temple. Still contracted, eh? Yes, I think you were right, Inspector. I could kick myself for overlooking it."

"You weren't expecting it," Knollis replied.

Temple looked from one to the other. "What's all this about? What's been happening to me?"

Knollis sadly shook his head. "We are sadly afraid, Temple, that someone put knock-out drops in your beer. You left the inn at three o'clock, and you were out cold when you were found at midnight last night."

"But I woke in bed!" Temple protested. "About four this morning, it was. I—I thought the missus had put me to bed when I got home!"

"The police found you, and put you to bed," said Knollis. He turned to the doctor. "Look, Dr. Clitheroe, if it was chloral hydrate he would be incapable of you-know-what, wouldn't he?"

"Yes, I'll give him a clear score on that."

"Good enough," said Knollis. "Now listen, Temple, and listen carefully. I'm going to be perfectly fair with you, and I'll expect you to help me in return. Manchester was murdered in the Green Alley at twenty to six yesterday evening."

Temple stared his incredulity. "Mur-murdered? Fred Manchester murdered? But who did it?"

"That," said Knollis, "is what I want to know, and I think you can help me to solve the puzzle."

"Me, sir?" Temple gasped. "How?"

"I told you that I'd be fair with you. Well, here it comes. On the face of the evidence at present available, it looks as if the killer had tried to make it look as if you were responsible."

"But—"began Temple. He sank back among his pillows. "I don't understand. It's this head!"

"For years now," explained Knollis, "you have been threatening Manchester behind his back. That is correct, isn't it?"

Temple nodded miserably. "I suppose it is, but I never meant it that way. I'd have done him a dirty trick if I'd had half a chance, but to—to kill him! No, sir. I didn't do it!"

"I believe you," Knollis said simply. "Nevertheless, you were pulled into the affair. You left the inn at three o'clock yesterday afternoon, and were not seen again until midnight. During that time your employer was murdered. You see the way the evidence points?"

"Yes, I do see," Temple said dully.

"Now tell me; you were in possession of an axe, an official A.R.P. axe, and you were also in charge of the equipment during the war?"

"That's right, sir. As for the axe, I've used it since the post closed. It came in handy for splitting logs, and hedge-trimming, and other odd jobs." He peered at Knollis. "You mean, sir, as he was done in with my axe?"

"I'm afraid so." Knollis nodded. "We found it in your dustbin, wrapped in a newspaper."

"God Almighty!" gasped Temple. "It does look as if—as if—"

"We can't always judge by appearances," said Knollis. "Now, what morning paper do you take?"

"The *Daily Courier*, sir," Temple said absently. He was still staring blankly at the window, and the elms beyond. "My axe! God Almighty!"

"Any evening paper, Temple?" Knollis pursued. "Eh? No, sir. No evening paper."

"Do you take any local paper?"

"Only *The Weekly Record*, sir."

"A Trentingham paper," Dr. Clitheroe explained. "Who is your newsagent, Temple?"

"Keyson, at the top end of the village. So he put it in my dustbin, eh?"

"Who did?" Knollis asked quickly.

A sly look came into Temple's eyes. "Why, him that killed Manchester, o'course!"

"Who was it?" asked Knollis in a firm tone. Temple's lips formed into a stubborn line.

"Who was it?" Knollis repeated.

"I—I don't know," Temple replied lamely. "I don't know—but nobody can stop me thinking, can they?"

"Somebody managed it quite well yesterday," Knollis said dryly.

"Happen they did, but I can think to-day, and I can keep my thinking to myself."

"I thought you were going to play fair with me," Knollis said in a disappointed voice. "I wouldn't get tough if I were you, because you are in a very precarious position, and I would be quite within my rights to charge you with Manchester's death. All the circumstantial evidence points to you as the culprit."

"It wouldn't be fair for me to mention a name when I've no proof," Temple grumbled. "I'm only guessing!"

"Have it your own way," said Knollis. "I have no need to rely on your help, because I can find what I want in other quarters. Now what about the axe? Where did you keep it?"

"In the woodshed, hanging between two nails just inside the door."

"The woodshed isn't locked—ever?"

Temple shook his head. "There's no reason why it should be, because there's nothing in there that anybody would want to pinch."

"When did you last see it?"

"The axe?" Temple asked. It was only too evident that he was stalling for reasons of his own.

"The axe? Of course, the axe!" Knollis snorted. "What the devil else do you think I'm talking about?"

"I thought you might have meant the shed."

"Now suppose you give me a square answer, Temple, or I'll have to find other means of encouraging you."

"Well," Temple replied cautiously, "I seem to remember seeing it there—in the shed—yesterday morning, but I wouldn't swear to it."

"Have you any reason to use the door into the annexe? Tell me that."

Temple shook his head. "It isn't often I do use it. Mrs. Redson complains about the muck that I take in on my boots. There is an iron scraper round at the other door."

"You did not use that door yesterday morning?"

"I'm sure I didn't, sir. I'll swear to that!"

"And you are equally certain that you did not bring the axe from the shed?"

"I'd no use for it yesterday morning, sir," Temple said fervently. "So help me, I hadn't. I was mowing the lawns yesterday morning."

"Manchester bawled you out, I believe?"

"That was over the hedges," said Temple. "He said I'd neglected them, and it was only a week since I'd spent three days on them! I suppose he just felt like it—probably had a row with the missus."

Knollis suppressed an exclamation of satisfaction at the leakage of this piece of information, and said: "He had many quarrels with his wife?"

Temple chewed his bottom lip, and gave a significant nod. "I get lit up once a week, but I have less rows in a year with my missus than he had in a month with his'n. Always rowing her, he was."

"How did she take them, Temple?"

"Dam' funny to me, sir. One time I heard them rowing in the rose garden. He walked past me cursing and swearing, and she stood with her hands clasped in front of her. I had to pass her with my barrow, and I tried to look away from her, but she smiled at me—and do you know what she said?"

"I haven't an idea," Knollis assured him.

"Well," Temple said firmly, "you can believe it or not, but she said Fred is so strong and masterful!"

"Did she now," Knollis murmured. "That is most interesting."

"Unnatural to me," said Temple.

"Can you suggest any sensible and normal reason why the axe should have been left against the door of the annexe?" Knollis next asked the gardener.

"No," Temple said slowly. "There's no reason at all. I used it the day before, but I take all my tools to the shed when I finish for the day, and I know that I put that axe away! I neither left it there, nor took it there."

"Can you suggest how it got into your dustbin, wrapped in a newspaper?" Knollis continued.

"*That*," Temple said firmly, "is your job, sir. I'm a gardener, and it isn't in my line at all."

"Your head seems to be clearing," Knollis remarked. "Dr. Clitheroe's pills must be potent ones."

Temple gazed blankly at Knollis for a second or so, and then shook his head. "There's something at the back of my mind, Inspector, that should help you, but it won't come out. Perhaps it will when my head's fully right again. Hm! No, it won't come."

"I think my patient should sleep," interrupted the doctor. "Have you finished with him?"

"Completely, thanks."

"Then I'll hand him over to Denstone."

They returned downstairs after Knollis had warned Temple to say nothing about the questions he had been asked, and the doctor warned him not to leave his bed for another twenty-four hours. As they returned to their cars, the doctor said: "You know, Inspector, I rather like your bedside manner."

"There are certain similarities between our respective crafts," Knollis replied slowly. "When all is said and done, we are both seeking the necessary facts on which to base a diagnosis. I have an advantage inasmuch as I have assistants. You have to work alone."

The doctor laughed. "By the way, where is your assistant?"

"Down at Baxmanhurst, checking over the few odds and ends left over from last night."

"You are going down to Baxmanhurst now?"

"No-o," said Knollis. "I want to find the newsagent, Keyson. He may be able to help me. Do you happen to know where his shop lies?"

"I'm going back to town now," replied Dr. Clitheroe. "If you care to drive behind me I'll point out the shop as I pass—although you can't miss it in this little place."

Keyson was a slim little man with eager eyes. As Knollis talked with him he continually passed a hand through his sparse black hair. "Scotland Yard, eh? Pleased to help you if I can, Inspector. What can I do for you?"

"You deliver copies of the *Trentingham Advertiser and Courier* round the village?"

"A dozen, all told, Inspector."

"Would you mind showing me the list?"

Keyson went to a rack and took from it a black-bound book. "Here you are, Inspector."

Knollis ran a finger down the list. "Only one copy to Baxmanhurst?"

"Only the one," Keyson replied.

"Matthew Temple does not have a copy?"

"Only the *Courier*. . . ."

Knollis straightened his back. "Wait! The *Daily Courier*, or the *Trentingham Advertiser and Courier*?"

"The daily one—the London *Courier*."

"Mm!" Knollis mused thoughtfully. "Now I wonder if anyone asked him . . ."

"Yes, Inspector?" the newsagent asked anxiously. Knollis laughed. "Sorry, Mr. Keyson. I was talking to myself again, a most dangerous habit in my profession. Now look; would you mind if I was to copy this list?"

"Not at all, sir. I'll do it for you. You see, I know all the addresses, and you may need them."

"Most kind of you. Care for a cigarette while you are doing it?"

"Thank you, sir," said Keyson.

"By the way," Knollis said as if it was an afterthought. "You have no competition in Bowland?"

"No, not as yet. I'm lucky—and it does make a difference to my income, I can assure you."

"I'm sure it does," Knollis agreed. "Look, Mr. Keyson; surely this is a remarkably low figure for the circulation of the *Trentingham Courier* in Bowland?"

Keyson smiled at him. "You are forgetting the nature of the paper, Inspector. Most of my customers prefer the picture papers such as the *Reflector*, and the popular papers like the *Fortress*. The *Courier* is a kind of provincial *Times*."

"I see," said Knollis. "Tell me, Mr. Keyson: do you deliver to Baxmanhurst yourself?"

"I do, yes."

"To the front door?"

"Why, yes. I usually open the door and sling them inside. I've done so for years, even during Sir Giles's days."

"Deliver them?" asked Knollis.

The newsagent stared at him for a moment, and then laughed. "Oh, I see what you mean! Well, there are weekly periodicals as well—gardening papers, and furniture trade papers, and the women's mags which Mrs. Manchester has on the order."

"I understand," said Knollis.

A few minutes later he left with his list, and coasted down the hill to Baxmanhurst, where Ellis was awaiting him.

"How's it going, sir?" he greeted him.

"Not at all bad, Ellis. How many of the Trentingham men are here?"

"Four. Three constables and a sergeant."

"Doing what?"

Ellis laughed. "Trying to look busy and efficient. The sergeant hasn't an idea to his name."

"Well, he's going to get one," Knollis said grimly. "I've a job for his man. Where is he?"

"In the garage, drinking tea. Mrs. Redson says she will have one for you when you arrive, because the Inspector is a fair proper gentleman, and not a bit snotty."

"That is distinctly an invitation," said Knollis. "But talking of idle policemen, what have you been doing?"

"Trying to take a cast of a fraction of a foot-print against the water-butt, but it won't take. Wasted an hour on it. I've got the measurements, though. It's a male print, wide-fitting shoe."

"Good enough," said Knollis. "Come round to the garage. We'll despatch these local men on the job, and then have a *tête-à-tête* with Mrs. Redson."

The sergeant saluted when Knollis walked in, and tried to conceal a cup of tea.

"That's all right, Sergeant. Finish it, and then there is work ahead. Here is a list of all the people in Bowland who take the *Trentingham Advertiser and Courier*. I want you to beg, borrow, or steal every copy of yesterday's issue on which you can lay hands, and each one is to be marked with the name and address of the person from whom it is obtained."

"Very good, sir. We'll get working on it straight away? What about the house here?"

"I'll attend to that. You see to the other eleven." He and Ellis then invited themselves into Mrs. Redson's kitchen, and were straightway invited to be seated, and wait just half a minute.

"How is Freeman this morning?" asked Knollis.

"Better in health than temper, sir," the cook replied. "She's got something on her mind has that girl! I thought that perhaps she and Smithy had been tiffing, but it doesn't look it by the way they was hugging when I came down this morning."

"I'm interested in yesterday's *Courier*," said Knollis. "Do you think you can find me a copy?"

Mrs. Redson finished pouring the boiling water into the teapot before she answered. "We've only one copy, sir, and that will be in the sitting-room. I'll get Freeman to fetch it for you. She'll be in within a minute or so."

Knollis and Ellis were tea-drinking and cake-eating when Freeman appeared, her eyes tear-stained and her hair sadly lacking attention. Mrs. Redson sent her in search of the paper, and poured out a cup of tea in readiness for her return.

"No news about the nasty business yet, sir?" she asked.

He shook his head. "No, we are still in the dark, Mrs. Redson. I don't suppose you've any news for me."

"Now what news could I have, sir?" she demanded.

"You never know," Knollis replied. "Some of the most valuable information we receive is stuff which people did not consider important."

"There now! Would you credit it!" she exclaimed.

Knollis's features expressed the same thought as Freeman entered the kitchen with the paper in her hand. "You've got it!"

"Yes, sir. It was in the sitting-room."

"You look as if you didn't want it," Mrs. Redson commented.

Knollis looked at the date on the front page. It was yesterday's issue.

"I wasn't expecting Miss Freeman to find it," Knollis said in a puzzled tone. "You are sure that only one copy is delivered to the house, Mrs. Redson?"

"That's right, sir. Isn't it?" she asked of Freeman.

"Quite right, sir."

Knollis gulped at his tea, as if he needed a stimulant. Then he pushed the cup and saucer on the table. "There must be some mistake."

Freeman sat watching him, wonderingly. A light of comprehension came into her eyes. "You mean that you were expecting it to be missing, sir?"

"Yes, just that," replied Knollis, and suddenly added: "Why?"

"Well, I almost forgot. It was missing!"

"Wha-at?"

"Smithy brought this one in from Trentingham. You can see how creased it is with being pushed down behind the cushion in the car."

"Phew!" gasped Knollis. "Now we can start again. What happened to the copy delivered by Keyson?"

"I don't know, sir. Miss Vaughan was asking for it last night, and I remembered that Smithy had brought this and left it on this table, so I took it in to her."

"At what time was that?"

"About half an hour after—after Smithy found the Master. She said she wanted something light to take her mind off things."

"That would be about ten-past six, Miss Freeman?"

"Dead on six, sir. The wireless was pipping, just before the news."

"She was in the sitting-room then?"

"Oh yes, sir."

"And Mrs. Manchester was there as well?"

"She hadn't moved out of the room, sir."

"Hm!" said Knollis. "Thanks!"

CHAPTER VIII
THE AVERSIONS OF SMITH

SMITH WAS WASHING DOWN the car in the garage when Knollis and Ellis sought, him. He gave them a more or less cheerful good morning, and then waited as if he was expecting the questions which Knollis had prepared for him.

"I understand," began Knollis, "that you have made a statement, and signed it?"

"Yes, sir," said Smith. "The Trentingham sergeant took it earlier this morning. He read it through to me, and I signed it as a correct account of my finding of the body of Mr. Manchester."

"It was similar to the verbal statement you made to me last evening?"

Smith looked surprised. "Of course, sir. Did you expect any difference?"

Knollis shrugged his shoulders as if the question was of no importance. "I merely wondered. Witnesses very often want to amplify their statements, or find that there are parts of it which need qualifying."

"No, I don't think I do, sir," Smith replied, but he stared hard at Knollis, as if he suspected that there was something behind the mere words.

"You are sure that you don't want to change your stated reason for going round to the cactus house last night?" Knollis murmured persuasively.

Smith's eyelids flickered. "Why should I?" he demanded almost defiantly.

"Because you gave the wrong reason," Knollis replied flatly. "You know that you did."

"I—" Smith began, and then clamped his mouth tight shut.

"Suppose you give me the real reason," Knollis suggested. "I shall find out, you know, and the truth now will save much time and trouble in the long run."

Smith was recovering his balance to some extent, but being incapable of adjusting it to a nicety he became cocky in his manner. "How could I give you a wrong reason?" he demanded. "Why should I tell you a lie—as you're suggesting? I gave you the right reason."

"You could have told a half-truth, or even a misstatement, if you were wanting to shield someone—say, a girl. It has been done in the past."

"I told you the truth!" Smith replied hotly. "I don't know what you are talking about."

"Steady now," Knollis cautioned him. "I am not talking through my hat, even if you think I am. You told me last night that you went to take a look round the cactus house because the queer plants always fascinated you."

"Yes, I did, and it's the truth," Smith replied.

"You know it is not the truth. You hate cacti!"

Smith threw his car-polisher into a corner, and sought for a cigarette, which he lit, and puffed at angrily.

Knollis waited patiently.

"You know, Inspector," Smith said stubbornly; "this is a lot of rot. I do like cactuses—but even supposing I didn't, well, what difference would it make? I found Mr. Manchester, didn't I? You know yourself that I hadn't a chance to kill him even if I'd wanted to. A man's a damned fool if he kills the goose that lays the golden eggs, and Manchester was my goose."

"Oh yes, you had plenty of time," Knollis replied quietly. "You have admitted that the doctor arrived fifteen minutes after the finding of the body, and the doctor says that he had been dead about fifteen minutes before he arrived. You could have killed him and then reported the finding of the body. I am not accusing you of doing so, and to be quite frank I don't think that you did, but I do want to know what led you into the Green Alley!"

"But I've told you at least half a dozen times, Inspector!" Smith persisted. "I went to look at the cactuses."

"And yet," Knollis said very quietly, "both Mrs. Redson and Freeman say that you hated the very sight of them, and were constantly saying that they should be burned out of the way. Don't you think it is time you made up your mind whether you like them or whether you don't? You're adult now, remember!"

Smith seated himself on the running-board of the car, and looked gloomily at his toes. "So that's it! You've decided I'm lying on the strength of odd remarks made by two women."

Knollis crooked a finger. "Come with me, Smith!"

Smith followed wonderingly, Ellis bringing up the rear. Knollis led them to the cactus house.

"So you like these quaint little plants, eh?"

"I think they are—well, cute!" replied Smith. "I've taken an interest in them ever since I came to work here."

"You'll probably grow them yourself when the opportunity arises—say, when you've married Freeman and have a house of your own?" suggested Knollis.

Smith wagged his head. "I certainly shall!"

"Such an interest is admirable," said Knollis. "By the way, what do you call this one?"

"Call it?" Smith asked vacantly.

"The name of it," Knollis said subtly.

"The—the name of it?"

"The name of it. What they call it. Name, brand, type, variety, species, genus, or what have you. They must call it something!"

Knollis waited for the answer, a queer smile lurking round his lips.

"I—I don't know that particular one," Smith stammered. "Mr. Manchester bought it only a few days ago. It is a new one."

Knollis picked out a small wooden label that was pushed into the pot beside the plant. On it was the Latin name of the cactus. "This is Mr. Manchester's handwriting?"

"Yes," Smith replied feebly.

Knollis turned the label over. "The date is in the same hand-writing. He bought it two years and three months ago. Still," he sighed, "you may not have noticed it before. It is a rather insignificant plant."

"I hadn't noticed it, sir! I'm sure I hadn't!"

"Continuing this garden quiz," said Knollis, "what is the large one at the back of the staging, the one with the tiny red bud?"

"It's a—it's a—it's a," said Smith, and moistened his lips with his tongue.

"Very interesting," remarked Knollis; "I have never seen an itsa before. A most remarkable plant. It is evident that you are a keen cactus enthusiast, and know quite a lot about them. No wonder you rush here at every available opportunity to gaze on them. All right, Smith, you can go. You're a pretty poor liar, aren't you?"

They left Smith gazing at the cacti, and went back to the kitchen. Knollis smiled on Mrs. Redson, and watched Freeman closely as she helped with the preparations for lunch.

"I hope you can drive a car, Mrs. Redson," he said chattily.

She turned from the table and regarded him with astonishment. "Me? Drive a car? Why, I hardly know one end from the other, sir. I couldn't drive a scooter." Then she stared at him. "Why?"

"We—ell," said Knollis reluctantly, "it looks as if I'll have to take Smith back to Trentingham with me. Most disappointing! If only people would tell the truth!"

Freeman span round, her back against the Welsh dresser, the edge of which she clutched with her hands.

"Smithy!" she cried out. "Take Smithy! Smithy didn't do it! I swear he didn't do it. He couldn't have done it!"

"Done what?" Knollis asked with feigned surprise.

"He couldn't have killed Freddy! I swear that he couldn't! You can't take him away!"

"I'm not saying that he did kill Manchester," Knollis replied. "I'm going to charge him with obstructing the police in the execution of their duty. He's holding information, and holding up the investigation. He told me that he found Manchester by accident, and that he had walked round to the cactus house because he liked to look at them, and that they fascinated him—and yet both yourself and Mrs. Redson told me that he hated them and declared that they should be burned out of the way. I mean, it's two against one, isn't it?"

Mrs. Redson's jaw tightened. "I'm surprised at you, sir. I thought you were a gentleman, and here you go taking the words out of a woman's mouth and using them against her man!"

"Mrs. Redson," said Knollis; "a murder has been committed. This is no time for niceties of behaviour, although I always try to observe them as far as possible. I have to find out why Smith went to the Green Alley, and I intend to find out if I have to charge Smith with his death. In other words, innocent though he may be, he will have to accept the consequences of his own stubborn attitude."

Freeman left the protection of the dresser, and slowly walked across the flagged kitchen floor. "I sent him there, Inspector!"

"Now why would you do that, Miss Freeman?"

"To—to wait for me. We were going for a walk."

"Very natural explanation," Knollis commented gravely. "You think a great deal about Smith, don't you?"

"I'm in love with him," she replied simply.

Knollis nodded. "I appreciate that, Miss Freeman. You are so much in love with him that you send him to wait for you in the only spot in the grounds which he detests. Very natural! You are no better a liar than is Smith."

"But—" began Freeman, and then put her hands over her face and began to weep softly.

"Can't you leave the poor girl alone?" the cook protested angrily. "Hasn't she had enough without this?"

"Has she?" Knollis asked with innocently raised eye-brows. "Why, what else has upset her?"

Mrs. Redson stared at him for a full twenty seconds, and then banged a dish angrily on the table. "Men!"

"I'm suggesting," said Knollis, "that Smith knew what he was going to find before he went to the Green Alley—and it wasn't cacti. I'm further suggesting that you, Miss Freeman, had pre-knowledge of Manchester's death. Neither of you will tell the truth, and so I'll have to charge Smith with obstruction, and he will only have himself and you to thank for it."

Freeman flopped into a chair and bent her head to the table. "I can't tell you! I can't!"

"So there is something to tell," said Knollis.

He turned to Ellis. "I want you to slip back to town and obtain a warrant. . . ."

Freeman's tearful face was lifted from the table. "I overheard it. Neither Smithy nor me had anything to do with it."

Knollis remained silent, while Ellis made a great to-do of buttoning his coat, clearing his throat, and taking his hat from the chair where he had laid it.

"I was in the dressing-room," Freeman said slowly, "and I'm sure that Miss Dana didn't know that I was there. Mr. Brailsford came into the room. . . ."

Ellis produced a notebook as inconspicuously as possible, and Knollis said: "Yes . . . ?"

"I heard him say: 'Well, the so-and-so has got it at last. He's lying in the Green Alley with a damned great hole in his neck.'

"Miss Dana gave an exclamation, and she said: 'We'd better call the police.' Mr. Brailsford said: 'Don't be a fool, Dana. He's dead now. Let somebody else discover him—one of the staff. You don't want to be suspected, do you?' Miss Dana then said. 'Why me?' and Mr. Brailsford gave a nasty sort of a laugh and left the bedroom."

"Yes?" Knollis prompted her again.

"Miss Dana went into the bathroom then, and I slipped downstairs to see Smithy. I told him that something horrible had happened in the Green Alley, and what was to be done about it? He wanted to know what it was, and I told him that I thought somebody had killed Freddy. He wanted to know how I knew, and I wouldn't tell him because of Miss Dana. He said he would go and look on condition that I told him all I knew about it later. I promised that, and he—he went and—and found him."

"And that is the whole truth?" asked Knollis.

"That's the whole of it, sir!"

"You've caused yourself a lot of unnecessary worry by keeping this back—and put your Smithy in a very awkward position. You are certain that you've told me the full truth?"

"I've told you everything, sir!" Freeman protested. "Honest, I have."

Knollis glanced from Freeman to the cook. "Why on earth are all you people in this house keeping so quiet about the affair?"

Mrs. Redson answered his question in a quiet and dignified voice. "Because everybody hated him, Inspector Knollis. Can't you see that Freeman thought that Miss Dana was mixed up in it, and was shielding her, and that Smithy thought Freeman was mixed up in it, and was shielding *her*!"

"Oh yes, I see all that quite clearly," Knollis replied, "but I wanted to hear you or Miss Freeman say so. Now, Miss Freeman; I'll want you to sign a copy of your statement. You'll be prepared to do that?"

"Yes, sir." She nodded. "It's all the truth."

"Good enough," said Knollis. "I'll now go and put Smith out of his misery."

They returned to the garage, to find Smith sitting with his chin balanced on his hand, and his elbow on his knee.

"You can relax," said Knollis. "Miss Freeman has explained the whole affair. When I've asked you a few more questions you can go and get her story at first hand. She told you that Manchester was lying dead in the Green Alley. Is that correct?"

"She's said that?" Smith asked incredulously.

"Yes, she's said that."

Smith rose, and brightened as he did so. "Well, it is the truth of it, sir, only I didn't know but what she was mixed up in it all, and whether she was or not I was going to keep my mouth shut."

"And you had to find a reason for going to the Green Alley!"

"Well," said Smith with expressive hands, "of course!"

"Ellis," said Knollis, "go find the sergeant and get the statement that Smith signed this morning. I think we should destroy it and start again."

"You mean that you won't do anything about me making a false statement, sir?"

Knollis granted him one of his rare smiles. "Your motive was a good one, Smith, and such loyalty is rare in the world I move in. I think we can forget the first statement, but this time we'll need the truth, the whole truth, and nothing but the truth. That understood?"

Smith smiled. "Understood, sir—and thanks."

"Come back to the kitchen. We'll check on the times. Ellis— wait for me in the study when you've got that statement."

"Very good, sir," said Ellis, and departed.

Back in the kitchen, Knollis asked Freeman at what time Brailsford had entered Dana Vaughan's bedroom.

"It must have been about twenty to six," she replied.

"And how long had you been in the dressing-room?"

"Only a few minutes, sir. There is a boudoir and a dressing-room attached to the bedroom, and of course Miss Dana doesn't use the dressing-room. I keep some of my clothes in it, in a built-in wardrobe, and I was getting out the dress I was going to wear for my walk with Smithy."

"Miss Vaughan wasn't in the bedroom when you went through the dressing-room?"

"No, sir. She came in just before Mr. Brailsford knocked on the door."

"And went to the bathroom immediately after he left. So that she didn't know you were there?"

"No, sir. I don't think so, anyway."

"Mm!" Knollis murmured. "She must not get to know that you were there. Is that understood? I am telling all three of you!"

They nodded in turn.

"Can you tell me where Miss Vaughan had been previous to entering the bedroom, Miss Freeman?"

"No, sir, I'm afraid I can't."

"She was perhaps in the sitting-room with Mrs. Manchester?" Knollis suggested.

"No, sir, I know she wasn't there, because I had looked in on the way upstairs. Madame was just opening her work-basket, and she was alone."

"That is not the work-basket that is usually in her boudoir?"

"No, sir, that is a workbox."

Knollis grunted. "Now, that copy of the *Trentingham Courier*—it was usually left in the sitting-room?"

"Every day, sir," Freeman replied. "Mr. Manchester used to read it over breakfast, and then I would take it to the sitting-room."

"No other daily paper entered the house?"

"None, sir."

"So that, guests or no guests, Manchester was in the habit of reading over breakfast?" asked Knollis.

"He used to read it aloud," replied Freeman.

"Charming manners!" commented Knollis.

"He had the manners of a pig—or he hadn't," interposed Mrs. Redson, "and I'm not sure which it was. That was him all over—no thought for anybody else but himself."

"Now I want you to think carefully," Knollis said to Freeman. "When do you last remember seeing that particular copy of the paper?"

"Well," she said slowly, "it was there at teatime, because I went in to tidy up while they were finishing tea."

"That would be at what time?"

"About ten to a quarter-past four. Tea is served at four o'clock in the dining-room."

"Formal tea, or afternoon tea?" asked Knollis.

"Afternoon tea—served on the wagon."

"The Manchesters seem to have some queer ideas," Knollis remarked dryly.

"You're telling us!" commented Mrs. Redson.

"And you can swear that the paper was in the sitting-room then?" Knollis asked keenly.

"Yes, sir, I can swear to that, because I had a look at it. There was a fashion article I was interested in."

"We're getting somewhere at last," said Knollis, "thanks to a little co-operation. Now more careful thinking, please. Can you say for sure whether either Miss Vaughan or Mr. Brailsford went in the sitting-room after tea?"

"They both went in with Madame after tea was finished," replied Freeman.

"The time?"

"Half-past four."

"Now," said Knollis, "Mr. Manchester was at home for tea, was he not? At what time did he leave for Trentingham?"

"I can help you there," said Smith, taking a step forward. "It was twenty to five by the hall clock. We got to town about ten to five, and made one call before driving round to the Guildhall."

Knollis turned back to Freeman. "Did Mr. Manchester go into the sitting-room?"

"No, sir, he went to the bathroom, and then straight out to the car. Didn't he, Smithy?"

Smithy smiled. "I can't say. I wasn't in the house."

Knollis grinned. "That is good enough. Cheer up, I've nearly finished with you all. I'm now interested in the hour after half-past four. Can either of you two ladies tell me the movements of the three remaining members of the household during that hour?"

"Excuse me, sir," said Smith. "Could you tell me why you are so interested in that paper?"

"I can, and I will," Knollis replied pleasantly. "The axe was wrapped in it, and thrown into Temple's dustbin. I'm trying to find who took it from the house."

"Then it is possible for the paper to have been taken after he was killed, sir—that is, a long time after?"

"Think it out for yourself, Smith," said Knollis. "Your young lady will corroborate the fact that Mrs. Manchester never left the sitting-room after being informed of her husband's death, so that whoever went in to take the paper would have been under the necessity of conjuring it away without her noticing it—a very risky proceeding if the killer intended the axe to be found in Temple's dustbin. Further to the point, the body and the place where it lay could not have been left unattended for more than a few minutes after you discovered it. No, Smith, the paper was filched before the killing, and kept in readiness on the killer's person."

"Yes, I see, sir." Smith nodded.

"I've been thinking about your question, sir," said Freeman. "Neither Miss Vaughan nor Mr. Brailsford stayed in the sitting-room for more than a few minutes. Both went to their own rooms."

"Thanks," said Knollis. "We've nearly finished. Did you, Miss Freeman, see Miss Vaughan between her leaving the sitting-room and you being present in the dressing-room when Mr. Brailsford called on her?"

"No, sir, I can't say that I did."

"And Mr. Brailsford?"

"I saw him twice. Once on the landing as I was going up the back stairs—"

"What was he doing?" Knollis interrupted sharply.

"We-ell," Freeman replied, "he looked as if he was about to go down the back stairs. He was leaning over the banisters when I got to the top. He grinned at me in that awful way he has, and said he hoped it was a burglar when he heard me start up the stairs, because it needed something to liven the place up."

"And the second time?" queried Knollis.

"He was in the hall when Smithy brought Mr. Manchester back from town. He said to me: 'Looks as if the Big Noise is home again. I'll skip out of the way.'"

"Hm!" said Knollis. "I thought he was supposed to be Manchester's personal friend?"

"He was, sir," said Freeman, "but earlier in the day I overheard him telling Mr. Manchester to dry up about the cat and the budgie and not be a beastly bore."

"I understand," said Knollis, "that on the morning of his death, which was yesterday of course, Mr. Manchester left the breakfast-table saying that he was expecting a telephone call. Do you know whether he received it?"

"That was Sunday, sir, and not yesterday," Freeman corrected him.

Knollis consulted his notebook. "Quite right; so it was. Still, did he get the call?"

"Not to my knowledge, sir, and I was backwards and forwards through the hall, serving the meal."

"Was Mr. Manchester—well, hovering round the telephone? You know, as if he was expecting it?"

"I saw him twice, sir."

"How many times did you go through the hall in one direction—say from the kitchen to the dining-room? Can you remember, or guess?"

"Oh, at least six or seven times, sir."

"And you saw him twice?"

Freeman's forehead developed a row of creases. "I don't understand, sir?"

"I'll try to help you." Knollis smiled. "You saw him twice, and yet he was not at breakfast on the four, five, six, or seven occasions when you entered the room?"

"No-o, he wasn't, sir. I hadn't thought of that before."

"And this was the morning on which the budgerigar was found dead in Mrs. Manchester's boudoir?"

Freeman stared. "You mean, sir, that it was him!"

"Now, now!" Knollis corrected her. "I never said anything of the kind. I believe you also told me that Miss Vaughan was late down to breakfast?"

Freeman considered the point. "No," she said at last, "I didn't tell you that, sir, although she was late."

Knollis again pretended to consult his notes. "Oh no, it was Mrs. Manchester who told me that. She also said that her husband was fetched to the 'phone."

Freeman shook her head vigorously. "He was not fetched, sir. He looked at his watch as I was serving the porridge, and rose from the table saying that he was expecting a call."

"Rather unusual for a Sunday morning, surely?" suggested Knollis.

"I suppose so," Freeman said in a puzzled tone. "I've never known him get calls so early on a Sunday."

Smith appeared to be as puzzled as Freeman, judging by his expression. "Inspector?" he said.

"Well?" murmured Knollis.

"That paper? Who could have taken it from the sitting-room?"

"There's only one person for it," Knollis replied vaguely, "and I know who it was!"

Smith opened his mouth in awe. "Oh!"

CHAPTER IX
THE INNOCENCE OF BRAILSFORD

DESMOND BRAILSFORD was not pleased to see either Knollis or the inevitable Ellis as they entered his room. The corners of his mouth took a downward curve, and there was a lowering of his truant eye. "Questions again?" he asked.

"The sooner they are asked, the sooner they are done with," Knollis replied cheerfully. "This is merely the routine check-up on statements See, where did you say you were at the time of Manchester's death? In your bedroom?"

"I told you that," Brailsford replied, "and I told you about hearing the voices under my window."

"You had your window open, of course?" Knollis suggested.

"Why, yes, the top sashes of both windows were well down. Otherwise I don't suppose I should have heard the voices at all."

"Quite," said Knollis. He glanced at his notebook. "You heard a voice like a woman's under the window. That was before Manchester was killed, of course?"

"Oh yes," Brailsford replied, and glanced suspiciously at the two detectives.

"Where were you when Manchester was killed?" Brailsford stared. "I—well, I must have been here, mustn't I?"

"That," Knollis said easily, "is what I want to find out. You heard the voices beneath the window, and yet, strangely enough, never heard a sound while Manchester was· being murdered. I find that rather queer, Mr. Brailsford. In fact I refuse to believe it. At what time did you hear the voices?"

"A few minutes after half-past five."

"Good enough," said Knollis. "The next time you went downstairs you were informed of Manchester's death?"

"Er—yes." Brailsford hesitated for a fraction of a second before making the reply.

"Who informed you that Manchester was dead?"

"Smith, the chauffeur."

"And you were in this room for the whole of the time previous to Smith informing you?"

"Yes. Haven't I made that clear?" Brailsford demanded heatedly.

"No," Knollis said flatly.

"I don't understand," complained Brailsford.

"I don't understand your story myself," said Knollis. "You heard voices at half-past five, and apparently closed your ears for the next twenty minutes, neither hearing Manchester being struck down, nor Smith finding the body. That strikes me as queer."

Brailsford's twisted mouth developed a leer. "That's the way it is, and I can't do anything about it, can I?"

"Oh yes, you can do much more," said Knollis. "You can tell me how you came to discover the body."

"Dis—cover the body? But Smith discovered the body, Inspector!"

Knollis flicked over the pages of his notebook.

"Hm! According to information that has been placed at my disposal, you went to Miss Vaughan's room about twenty to six, and the following conversation ensued . . ."

He read the facts as related by Freeman, but without stating their source. He then put the book in his pocket and said: "Well?"

"I—I—" said Brailsford, and then made for the door exclaiming: "Dana's done this—the double-crossing bitch!"

Ellis nimbly stepped between Brailsford and the door, smiling at him. "I wouldn't leave just yet, sir. I don't think the Inspector has finished speaking to you."

"You can't get away with this!" stormed Brailsford.

"Whether I can, or whether I can't, please attend to the Inspector," smiled Ellis.

Brailsford turned on Knollis. "You are trying to work something across me. You are trying to suggest that I did him in. Well, I didn't, but I'm glad that somebody did. I know nothing about it!"

Knollis smiled on him, and turned to the window on the north wall. He first examined the sill, and then tried to push up the lower sash, which refused to be moved. He next pulled down the top sash, but it came down a mere fifteen inches all told.

"Rather high windows," he commented. "Even standing on the sill I would not be able to see over the top sash and down into the Green Alley. I also notice that your bedroom chairs are considerably lower than the sills. Deduction? That you didn't discover Manchester's body by looking from the window. Therefore you either went downstairs to the Green Alley, or were told by a second person."

He looked straight into Brailsford's eyes. "By withholding information you become an accessory after the fact, and as such liable to prosecution. You knew that Manchester's body was lying under your window, didn't you?"

Brailsford took a loose match from his pocket, broke it in halves, and chewed them viciously. "You're making it devilish awkward for me!"

"I haven't really started yet," Knollis said happily. "You'll be surprised what I can do when I get warm. Now suppose you give me the full story—unless you would care to accompany me to Trentingham."

Brailsford glowered. "What do you want to know?"

"Where were you between half-past twelve and half-past one yesterday noon?"

Brailsford jumped as Knollis shot the unexpected question at him.

"I—why, I was in the house. It was lunch-time. Freeman, Redson, or Smith can prove that."

"And between one-thirty and three o'clock?"

"I went for a walk in the village—to the newsagent's as a matter of fact. I wanted some magazines."

"Surely the house supplies them for guests?" Knollis enquired.

Brailsford rolled his eyes in a manner that indicated that he was sick of silly questions. "I wanted my own type of magazines, not caring to read furniture-trade journals and gardening papers."

"You do drink?" said Knollis.

"Yes, moderately. Why?"

"I merely wondered," Knollis replied. "So you went down the back stairs after hearing Manchester being killed, and rushed into the Green Alley to find his body?"

"I never said that!" Brailsford protested.

Knollis smiled soothingly. "No, you didn't say so, but that is what happened, isn't it?"

"You are wrong, Inspector. I wouldn't have gone down the back stairs in any case. Definitely against all the etiquette of the house."

"I'm not supposed to know that," said Knollis. "I'm only a detective."

"Of course," Brailsford said leniently.

Ellis grinned, and winked at Knollis.

"So you came down the main stairs, along the passage, through the annexe, and out into the Green Alley. Is that more like it?"

"Well—yes," Brailsford admitted reluctantly. "And there he lay, smothered in blood. I was going to him when I heard retreating footsteps behind me, and turned to see someone vanishing behind the house. I rushed to the corner, but he had gone."

"Interesting!" said Knollis. "You heard footsteps on the grass!"

"Well, I did!" Brailsford said defiantly.

"And you say the person was a man?"

"I think so, anyway."

"That's very queer," said Knollis. "You heard a woman speaking to Manchester, heard sounds which make you curious, and rush down to see a man rushing from the scene. Anyway, we can ignore that temporarily. Which way did he go?"

Brailsford shook his head. "I don't know, Inspector. I can only suggest that he went in the house by the back door."

"There's no back door," said Knollis. "Try again." Brailsford assumed an expression of innocence. "There isn't? Well, that is surprising, but of course I wouldn't know, because if there is one it would be in the staff quarters, and one doesn't go in them, near them, or round them. Definitely not done."

"Really!" said Knollis. "As he didn't go into the house through a doorway that wasn't there, can you make any other suggestions which may help me?"

"Well," Brailsford said cautiously, "he could have gone into the woodshed at the back of the house—it is against the boundary wall on the west side."

Knollis nodded solemnly. "Perhaps you have something there. Very useful suggestion, Mr. Brailsford, if I might say so."

"Oh well, if I can be of any use . . ."

"You didn't pursue this fellow?" Knollis murmured. "Rather queer, surely?"

"Well," said Brailsford with an uneasy laugh, "I suppose it does look that way now, but what with the shock of finding Fred, and the hope that he was still alive, and that I could do something for him—well, you must see for yourself . . ."

"Of course! Of course!" Knollis appeared to agree. "There was Fred. He was dead? I mean he didn't give you any last-minute message, or anything like that?"

Brailsford regarded Knollis suspiciously, but he was perfectly serious to all appearances. Brailsford shook his head, very sadly. "He was dead as the proverbial door-nail, Inspector. He never said a word."

"Too bad!" Knollis murmured.

Brailsford leered, or perhaps he only smiled. "I didn't know what to do, and so I dashed upstairs to consult Miss Vaughan."

"Using the main stairs, I hope," said Knollis.

"Oh yes, naturally!"

"You know," remarked Knollis, "I can always admire a man who can respect the conventions even during fearful stress. It marks him out as a gentleman."

"Well," Brailsford sniffed, "if it's bred in one! I mean, you just don't notice because you wouldn't think of acting in any other way."

"Quite so," said Knollis. "I envy your advantages. Now you consulted Miss Vaughan. May I ask why you went to her?"

Brailsford fumbled for a reply. "We-ell, you see, Inspector, she's been mixed up with murder—on the stage—for three and a half years, and I thought she might know something about what one does on such occasions."

"And she couldn't help you?"

"Well, she suggested that we send for the police."

Knollis nodded. "A sensible suggestion. And you opposed the idea, hinting that she herself might be suspected. Peculiar remark to pass to her after asking her advice, surely? Are you certain that you went to ask her advice?"

"What else could I have gone for?"

"That is where I am interested," said Knollis. "We will ignore that for a time. Why should Miss Vaughan stand in danger of being suspected?"

Brailsford shuffled, and made a good pretence of being embarrassed by the question. "Oh come, Inspector! You can't expect me to answer questions of that nature!"

"I can," said Knollis, "and I am waiting for the reply. Why should she be suspected? She hadn't been downstairs—or had she?"

"As a matter of fact, she had," Brailsford replied slowly. "She went down to find Tanroy, but he had gone. Now whether she saw Fred while she was down is something I can't say, and I'm not going to guess, nor have such an eventuality suggested to me."

"Very wise!" Knollis remarked quietly.

"The main trouble with having Dana mixed up in the finding of the body was her illness," Brailsford went on. He spoke reluctantly, as if the information was being forced from him under pressure. "You'll know all this, or I wouldn't mention it. Her sleep-walking, and all that, and those waking dreams she had before she packed up. I mean, it all looks so horrible for her, doesn't it?"

"It does! It does!" Knollis murmured sympathetically.

"I mean," continued Brailsford; "there was a hell of a row after she tried to strangle her maid, and it was only influence and wangling that persuaded the maid not to make a case of it."

"Terrible!" commented Knollis. "It must be quite disturbing to live in the same house with her."

"I always keep my door locked at night." Brailsford laughed. "I take no risks whatsoever."

"I can well believe that," said Knollis pointedly. "By the way, I take it that you are prepared to make a statement with regard to the finding of the body, and to sign it?"

"If it will help you, yes."

"Decent of you," said Knollis. "You won't forget to mention the man who vanished behind the house?"

"Oh dear, no! I suppose that is vital?"

"You'd be surprised," said Knollis.

He looked across to the door. "Ellis! Will you see if you can force up that lower sash? It's only a test," he assured Brailsford.

Ellis passed over to the window, and grunted and pushed manfully, but all to no purpose.

"Perhaps Mr. Brailsford will help you?" Knollis suggested.

Brailsford was only too willing. While his back was turned, Knollis extracted a cigarette from his own case, and polished the silver surface with his handkerchief.

"Oh, never mind! Leave the darn thing, Ellis."

As Brailsford turned away from the window Knollis extended his case with a muttered apology. "Do help yourself, Mr. Brailsford! I forgot my manners!"

Brailsford fell for the oldest trick in the detective's repertoire, and handed the case back, complete with his finger-prints. Knollis dropped it in his pocket. "Thanks for your help, Mr. Brailsford. We have had a useful chat, but I must ask you to keep to yourself everything we have talked about. You will appreciate the reason."

Brailsford laid a finger to the side of his nose. "You trust me, Inspector!"

As Ellis closed the door behind them he said: "Mm!"

"Mm!" Knollis echoed.

"What about him?" asked Ellis.

"I'd like to take hold of the back of his neck and kick his behind," said Knollis. Then he smiled. "It isn't often I get so vicious, is it? Oh well, let's have another chat with Miss Vaughan. To-night, you will take the London train, conveying my cigarette case with you. You will see if he is in the records, and also find Miss Vaughan's late maid, and her doctor. If the doctor won't come clean with you, ask either Inspector Burnell or Inspector Frecklehurst to take over at that end—seeing the Super first! I want the whole of Miss Vaughan's case-history, and I won't take anything less. Got that, Watson?"

"Every bit, sir," replied Ellis. "There is a question in my mind."

"Got an idea?" asked Knollis. "Let's have it."

"Have you noticed that the people in this house only meet at meal-times?"

Knollis's expression was a queer one as he stared at his sergeant. "Do you know, Ellis, that I hadn't noticed it—but you are quite right!"

He seated himself on a linen chest and grunted. "Now I wonder why that is? Interesting!"

"You did say," Ellis pointed out, "that Freeman and Smithy were the only two people in the house who loved each other."

Knollis nodded. "Yes, I did! I hadn't taken the notion any further. I observed, and didn't reflect, which isn't a bit like me. Well, thanks for the notion, Ellis. I'm grateful. I'll think about it, as I'll do with Brailsford's phoney story."

"You ribbed him very nicely, sir."

Knollis allowed himself a smile. "I'm going to write a book one day, Ellis. I shall call it *How to Twist Friends and Flannel People.* Poor old Brailsford sucked it up like a sponge—or did he? He's deep, Ellis, deep as the very devil. You know, he's provided us with one of the worst dilemmas we meet in this game."

"Such as?" Ellis asked laconically.

"The lack of an alibi. If there is anything worse than an alibi which proves that your man wasn't there, it is the lack of evidence proving that he was there when he has no alibi at all."

"Yes," Ellis agreed. "There is a chance of breaking down an alibi, but you're completely beaten when you haven't a witness of any sort."

Knollis rose. "Miss Vaughan, Ellis."

He walked to her door, and knocked upon it. It was opened by Freeman.

"Ah, Freeman the ubiquitous!" Knollis greeted her.

"That doesn't sound nice," she retorted.

"I assure you that it is nice," Knollis said in reply. "Can I see Miss Vaughan, please?"

"I'll ask, sir, if you'll wait a minute."

Miss Vaughan deigned to see them. She laid her novel face down on the divan, and once more became an actress with a scene to be played.

"You wish to speak to me?" she asked vaguely.

"Er—yes," Knollis replied lamely. "You see, Mr. Brailsford tells me that he found Manchester's body, and came to ask your advice about what he should do with it. You can verify his statement?"

He saw Freeman start, but he also saw Ellis catch her eye and give her a comforting wink.

"Yes," Dana Vaughan replied, "if he says that I can verify it, Inspector. He did come to see me, about twenty minutes to six it would be."

"He also tells me that you went down to the Green Alley some time previously to look for Sir Giles Tanroy. Is that statement correct?"

Her nostrils suddenly became pinched, and it was only too obvious that she was trying to control herself. "He—told—you—that!" she said slowly.

"He did, Miss Vaughan. My sergeant was a witness to the statement. I presume that he was correct?"

"Sir Giles? No, no! I didn't see him."

"Ah!" sighed Knollis. "In that case, we may assume that it was you whom Mr. Brailsford heard talking to Mr. Manchester under his window!"

Dana Vaughan jumped to her feet, her eyes shining indignantly. "I didn't go down to the Green Alley, Inspector. I never left this room. Freeman—you were with me all the time, were you not?"

Freeman, thus appealed to, looked from Dana Vaughan to Knollis, and thence to Ellis. "I—I wasn't here all the time, Miss Dana. You know that I wasn't!"

"But you were, Freeman. You were!"

"Please make up your minds," Knollis said impatiently. "Miss Freeman has made one statement which accounts for all her movements between four o'clock and six o'clock, and nowhere in that statement does she mention spending more than a few minutes in your company. Did you, or did you not, go down to the Green Alley, Miss Vaughan? And I must have a truthful answer."

She drew herself up with regal indignation. "You dare to suggest that I should be guilty of a lie!"

"Not necessarily a lie," Knollis replied diplomatically. "A half-truth, or an evasion, or even a mistake. Now you did go down to the Green Alley?"

She hesitated, for perhaps a second, and then lowered her head gracefully. "Yes, I did, Inspector. I went down about five minutes past five, and returned some time later."

"Then you saw Sir Giles?"

"No, I did not."

"May I ask how you passed the time before you returned to this room, Miss Vaughan?"

"I cannot answer that question, Inspector. My movements, as you call them, can have no bearing whatsoever on the matter you are investigating."

Knollis bowed his head. "Perhaps you will answer one other question. On Sunday morning last, did you happen to call in Mrs. Manchester's bedroom on your way down to breakfast?"

"I did, Inspector, in the hope of catching Mrs. Manchester and going down with her."

"I see," said Knollis. "I suggest that she was not there?"

"She was not."

"You were the last down for breakfast? Is that correct, Miss Vaughan?"

"That is also correct, Inspector."

Knollis took out his notebook, and consulted it.

"Am I correct in assuming that the budgerigar was dead when you were in the room?"

Dana Vaughan shook her head. "The budgerigar was not dead, Inspector. It was enjoying an early morning bout of liveliness."

"You actually saw the bird?" asked Knollis.

"Yes, I went through to the boudoir when I saw that Mrs. Manchester was not in the bedroom, and the bird was in its cage, and quite happy."

"And," said Knollis, "you will pardon the implications of this question, but was it alive when you left?"

"I do not kill pet birds, nor anything else, Inspector!" she replied loudly.

"Thank you," said Knollis. "Do you happen to walk in your sleep, Miss Vaughan?"

"I have never been aware of doing so," she replied with a puzzled frown. "Why do you ask?"

"And you have never suffered from loss of memory?"

"Me? An actress, Inspector!"

Knollis smiled. "It would seem incredible, would it not, Miss Vaughan? Nevertheless, I have good reasons for asking you."

"You ask very impertinent questions, Inspector."

Knollis nodded as he turned to the door. "Yes, Miss Vaughan, but you must remember that Death has no manners as a general rule. In this instance he was a reformed character, and knocked twice before entering."

CHAPTER X
THE CURIOSITY OF KNOLLIS

KNOLLIS LUNCHED in Trentingham, and then went to the Guildhall to report to Colonel Mowbray. The Chief Constable was showing signs of anxiety, and asked with some exasperation in his voice if Knollis was any nearer to a solution of the case.

"We are still in the fact-finding stages of the case," Knollis replied quietly. "This is the stage where we are only possessed of facts, lies, and mistaken impressions all supplied without labels, and mixed up in one box for the poor detective to sort out. I'll give you what I have at the moment. May I borrow your ruler and a sheet of paper?"

He took out a pencil and drew a square, and a compass indication beside it. On the north side of the square he drew a small oblong.

"This is supposed to be Baxmanhurst," he said with a smile, "even if it is not recognisable as such. To save confusion, and more work, I'll shade the upstairs rooms that are vitally concerned; that is, the bedroom on the north-east corner, and the next one to it, which is Dana Vaughan's three-in-one suite. The sitting-room lies directly beneath those shaded rooms. Here is the cactus house. This is the garage, and here we have the woodshed. X, as usual, will mark the spot where the body was found."

"That's quite clear," said the Chief Constable.

"Now according to the original statements," Knollis explained, "Mrs. Manchester was in the sitting-room under those two bedrooms. Brailsford was in his own room on the corner, and the Vaughan woman was also in her own room. Smith was in the kitchen, with Mrs. Redson. Freeman was either in the kitchen, on her way to Miss Vaughan's room, or actually in that room. Temple was unconscious in the woodshed, and—oh yes, Sir Giles was on his way home through the hurst, which lies to the south of the house, and is a quarter of a mile long and two hundred yards wide."

"So, on the face of it, all the people of the house were safely disposed?" the Chief Constable remarked.

"That is the way it looks," said Knollis, putting emphasis on the last word.

"Have you taken into account the possibility of a stranger having done the job?"

"I have," Knollis said frankly, "and I am still satisfied that one of those six people killed him."

"Seven," the Chief Constable corrected.

"Count Freeman out, sir. She's the only person who couldn't have done it."

The Chief Constable fiddled with his monocle. "Six suspects, eh? That makes it rather hard going, Inspector!"

"It looks tough until we start checking the statements, and then we find that the original view has to be modified. The modifications are the result of this morning's work."

The Chief Constable edged forward in his seat. "Come on, man. Let's have the story."

"We start with the morning paper in which the axe was wrapped," said Knollis. "In fact we can start with the axe itself, because it is going to be the eventual means of getting our man—or woman." ·

"But Clitheroe says that a woman couldn't have swung the thing!" protested the Colonel.

Knollis laughed shortly. "Wasn't it Napoleon who said that the word *impossible* was only to be found in the vocabulary of fools?"

The Chief Constable looked surprised. "True! True! You are a wide reader, Inspector?"

"So-so," Knollis replied casually.

"Hm! We'll assume then that a woman could have killed him. What comes next?"

"Here is the picture as I see it at the moment, sir. Smith brings Manchester back from town to Baxmanhurst. Manchester is expecting a visit from Sir Giles. Now Sir Giles has already arrived, and has walked round to the cactus house to pass the time. That is five-ish. He gets fed up with waiting, and walks off through the hurst, so that when Manchester seeks him he is not to be found. Miss Vaughan admits, now, that she went down to the Green Alley, and refuses to give a reason or to state how she passed the time—that is a blank we have to fill in for ourselves."

"Interesting point, that," said the Chief Constable.

"Here is a more interesting one," went on Knollis. "Brailsford says that he heard voices under his window just before the time we have assessed for Manchester's death. In his own words: *Someone was talking under my window round about*

*the time that Fred was killed. One was definitely Fred's. The
other sounded like a woman's voice."*

"That surely coincides with the Vaughan hiatus."

"It appears to do so," Knollis replied ambiguously. "At a
quarter to six, Brailsford entered Vaughan's room and told her
that Manchester was dead. He advises her to let a member of
the staff find the body, adding significantly that she surely does
not want to be suspected. That suggests to me that Brailsford is
satisfied in his own mind that it was Vaughan who was talking
to Manchester. I have examined the windows, and found that
Brailsford could not have seen the body from his room. Therefore, he must have gone down to the Green Alley. He admitted
this after a certain amount of pressure had been brought to bear
upon him. He also asserts that he saw a man vanishing round
the back of the house, that he was so upset that he did not give
chase, and that he slunk back to his room, warned Vaughan, and
otherwise kept quiet."

"Freeman was in the dressing-room, unknown to Vaughan,
and overheard the conversation. She appears to be devoted to
Vaughan, and had no intention of giving her away if she was
mixed in the affair, so she went down to the garage and told
Smith that there was something horr—"

"Something nasty in the woodshed?" the Chief Constable
chuckled.

"This is Baxmanhurst, sir, not Cold Comfort Farm," Knollis
reminded him. "No, she had heard that there was something
horrible in the Green Alley, and would he please 'discover' it for
her, and not let anybody know that she was aware of its presence. She was scared stiff, and would not tell him how she had
come to learn about it. Smith discovers the body, and rings for
us and the doctor."

"A clear enough picture—or is it?" asked the Colonel.

"The colours overlap," said Knollis, "and they have to be sep-
arated so that we can assess the true value of each. On the face
of it, Temple is responsible, and yet according to all the medical
evidence available he was out, stone cold."

"Brailsford could have done it," said the Chief Constable. "Yes, he could have killed Manchester when he went down."

Knollis nodded. "I've thought of that, sir, but if he is the guilty party he left himself remarkably open. Why didn't he arrange an alibi for himself? It would have been fairly easy."

"Quite so. There is that objection. So at the moment Temple is our star turn?"

"No, I don't think so," Knollis replied. "He may be causing us the most trouble."

"What about the axe and the newspaper?"

"Ah, the axe!" Knollis exclaimed. "That is interesting. It wandered from the woodshed to the annexe door, and from the Green Alley to Temple's dustbin. If anybody can explain who conducted it on those two journeys I can complete the case—providing that it is also explained who took the copy of the newspaper from the sitting-room. Freeman says it was there at tea-time, because she was tidying up, and read an article in it. After tea, it was missing, and she commandeered Smith's copy to replace it. Now Brailsford and Vaughan were in the room together after tea, and I don't want to ask either of them if they saw the other pick it up, because of starting a train of thought which might develop against us."

"Yes, I see," said the Chief Constable. "Either of them might warn the other."

"There is one other peculiar point," went on Knollis. "If the axe was placed in Temple's dustbin, as we know it was, then how the deuce did anyone but Temple manage to put it there? Surely Mrs. Temple would have been suspicious if she had seen one of, say, the guests messing about round her out-offices?"

The Chief Constable stared moodily at his pipe, and slowly filled it from the humidor. "The thing looks horribly complicated, Inspector. I'm beginning to think that Manchester was right when he said that my men weren't up to such an investigation—although he didn't know then that his corpse would be the centre of attraction. By the way, Inspector; what about those silk cords?"

"Not a darned thing," said Knollis in a disgusted voice. "They were taken from Mrs. Manchester's work-box, and that is all I know about them."

"You think they hold any significance?"

"They suggest nothing that has come within my experience," Knollis said with complete frankness, "and yet I am sure that there is a significance. They were blue, they were silken, and they were appropriate lengths for the necks they surrounded. Why Manchester's was crammed into his pocket, I cannot conceive—although of course the bloody state of his neck would have obscured the colour. I wonder if that has any meaning?"

His voice trailed away, and his eyes vanished behind narrowed lids. "Yes, that may be it," he said after a minute or so.

"What might be what?" demanded the Chief Constable.

Knollis awoke. "Look, sir! If the cord had been placed round Manchester's neck, the effusion of blood would have dyed it. It would have been red instead of blue."

"Yes?" murmured the Chief Constable.

"In which case the blue colour must be the vital factor. The significance lies in the colour. Now what the devil is it?" he demanded testily. "I need a Brewer."

The Chief Constable stared. "If you need a drink to stimulate your brain . . ."

Knollis made a gesture of impatience. "I mean Brewer's *Dictionary of Phrase and Fable*. That might help."

The Chief Constable spoke into the blower. "Have you got a copy of—what is it, Inspector?"

Knollis repeated the title.

The Chief Constable gave it, and waited. He lifted the switch. "They are bringing a copy."

When it appeared, Knollis thumbed the pages over until he reached *Blue*.

"*Blue-Apron Statesman, Blue-bag, Blue beans, Key, Billy, Blood, Boar*—there's everything blue here from apes to zephyrs. *Chickens, John, Murder, Peter, Flyer, Ribbon*—we may be getting warm. *Cordon bleu*, term used to denote the highest honour attainable in any profession or walk of life. That takes us to Blue Blood again. Now I wonder . . ."

"Yes, Inspector?"

"Nothing, sir," replied Knollis. "I was just wondering about an idea. . . ."

"I noticed it," the Chief Constable replied dryly. Knollis looked up and smiled. "Sorry if I am in a provoking mood, but when I get an idea I like to mull over it. It seems to disappear if I talk about it."

He stared keenly at the Colonel. "Yes, I think I've got something—two somethings, if you know what I mean."

The Chief Constable repolished his monocle and fixed it in his eye. "I enjoy working with you, Inspector! You are so interesting. Of course, you don't have to take me into your confidence if you don't want to do so."

Knollis was not aware of the Chief Constable's sarcasm. An idea was teasing him, and he was far away from Trentingham's Guildhall. He suddenly rose, and grabbed his hat. "I'll be back later, sir," he said perfunctorily, and hurried down the stairs to the car which was constantly at his disposal. Ellis was idling at the wheel, and looked up with a quizzical expression as Knollis strode across the pavement.

"Something doing, sir?"

"Drive me out to Knightswood, Ellis," said Knollis. "I think I've got hold of something."

Ellis knew better than to ask questions when Knollis was in his present mood. He drove out to Knightswood, turned down the red gravelled drive, and pulled up outside a house so much like Baxmanhurst that it was difficult to believe that they had not been built from the same plans. Sir Giles walked across the lawns to meet them as they stepped from the car.

"Hello, Inspector!" he greeted Knollis. "I had an idea that you would want to see me again. My movements were not very satisfactorily explained, were they?"

"If you mean that they were suspicious," said Knollis, "I am not with you. The only unsatisfactory point about your statement was that you didn't tell me the full story."

Sir Giles played with the silk scarf that was twisted round his neck. He was handsome, although it was doubtful whether he was aware of the fact, and Knollis liked him for his frank smile and direct eyes.

"I didn't tell you all, eh?" he said. "So that's it, Inspector. What did I miss out. I'll help all I can, and I do mean that."

"Then you'll let me question you in my own way, and not resent it," said Knollis.

"Why should I resent it?"

"Why should you, indeed?" Knollis replied. "Now, Sir Giles, I'd like to know how you feel about those people living in Baxmanhurst."

Sir Giles offered his cigarettes, and when the three men were smoking he stared at his shoes for a moment, and then suddenly raised his head to look straight at Knollis.

"I don't like it! I don't like the times. I'm twenty-nine, and this thing has been working-up for generations before my birth. It's a social revolution, or so we have learned to call it. I suppose it started with Wat Tyler and all the other village Hampdens, and is just reaching its culminating point. I'm depressed about it, too, because I can't see where it is going to end.

"And what does it amount to? Simply that one aristocracy has given place to another. An aristocracy of birth and manners has given place to one of money and dictatorial power. I wonder if you see what I am driving at, Inspector? These people like Manchester have been yelping at our heels for hundreds of years—they weren't sturdy enough to bark—and now they have turfed us out of our homes, and collared our heritages, they are trying to live exactly as they accused us of living—the same old ways which they affected to despise. Does that sound snobbish?"

"Please go on," Knollis said quietly.

"Well, if it does, it does. It's all a matter of angle, or what the Americans call *slant*. As I see it, we've been twisted. For all these years these people have been trying to hound us out—but I've said that, haven't I? It's the French Revolution all over again, bloodless, fortunately, but nevertheless the French Revolution with all the same mob-cries and shibboleths. *These people have power! These people have wealth! Take it from them!* And then, once we were ousted, the mob tries to ape our ways. Tell me, frankly, wherein lies the difference between Frederick David Manchester and Fouquier-Tinville?"

Sir Giles flicked his ash to windward. "You know, Inspector, people of Manchester's calibre are worse than we ever could have been. Our so-called power, our undisputed wealth, was used on and for the common people, but it was used in conformity with a code. Now I ask you; what code had Manchester? He didn't know the word, nor even the ideas that it represented. No, I didn't like Manchester, and I don't like the class he stands for. Put him in the Commons, and you'd have a Robespierre, or a Danton, or a Marat, and the times are too milk-and-watery to provide a Charlotte Corday. In the eyes of these people I am a blasted aristo, and yet have to work for my living, while the symbol of democracy up at Baxy can golf all day, rob rich and poor alike under cover of the laws of the land, and call himself a worker because he attends a board meeting once a month."

He sighed. "Oh well, old orders do change, and perhaps this present one will not last as long as ours did. You're right, you know! You suspect me of hating Manchester and all his works, and I do, most heartily."

"Your antagonism would not have led you to wipe him out?" Knollis asked quietly.

Sir Giles shrugged, and kicked his cigarette end to the path. "What would have been the use of that? Why bash one poor idiot over the head when five million more are crowding into the Tuileries to get their pound of flesh? Birth control is the only answer to the threat of a race of Manchesters. And if they won't stand for that, then we must try education."

"You are totally undemocratic?" suggested Knollis.

Sir Giles stared at him. "Good lord, no! Have I given you that impression? I'm the most patriotic cove alive. I'm only moaning about the sharpers of democracy, the men who do all the shouting and take all the gain, who gain all the votes by telling the mob that they are being fooled, and then proceed to rob those who have voted them in. Good lord, no! Don't get me wrong, Inspector! The worst I can say about the common man is that he is too trustful, or too big a fool, for this earth. He's bovine-minded, and will trot from his pasture twice a day to be milked by people like Manchester. Anthropologists call him *Homo sapiens*, but they should call him *Homo erectus*. He's got on to his back feet, but he hasn't even started to think. I've mixed my genders, but still—!"

"That clears that up," Knollis said thoughtfully. "Now tell me, Sir Giles: Manchester sent for you?"

"Ye-es," Sir Giles replied hesitantly, "I suppose it did amount to that. I had mentioned this flying-club effort to him, and he said that he would think it over and let me know. Well, he let me know! He sent a note saying, almost, that he was now prepared graciously to receive me, and would I attend his court at five o'clock on the stated date, when he would have great pleasure in informing me of his decision."

"You reared up at that? Was that your reaction?" Sir Giles grinned. "I believe I did pass a few foul remarks about him when the note arrived, but I was a beggar-on-foot, so I had to eat humble pie. I went. He wasn't there. The rest of the story you know!"

"I don't think I do," Knollis corrected him gently.

"Oh, I remember," said Sir Giles. "You think that I missed something out, don't you? You need a minute-by-minute itinerary. No, don't say anything. Let me start by entering the drive and working my way out by the hurst, and narrate every movement in between. That's what you want, I think."

Knollis nodded. "I wish all my witnesses would grasp my needs as easily."

"Oh well," laughed Sir Giles, "I'm a frightfully intelligent type, and can read words of three syllables!"

"Then get on with it," Knollis chuckled.

"Well, then I went down the drive, on foot, and up to the front door. Freeman let me in, and I was shown to Milly's sitting-room—that room is a psychological relic of her bringings-up, and she never got above a sitting-room mentally or emotionally. The idea of a lounge or a drawing-room never entered her head. Milly keeps both feet on the ground, and her head is far below the clouds. However, I was shown in, and she said that Freddy had gone to town and would be back shortly. I talked with her a few minutes, but it was mainly Jones's pigs, Temple's flowers, and such-like, so I picked up the paper and excused myself by saying I would have a look round the cactus house. I really intended to park myself in a convenient spot and read what I had missed over my breakfast. There was a draught blowing all round the building, and so I did go to the cactus department, and stooged round for a few minutes, but it was a bit close in there. I got fed up with waiting—ten minutes is my limit—and buzzed off through the hurst, as narrated heretofore. And that, I think, covers everything."

"No, it doesn't," said Knollis. "You have solved one puzzling problem for me, and here is the vital question: *what did you do with the paper when you left?*"

"The paper?" exclaimed Sir Giles. "Why, I bunged it between the wall and the spout—the downright, fall-pipe, or whatever they call it. Y'know, the one against the annexe door—or perhaps you don't know it?" he added.

"You are certain of that?" Knollis asked quickly.

"As certain as I am of going to heaven," Sir Giles replied. "But perhaps that is the wrong qualification. I'm willing to go into the box and swear to it, if that will satisfy you."

And then he gaped. "Lord! The ruddy axe was wrapped in a *Courier*, wasn't it?"

Knollis heaved a great sigh. "I've spent all day chasing that paper. Thank heavens for you! You are sure that it was a *Courier*—the *Trentingham Courier*?"

Sir Giles raised a hand, palm outwards. "So help me, Brother Juniper, it was!"

Knollis was silent for a minute or so, and Sir Giles brought him back to life by the offer of another cigarette.

Knollis brusquely refused the offer. "You mentioned Mrs. Manchester's background—her bringings-up, to quote your own words. Who was she before she married Manchester?"

Sir Giles grimaced. "You mean that you don't know? I could have told you before, only I imagined that you fellows would know all that. I don't mean that to sound offensive, incidentally. Anyway, there is good reason for you not knowing it, for it is more or less a secret, and I don't think Milly would broadcast it."

Sir Giles was still holding his case open, so Knollis took one and lit it. "Don't rush to the denouement, will you?" he murmured acidly. "I'm not in any hurry."

"It will prove a bit startling if I rush it," Sir Giles replied amiably.

"Listen, Sir Giles! You naturally know about the deaths of the cat and the bird, and the blue silk cords that were found round their necks. Have they, in your mind, any significance associated to your antagonism with Manchester? I mean, Manchester regarded you as a blue-blooded so-and-so—this is a time for frank speaking, so do excuse my crudeness! Well, that being so, could those cords be intended as a pointer to you? I should tell you here and now that Manchester regarded you as a possible cat-killer."

Sir Giles waved an arm. "Manchester was a prize bloody fool. For your questions, well, I'm no detective, but I had a hunch about the link as soon as I heard about the cords—the link between Milly's upbringing and these three deaths."

Knollis gave a sigh of impatience. "For heaven's sake tell me; WHO WAS MILDRED MANCHESTER?"

Sir Giles wrinkled his brows. "Now what's the name of the hangman fellow—hm! Darned if I can remember his name!"

"Teddy Jessop," Knollis replied sharply.

"Before Jessop! His name is on the tip of my tongue."

"You mean Marlin?"

Sir Giles snapped his fingers. "That's the fellow. Milly is his daughter."

"What!" shouted Knollis.

"It's true, old man. Perfectly true."

The unconscious association of ideas plays queer tricks with us at times, and Knollis was an immediate victim. "Well, I'll be hanged!" he said.

Sir Giles slapped his leg and gave a great laugh. "Then you'll have to apply to Jessop, because Marlin died in mysterious circumstances seven years ago."

Knollis sought for information in his well-stored mind. "Ye-es," he almost whispered; "that's right, he did.

The Coroner brought in a verdict of Death by Misadventure.

"His home was only five miles from here, you know," said Sir Giles. "I am a bit pally with the johnny who was in charge of the case."

"Five miles from here," Knollis murmured absently. "Quite a small hamlet."

"Marlin's daughter—and three cords. . . ."

"And if a man prevail against him that is alone, two shall withstand him; and a threefold cord is not easily broken," quoted Sir Giles.

Knollis started. "That's from the Bible!" he announced.

"Ecclesiastes, chapter four, verse twelve," said Sir Giles. "I occasionally read the Lessons in church, and that verse, or part of a verse, fixed itself in my mind. I couldn't get rid of it for days and days. Perseveration, the psychologist blokes call it. Er— look, Inspector, would you like me to take you up to Marlin's old place?"

Knollis considered the matter. Then he laid a hand on Sir Giles's arm. "I'd appreciate it."

CHAPTER XI
THE DEATH OF A HANGMAN

THE INSPECTOR OF POLICE at Frampton was looking forward to nothing more exciting than the usual daily routine when he seated himself at his desk at nine o'clock on the following morning. His complacency was shaken when the Station Sergeant announced that two gentlemen wished to speak with him. "One of them is Sir Giles Tanroy, and the other is an inspector from the Yard."

The Inspector glanced at the cards, and said: "Oh lord! Now what's gone wrong!"

Knollis soon put him at his ease, and assured him that he was only performing a policeman's normal function, that of asking innumerable questions—"An occupation to which we seem to be eternally fated."

"Yes, that's the whole of our life, more or less," the Inspector replied. "By the way, my name's Frank Johnson." He then looked enquiringly at Knollis, and waited.

"It's this Bowland case," Knollis explained. "There seems to be a tie-up somewhere with the death of Marlin, the ex-hangman. What can you tell me about him?"

The Inspector beamed. "I thought it would come up again one day, and you couldn't have come to a better man if you want to know about it, Inspector Knollis. I handled the affair, and I know all about it. I knew Marlin ever since he was so high, and a more unhappy man never lived."

"How did he die?" Knollis asked laconically.

"Fell down the cellar steps and broke his neck. Death from Misadventure was the verdict, but I wasn't satisfied in my own mind because, you see, I think he was murdered."

"Why?" Knollis enquired.

Inspector Johnson glanced at Sir Giles. "He hasn't told you my idea? We've often talked it over; that's why I ask. Sir Giles is not a bad criminologist—as an amateur."

Sir Giles bowed gravely.

"Sir Giles has told me no more than that you were in charge of the case."

"In that case, I repeat that I think he was murdered. I said so at the time, but Sir James Fell—Colonel Mowbray's predecessor—practically told me to keep my mouth shut and forget all the fancy ideas I had. I had no wish to be retired for any cooked-up reason, and so I obliged and obeyed, but I still think that Marlin was pushed down the steps!"

"What gave you that impression, Johnson?"

The Inspector left his desk and went to the safe. He returned with two photographs.

"I took these myself. I needn't explain that one is a photograph of Marlin's body lying at the foot of the steps, and the other is a close-up of his supper-table. Any questions at this stage?"

Knollis shook his head. "Tell me the story in your own way. I think we understand each other."

The Inspector relaxed in his chair, and clasped his hands across his stomach. He was a stoutish man, and blew out his cheeks before beginning: "Let me tell you Marlin's story. He entered the Merchant Navy in nineteen-thirteen, and went right through the last war on a minesweeper without getting a scratch. Three months after the armistice he was still sweeping off the East Coast when he hit his first mine. He was picked up by a sister ship, and taken to hospital in a serious condition. His life was saved, but—did you ever meet him?"

"No," replied Knollis. "I know Jessop, but I never met Marlin."

"Well, he came out of dock with a badly disfigured face. He really was a mess! There was no such thing as plastic surgery in those days, of course, and Marlin came back to his native village, two miles from here, a soured and despondent man."

"And turned hangman?" asked Knollis.

The Inspector shook his head. "You are going too fast. No, he turned day-gardener. Most of the gentry in the district were sorry for him, and they gave him all the work they could. Now he had one small daughter, Mildred. She would be about three then—I'm only guessing from my memory."

He shrugged his broad shoulders. "The next part of the story is rather nasty, but you need it to complete the picture. His wife was both shocked and repulsed by his physical appearance, and she refused to—well, have anything to do with him. That made him more bitter than ever, and acting on his own advice he took her to court for restitution of conjugal rights. That is why I know so much about him. The case went in his favour, and the usual moralising magistrate dressed Mrs. Marlin down well and truly, pointing out that her husband was more or less of a hero, and that his disfigurement was the result of fighting to protect her and the child. She left the court in an hysterical condition, and had to have medical attention, but she returned to her home."

The Inspector grimaced. "A son was born eleven months later, and he was born with a twisted face—"

"My God!" Knollis exclaimed. "That—never mind!"

"What on earth is striking you?" Inspector Johnson exclaimed in turn.

"Go on, man. Go on," said Knollis. "I'll do my explaining later."

"Well, as I said, the boy was born with one side of his face twisted to hell—just like the old man's. For the next fortnight Mrs. Marlin lay in bed and wept, and screamed, and moaned, and went silent in turns. Two days after she left her bed she drowned herself in the village pond, and I came into their lives and deaths again."

He paused to relight his pipe before continuing his story.

"The next phase started with the inquest. The Coroner, also a moralising so-and-so, took it out of Marlin this time. He dwelt at some length on the frail mental and spiritual make-up of Woman, and quoted a piece about dealing gently with your brother Man and still more gently with your sister, Woman. He denounced Marlin for taking his wife to court, and then denounced him for taking her to bed. It sounded a bit like the curse in the *Jackdaw of Rheims*. He cursed him in sitting, and lying, and eating, and drinking, and every other way he could think of. Could he not have taken his time and re-wooed her? Could he not have done this, and that, and the other? His sermon made me go red in the face, and I'd been married eighteen years then! Marlin walked out of that court with his jaw clamped as tight as a vice, with a verdict ringing in his ears of *Suicide While of Unsound Mind*, with a rider to the effect that Marlin's treatment was directly or indirectly responsible for the state of her mind."

"And then?" Knollis almost whispered.

"Marlin kept to his house for a full month. A nurse was found for the boy, and a part-witted girl who could not think was taken on as housekeeper. Marlin was a handy sort of fellow who could turn his hand to nearly anything, and he opened a shop as boot-repairer. Six months later I received a confidential enquiry from You-Know-Where about Marlin's character. He had applied for the position as executioner's assistant. He gave as his reason the necessity of withdrawing from public life, and he had given his service records and all that to help on his application against those applicants from the ranks of the prison warders. Well, what did I know against his character? Nothing from our point of view. He had lived a clean life, he was trustworthy, silent, and honest. I wanted to help the poor devil, and so I gave him a clean bill."

"Some story—what?" Sir Giles murmured to Knollis.

"Damned horrible!" said Knollis. "Go on, Johnson!"

The Inspector fiddled with his pipe. "It was difficult, I admit, but as I saw it the affairs of his marital life were nobody's concern but his own. What was it that Shaw said about marriage?"

"Something about giving the maximum provocation with the maximum opportunity, wasn't it?" Sir Giles suggested.

Johnson nodded. "Something like that."

"What happened to the children?" Knollis asked.

"The kids? They went to the village school until they were fourteen. Mildred then went to one of the near-by houses as a maid, and three years later the boy got a job with a local butcher."

"He did, did he?" Knollis murmured grimly. "What was his Christian name, Johnson?"

"Daniel—and that was another sidelight on his father's character. It was his idea of a joke. Marlin asked me to be the godfather, because he said that I was the only person who had stood by him in his troubles, which was a mis-statement. I asked why he was going to call him Daniel, and he said he'd have to dare to be a Daniel, and dare to stand alone, with a face like that! So Daniel it was—although we never told the reason to the parson. Somehow, I don't think he'd have stood for it."

"Definitely a ghastly type of humourist." Sir Giles grimaced. "I don't think I should have liked Marlin."

"Well, perhaps not, Sir Giles," said the Inspector, "but you must look back to the beginnings to see the affair straight. All that followed was the logical effect, or effects, of that first cause—the blowing-up of the minesweeper, and it was inevitable. Anyway, Marlin came to see me and asked me to keep quiet about the executioner job, which I did. A couple of years later old Lenten died, and Marlin stepped into his position as hangman."

"And the children?" Knollis asked again.

"Mildred learned the truth when she was eighteen, and by accident. Marlin left some papers lying around. She wept her eyes out, and left home. Daniel cleared out six months later, as a boy of fifteen or so, and I've never laid a glance on either of them from that day to this. Marlin stayed on in the village. He became a taciturn sort of fellow, half-feared and half-admired, because by now the village knew of his other trade. He was a good boot-repairer, and he made a steady income. Most nights he would slink into the local, and occupy a corner which became his own, and in which nobody else would dare to sit, and so the years rolled on, as they say in books. And then came the night when one of my constables 'phoned through to say that he had found Marlin lying at the foot of the cellar steps with his neck broken. You know the rest!"

"I'm afraid I don't," said Knollis. "Tell me; how did the constable come to discover him?"

"He was on night patrol, and found the cottage lit up and the front door standing open. He went in, and saw the table set for supper. Marlin had apparently left the meal half-way through to go down the cellar—a fact corroborated by the post-mortem examination of his tummy. There was no apparent reason why he should have gone down the cellar at that moment. There was a full scuttle of coal beside the fire in case he wanted to build it up. There were two bottles of beer on the table, together with a glass, so it wasn't beer he was fetching! No food was kept in the cellar, so it wasn't that. As far as I could make out there was only one reason why he should have left his meal and gone down at that particular moment. . . ."

"And that was?" asked Knollis.

"He was lured down by a noise, or a voice."

Knollis stared at the ceiling. "Did you discover anything that might substantiate your theory, Johnson?"

Inspector Johnson regarded the photographs intently. "Those photographs are my best answer, plus one other fact. You know how cellar gratings are fastened from the inside by a chain that is locked through a staple on the wall? That was hanging loose, as if someone had—but let me give you my reconstruction of the whole affair. The rear kitchen window is one of those old-fashioned slide-aside things, and the brass thumbscrew which fastens it was missing. Suppose that someone entered that way, and unfastened the chain in the cellar, and then left again by the window? Suppose that he waits until the old boy was having his supper, which was half-past ten-ish, because he stayed at the local until after closing time that night; suppose that he waits, then, and then quietly lifts off the grate and lowers himself into the cellar—"

"Or has a confederate who lifts the grating, rattles the chain, and so lures the old boy to the top of the steps," interrupted Knollis, his quick mind seizing on the possibilities.

"And then," went on Inspector Johnson, "as the old man starts to descend the steps—"

"The major partner in the crime pushes him," said Knollis.

"One person could have done it," said Johnson.

"How?" asked Knollis, creasing his brows.

Johnson smiled. "That was what I was trying to tell you, only you would jump to conclusions! I found a length of stout cord behind the cellar door. Now the door opens outward. That is, you pull it towards you to open it. Assume that it was already open, and the cord is hanging slack? The old boy stands at the top of the steps, wondering about the noises in the cellar. The house was only lit by lamps, and he might as well have been in the darkness for all the light that filtered from the living-room. And so he stands, listening, and the fellow at the bottom gathers up the slack in his hands, and then gives a heave! The door slams on Marlin's back. There is no handrail or other projection at which he could cling to save himself, and so he falls head-first down the steps. The murderer makes sure that he is dead, mounts the steps, detaches the cord, and leaves by the rear window—reached by an unlighted passage and a kitchen in which no lamp is burning."

"I see . . ." Knollis said slowly. "And you never heard of either of the children being in the district at that time?"

"No," said the Inspector. "I tried to trace them, but was unsuccessful. I was told by one of the local gentry that he and his wife had got a position for her with a family by the names of Gates, in Berkeley Square, but when I enquired Mrs. Gates said that Mildred had left, and she did not know where she had gone."

"The date of Marlin's death?" asked Knollis.

"September the fourteenth, nineteen-thirty-eight."

"Thanks. Now where can I find Sir James Fell?"

"I can take you to him," said Sir Giles. "He's a doddering old fellow of eighty-odd years, and a bit crusty."

"Well, Knollis," said Inspector Johnson, "if there is anything more I can do for you, just let me know. I'll leave you to decide whether there is anything in my theory or not. You are the murder-specialist, and I'm only the poor country bobby with a penchant for recovering stolen bikes."

Knollis grinned as he rose. "You are too modest, Johnson! Thanks for everything."

"By the way," the Inspector said slowly. "You haven't told me how this Marlin affair ties up with the Bowland job."

"Sir Giles will tell you that," Knollis replied. "I nearly jumped out of my boots when he supplied the link."

Johnson looked anxiously at Sir Giles.

"The daughter of the murdered man, before she married Manchester, was Mildred Marlin," Sir Giles said dramatically.

"Hell, no!" Johnson exclaimed.

"Hell, yes!" Sir Giles corrected him. "It's true."

"How did you get to know?" Knollis asked curiously.

"Dana Vaughan told me on the q.t."

Knollis's jaw dropped. "Dana Vaughan! How the devil did she know?"

Sir Giles grinned, almost stupidly. "I thought you'd ferreted all this out, Inspector. As you haven't, I'd better tell you the whole story. Do you know who wrote *The Hempen Rope*?"

"Er—Leslie Danvers, surely?"

"Exactly," replied Sir Giles, "and Leslie Danvers is Dana Vaughan. The play is based on the lives of Marlin and his daughter."

Knollis cast his mind back to the play, which he had seen three times. "Yes-es, it sounds possible," he admitted, "but I'm damned if I get it yet."

Sir Giles chuckled. "Well, you're the detective, and I'm not propounding a solution to the riddle. I'm only supplying the facts. And here are a few more. Dana, Mildred, and Freddy all met on a Mediterranean cruise some five years ago. Mildred had apparently progressed from 'tween-maid to governess, and had the entree to all the best houses. That is why Freddy married her. He wanted to be a Somebody, and he thought that she was a suitable stepping-stone."

"He didn't know that she was Marlin's daughter?"

"Of course not!" exclaimed Sir Giles. "Milly wanted money, and lots of it. If you were in that position, and had her outlook on life, would you tell the prospective bank-balance that your father was a hangman? Would you blazes!"

Knollis licked his lips. He crammed his hat on his head. "Take me to Sir James Fell—and thanks again, Johnson. I'll remember you in my report, and if I can get your case reopened, I'll do it."

"Thanks!" Johnson called after him.

Sir Giles drove, and sent the car chasing down the main road to Trentingham at a pace that alarmed Knollis.

"Happy?" asked Sir Giles.

"It depends what you mean by happiness. . . ."

"That is Joad's line!" Sir Giles replied. "Perhaps I should have asked you if you were satisfied with life."

"More satisfied than I was a few hours ago, but is it necessary to travel at this astounding pace? We are doing over seventy."

Sir Giles slowly eased his foot from the accelerator, and the car attained a respectable forty.

"Sorry," he said. "I'm a victim of the age. It's the instinct of imitation, *vide* MacDougal. The first time I was aware of it working in myself was a few months ago when I went to London. When I left the station I was astounded by the way in which Londoners rushed about, as if the bus coming up the road, or the Tube train coming out of the tunnel, was the last one for hours instead of the last one for two minutes. I felt sorry for them for allowing themselves to be caught up in such an idiotic race. Two days later I discovered myself running down an escalator to catch a train that wasn't even signalled in. Silly, isn't it? One sheep goes through the gap in the hedge, and all the others follow. There's a moral in it somewhere."

Knollis nodded sadly. "Yes, I'm afraid that the human race is more notorious for its stupidity than for anything else. I was reading an article on Edgar Wallace the other day, and the author was lauding the wordage he had turned out. It set me thinking about Charles Dickens, and the number of books he wrote with a quill pen. We seem to be rushing to destruction as fast as our legs can take us."

"I wonder when it all started," Sir Giles murmured pensively.

"Oh, that's a simple question," Knollis replied. "It started on the day when Crippen's description was wirelessed across the Atlantic. That dramatic event started the ball rolling, and it has been gaining speed ever since."

"And that is Sir James's house showing white through the trees. Want me to come in with you?"

"If you will, please," said Knollis. "You can act as my ice-breaker. Hang you, Sir Giles! You nearly had that gate-post! Have you no pity for my nerves?"

"*Mea culpa! Pax vobiscum!* The brake is applied, and the gentleman may step out all in one piece."

"Which is more due to Providence that to the driving of Sir Giles Tanroy," said Knollis. "Nice place Sir James has!"

Sir James Fell was an aged gentleman with very little hair, a drooping white moustache, bent shoulders, and a shortage of teeth. He appeared to be in the early stages of senile decay.

"Scotland Yard?" he grumbled. "I hoped that I had finished with the police. I want peace, dammit, for my last years. What is it you want, anyway?"

"I understand that you were the Chief Constable of Trent-ingham at one time, Sir James," Knollis said in a soothing voice. "Also that you remember the death of Marlin, the hangman."

The old man blinked blearily. "So that's turned up again! Yes, I remember it—what the devil do you want to know about it?"

"I've had a chat with Inspector Johnson, at Frampton, and it seems that he had certain suspicions."

"Certain suspicions!" bawled Sir James. "The man was mad. Said that Marlin had been murdered! Murdered indeed!"

"I consider that he had reasonable grounds for his suspicions, Sir James!" Knollis said firmly.

The old man looked up, blinked again, and wiped his moustaches away from his mouth with the back of his hand. "You do, eh? Well, so do I if it comes to that. Either his son or his daughter did it. Nobody else had a motive."

"Then why on earth—"began Knollis.

Sir James cut him short. "I know! I know! You are going to accuse me of dereliction of duty, and want to know why I didn't take up Johnson's evidence. I'll tell you, eh? Duty is duty, but there are times when other considerations must be entertained. Hadn't the two children suffered enough from the old rascal's twisted mind? Hadn't they, heh? Perhaps you don't agree, but I don't care! You can institute an enquiry into my handling of the case if you like—and what good will it do you?"

Knollis coughed behind his hand.

The old man nodded. "Cough away, Inspector! I'm old, now, and my memory is failing. So are my other powers. If you take me into a court of law I'll gibber and saliva. Everybody will cry you down for bullying such a poor and decrepit old man."

He chuckled.

"There are many compensations for old age, Inspector! If I don't want to hear, I don't hear, and they think I'm deaf, and don't worry me further. My eyes are too weak to read what I don't want to read, and my legs won't walk where I don't want to go. Be old, and be wise, Inspector! I know nothing. Johnson is a clever man who never got his chance, but you've left it too late. May I bid you good day?"

Knollis and Sir Giles made their adieux. Once more seated in the car, they turned to each other and laughed. "Stalled, by jiminy," said Sir Giles.

"We can't do much with him," agreed Knollis.

"I take it that you are going to try to find Mildred's brother next, Inspector?"

Knollis looked at him in astonishment. "You really mean to say that you haven't seen the obvious? You don't know where Daniel Marlin is?"

Sir Giles started, and the car leapt across the road. He drew it back to the left again, and then brought it to a halt beside the grass verge. "Good lord!"

Knollis ignored the erratic driving, and pushed his hat to the back of his head. "I have to prove it, of course, but if Daniel Marlin isn't Desmond Brailsford I'll eat this hat."

"You know," said Sir Giles, "I never thought of that one. You don't suppose that the twisted features of both could be a re-markable coincidence?"

"I don't believe in coincidences," said Knollis. "The modern definition of the word is almost synonymous with the word *miracle*, whereas it really means exactly what it says: coincidence. Unless I am very much mistaken, it is no accident, nor yet a fluke of fortune, nor a miracle that brother and sister are living in the same house. There is a reason for it somewhere, and I am going to find out what it is."

CHAPTER XII
THE MATTER OF TEMPLE'S BEER

KNOLLIS PICKED UP his own car at Knightswood, and drove to the village inn. It was open for the noon session, and the land-lord was able to supply him with cold lunch. Knollis placed his notebook on the table beside him and studied it as he ate. An idea occurred to him. He unscrewed his pen and wrote at the foot of the notes: "It isn't what people say that is important, but the significance behind their words." He studied his home-made aphorism and was satisfied that he had written the truth. A puzzled frown came over his lean features. Why had he written it? Was there, yet once again, some statement, or part of a statement, that had a significance which he had not realised? This was his third murder case, and in each of the previous two this queer tendency of his mind to work for him without conscious direction had surprised him.

He tossed all the facts of the case over and over as if he was searching in a newly mown hayfield for some small item which he had lost. He was mainly concerned at the moment with the manner in which Temple had been doped. That might have seemed queer to a layman, considering that he had just heard a story which laid bare vital evidence regarding the mentality of the Marlin family, and it could logically have been expected that he would follow up the evidence without delay, but Knollis was learning the full capabilities of his own mind, and learning that the new ways being indicated to him were safe ways, and useful ones. And so he had put the whole Marlin story into his mind, and intended that it should stay there for some hours before he further examined it. Whatever the nature of the queer depths of his mind, it seemed that they were more capable of sorting and classifying his material than was he, as a conscious and reasoning being.

Temple, then, was to be the subject of present thought. How had the dope been administered? It would be a risky proceeding in a public house, which, if not actually full, was reasonably so. And yet, at the moment, he could see no other possibility, and it must be explored.

He rang the bell, and requested the landlord's presence, if it was convenient. The landlord wasted no time in accepting the invitation, probably hoping to learn more of the Baxmanhurst case than was yet public property.

"You wanted to see me, sir?" he asked eagerly.

"I do," said Knollis. "Perhaps you will have a drink with me while we are talking?"

The landlord would, and did. Knollis asked him to close the door, and then pushed back his plate and folded his arms on the table.

"You can distinctly remember Temple's arrival on Tuesday afternoon?"

"Distinctly. As I told you before, sir, he came in about one o'clock."

"Where did he sit?"

"He didn't, at first," the landlord replied. "He stood against the counter. You'll have noticed that the bar is placed centrally, with windows giving on to the tap-room, saloon-bar, passage, and smoke-room. Temple was in the tap-room, and he stood there for his first two pints, carrying-on about Manchester. I judged that there had been another row between them. He said that he had told him off good and proper. I didn't believe him, because I've generally noticed that when a fellow has worked off his steam in a row he hasn't any left for telling him off when he isn't there."

"A penetrating observation," said Knollis. "You think as I do, that Temple stood there and took it without saying a word?"

"I certainly do, sir. Anyway, I put up with him for two pints, and then asked him to sit down because he was getting in my way while I was trying to serve. He went and sat in the corner against the fireplace, and stayed there until three o'clock, when I called time."

"Was he drinking with anyone?" Knollis asked. "No, sir. He was snubbed by being told to move from the counter, and he just sat and sulked."

"Now tell me," said Knollis; "were any other members of Baxmanhurst in here, either staff or otherwise?"

The landlord considered. "No," he said eventually, "I don't think they were."

"Mr. Brailsford, for instance?"

"That's him with the twisted face. No, I'm certain he wasn't, or I'd have noticed him. He seldom comes in alone, anyway. He's usually with Manchester on a Saturday night."

"Oh!" Knollis said glumly.

"You were hoping he'd been in, sir?" the landlord asked quietly.

"Expecting, not hoping," Knollis replied. "Look, I take it that you know how to keep your mouth closed? I don't mean that remark offensively."

"A landlord has to keep his mouth shut, or he'd soon lose his custom, sir. He has neither religion nor politics—nor opinions, for that matter."

"I suppose that is true," said Knollis. "Very well, I'll take you into my confidence, because I think you can help me. You are satisfied in your own mind that Temple was not in a state that you could describe as any worse than fuddled?"

The landlord thought for a moment, and then nodded. "Fuddled is how I would describe him. No worse, certainly."

"Temple," said Knollis, "was doped."

The landlord started. "Doped! In here!"

"That is what I am trying to discover," Knollis explained. "He left here at three o'clock, and apparently went to the woodshed at the rear of Baxmanhurst to sleep off the beer. It was midnight when he was found, and he was still unconscious. Somebody, somewhere, and somehow, had given him knock-out drops."

The landlord bridled. "It wasn't done in my house! I'll swear to that!"

Knollis shook his head. "You can't swear to it. No matter how well you may conduct your house, you can't be responsible for the actions of all the people who come into it. Now can you—reasonably?"

"No-o, I suppose not," the landlord admitted reluctantly. "And yet—"

Knollis brushed his objections aside. "I can quite well appreciate your attitude, and yet the fact remains that Temple was doped somewhere, and he did drink his beer in this house. That is why I asked you who was drinking with him."

"Wait here," said the landlord. He left the room, to return a few minutes later with a sturdy, red-faced British working man in cord trousers.

"This is Jake Meadows. He was sitting next to Matt Temple on Tuesday, weren't you, Jake?"

"That's right. He came next to me when he moved from the counter," said Meadows.

"He was talking to you?" asked Knollis.

"Only for a few minutes. He was grumbling about being moved. Then he settled down and scowled at the table for the rest of the time, except when he went up for more beer."

"No one approached him to speak to him?"

"That they didn't, sir. There were about fourteen of us in the tap-room, and I know 'em all. All of them know Matt, and they don't interfere with him when he gets one of his bouts on."

"Damn!" said Knollis. "Thanks, Meadows. And thank you, too," he said to the landlord. "Please draw a pint for Meadows at my expense."

He was left alone once more, and his eyes narrowed as he went through the pages of the notebook again.

"If he wasn't doped here . . ." he said aloud, and then pushed back his chair, went to pay his score, and drove down to Baxmanhurst.

It was now that he paid his first visit to the woodshed, although the Trentingham men had already examined it. It was a crude affair, knocked together from any old planks and posts which had laid about when it was being built, and the door swung open crazily as Knollis twisted the home-made wooden turn-button. The farther wall was stacked high with firewood. The left wall was well supplied with three-inch nails from which hung shears, hoes, spades, and the rest of Temple's gardening impedimenta. Two sacks lay at the foot of the right-hand wall, behind the door, and obviously constituted Temple's sobering-off couch.

The light was dim in the shed, and Knollis returned to his car for a torch. On his return he examined the earthen floor thoroughly, scraping a handful here and a handful there, and sniffing it. At last he seemed to find what he wanted, for he emptied the contents of his matchbox into his pocket, and refilled the box with earth. He went out, found a constable, and sent him post-haste to Trentingham in the car, instructing him to take the sample of earth to the laboratories and ask the staff to analyse it and let him have the result as soon as they conveniently could. "And bring my car back!" he added. "I may need it in a hurry. The game is warming up."

He then went to the kitchen, knocked on the door, and accepted Mrs. Redson's invitation to enter.

"Like a cup of tea, Inspector?" she asked. "I just happen to have made one."

"It's a fine habit you have." Knollis smiled. "I could drink one, and while you are pouring it out I'd like to talk to you about beer."

Mrs. Redson turned to him with astonishment written across her kindly red face. "Beer? I never touch the stuff. Mind you, I don't mind a nice milk stout, but beer! Ugh!"

"Is there any beer in the house, Mrs. Redson?" asked Knollis.

"Oh yes, we have a dozen-case every week. The Master used to have a bottle with his lunch."

"Mr. Brailsford drink beer?"

She shook her head. "He's all for whisky."

"And the ladies?"

"Madame won't touch any intoxicants. She has cider. Miss Dana has port and sherry," she replied. She looked closely at Knollis. "This another official matter, Inspector?"

"It is," Knollis admitted. "I think you can help me a great deal if you will."

"Well, I will; you know that. I was just a bit vexed by the way you treated Freeman and Smithy the other day, but I got thinking it over and saw that it was just your job—like cooking's mine. There's times when folk don't like the way I go about my cooking, but I always get good results, and I reckon it's the same with being a detective."

"That's good thinking," Knollis said quietly. "Yes, you can help me. Can I see your beer supplies?"

"The stuff's in the larder, along the passage. You'd better come with me and have a look."

She led the way, and pushed open the larder door, at the same time switching on the light. "Them two cases."

"One is composed of empties, I see," said Knollis.

"Well, there was one bottle left in that case when the man came on Friday morning, so he left the whole case till next time."

"So that the last bottle would be consumed on Friday, for Manchester's lunch?"

Mrs. Redson nodded. "That's right, sir. I fetched it myself and put it on the tray with the glass. The Master liked to draw and pour his own. Always said as a woman couldn't do it properly." She sniffed.

Knollis ticked off the days on his fingers. "Saturday, Sunday, Monday, and Tuesday. So there should be four empties in the new case?"

"Ye-es, that's right."

"And there are five," Knollis said shortly.

Mrs. Redson bent over the case to take out the empties, but Knollis caught her hands. "Please don't touch them. Finger-prints, you know!"

She stared at him. "You are queer this afternoon, Inspector!"

Knollis put his mouth against her ear. "Temple was doped on Tuesday, and nobody knows but you and myself, and nobody else must know."

"Good heavens! You mean that somebody put something—but he doesn't have any out of the house, Inspector!"

Knollis closed the door with his foot, and spoke in a normal tone. "He shouldn't have hid, but I think he did. Some time after three o'clock on Tuesday afternoon somebody took him a bottle to the woodshed—and it was drugged." He paused a moment, and added honestly: "I think."

"How are you going to find out?" asked Mrs. Redson.

Knollis grinned. "That is what is worrying me. The first stage is to take these into the kitchen and examine them in daylight. Perhaps you will open the door for me, please?"

He manhandled the case of beers and empties to the kitchen, and planted it on a chair close to the sink. He put on his gloves and carefully took out each of the empty bottles in turn, tipping it so that no more than a drop of the residue fell on the white porcelain surface of the sink. The first three bottles in no way interested him. The fourth one did, for it was clear water that dripped from its lip. He quickly tested the fifth, but put it back in the case.

Mrs. Redson, standing beside him, watched the experiment closely. "Looks as if that one has been rinsed out, Inspector, doesn't it?"

Knollis nodded grimly. "It does!"

"Now why should anyone want to rinse out a beer bottle?" she ventured.

"Why, indeed?" Knollis answered. "Have you an old duster you don't care about?"

"I think I can find you one. Wait a minute."

Knollis wrapped the bottle in the duster, and dropped it back into its compartment in the case.

"Now for that cup of tea, Mrs. Redson."

"I don't understand it at all, Inspector," she said when they were sitting at the table together. "I was in here most of Tuesday afternoon, and I can't remember anybody going to the larder."

"And yet somebody must have done," Knollis remarked. "You can't account in any other way for the fifth bottle having been consumed? What about Smith? Does he drink?"

She nodded. "He does, but he won't touch bottled stuff. Says it's too gassy, and blows him up. Freeman is teetotal."

"Temple wasn't in the house?" Knollis suggested.

"Not after one o'clock, and I do know that he never went to the larder. Temple knows his place in my part of the house!"

"Yes, I'm sure of that," Knollis said with a smile. "Now look, Mrs. Redson; is there any means of checking the number of empties there were at lunch-time?"

"No-o," she said hesitantly. "I didn't count them, of course, but I think I should have noticed if that extra one had gone then. That might sound daft to you, but you don't know how used I am to keeping an eye on my larder stocks. I sort of notice without noticing, if you know what I mean!"

"I understand perfectly," Knollis assured her. "Now the next thing is to try to trace the one who took it, and returned it. Is there any time of the afternoon when the kitchen is completely deserted?"

"Well, yes, there is. I was in most of the afternoon, as I told you, but I went for a wash and change about—see, it would be just turned three."

"That would account for half an hour perhaps?" said Knollis.

"Ye-es, I suppose so, Inspector."

"Where was Freeman?" Knollis asked quickly.

"She'd be in her room. She has a rest in the afternoons, because I finish after dinner at night, and she attends to anything else that might be wanted."

"But Tuesday was her evening off," Knollis pointed out.

"I know, but she still has her afternoon hour."

"And Smith?"

"He was washing the car down, because the Master had told him they were going into town, and Smithy is awful proud of the car."

"I see," said Knollis, "or perhaps I don't!"

He went out to the garage. Smith was relaxing in the back seat of the car, reading a magazine. He scrambled out on seeing Knollis, and straightened his uniform jacket.

"Relax again," said Knollis. "I only want to ask you a very simple question. Were you in the kitchen, or the staff passage, between three and four o'clock on Tuesday afternoon?"

"Between three and four?" Smith repeated, and puckered his brows. "I don't think so, sir, although I wouldn't swear to it."

"Tell me," said Knollis; "tea is at four o'clock in this house. How is it that you didn't have yours before you drove to Trentingham?"

"Well," Smith replied, "the staff don't get tea at the same time. I mean, Mrs. Redson and Freeman are serving the others. We usually get ours half-past four-ish, but I'd a bit of trouble with the car, and Freddy wanted to be down in town by five, and so I had to scrub my tea and get weaving on the car."

"What was wrong with it?" Knollis asked.

"Brakes wanted taking up. Freddy—Mr. Manchester—had been taking it out lately, and he seems to drive on the brakes instead of the hooter."

"So you can't remember going into the house?"

"I can't remember doing so, and I don't think I did, either. I'd no need to go in, and as I say, I was extra busy."

"You didn't slip in for a chat with Miss Freeman, by any chance?" Knollis suggested.

"Freeman would be upstairs then, sir."

"Quite," said Knollis. "I'm trying to find who went to the larder between three and four. I don't suppose you can help me?"

Smith's face reddened. "I've told you, sir, that I wasn't in the house!"

"I'm not disputing it," Knollis said smoothly. "I merely wondered if you had seen anyone enter the staff door. You didn't?"

"I never saw anybody."

"Thanks," said Knollis. "Please carry on with your magazine."

He strolled round the grounds until the constable arrived from Trentingham with the car, and then he sent him back again with the beer-case and a suitable message to the laboratory staff. "Tell them I suspect that chloral hydrate has been in the wrapped bottle—knockout drops, if you can't remember the name. Bring the car back here. I'll be somewhere in the village, and will collect it later."

He went across to Gate Cottage. Temple was downstairs, seated by the fire, and looking sorry for himself. Knollis greeted him cheerfully, and at Mrs. Temple's invitation took the opposite seat. She then left them.

"I hope you're satisfied about me not being—you know," said Temple miserably.

"There are only a few odd points which need clearing up," Knollis answered, "and if you can clear them, then you have no need to worry. First; did anyone pay for a drink for you while you were in the Anchor on Tuesday?"

Temple shook his head. "Not a soul, sir."

"Who sat next to you?"

"Why," Temple said slowly, "there was only Jake Meadows. I was sitting in the fireplace corner, you see."

"Meadows didn't buy you a drink?"

"He never does," said Temple.

"You didn't happen to see Mr. Brailsford while you were there?"

"I don't think he came in, sir. It isn't often he gets in before night, and then it is with Mr. Manchester."

"I see," said Knollis. "Now on your return to Baxmanhurst, did you meet anyone you knew—anyone connected with the house?"

"Ye-es, I did meet Mr. Brailsford. Actually, he caught me up. He'd got a bundle of papers under his arm."

"Did he speak to you?"

"I can't remember as he did," replied Temple. "He looked at me, and went down the drive to the front door."

"And you went to the woodshed!"

"Yes, that's right."

"Have you a good memory, normally, Temple?"

"Fairish, sir."

"Good," said Knollis. "Now tell me; what is the last thing you remember in the shed?"

"Getting down and getting to sleep, sir."

Knollis stared at him slowly. "I hadn't thought of that," he murmured. "Listen, Temple; did you fasten the door on the inside before you got your head down?" Temple considered. "Yes," he said after a minute. "The door swings inwards unless it's fastened, and I seem to remember that I leaned a shovel against it."

"You didn't wedge it so that it couldn't be opened from the outside?"

"It can't be done, sir. I've meant putting a catch on the inside for long enough, but somehow it doesn't seem to have got done."

Knollis scribbled a note and then looked up at Temple again. "The drink you had in the Anchor? That was the last you had that day?"

Temple scratched his head, and appeared to be puzzled. "That's what I can't make out, sir. It's what I was trying to get a hold of last time you saw me. I think it must have been a dream . . . !"

"Tell me," Knollis said shortly.

"Well, it's daft, sir, and I'm feeling ashamed of myself about the whole business, but I had an idea that I woke up and found a bottle of pale ale beside me, and that I'd drunk it, and then thrown the bottle across the hut. I can't say for certain, because I haven't been across to see if the bottle is still there!"

Knollis nodded. "There is no bottle there, Temple. It looks as if it was a dream, after all. Dreams are so vivid, aren't they?"

Temple shook his head sadly. "They certainly are, sir. And this one was extra."

"I don't suppose you know what brand of beer you drunk in this—er—dream?"

"Well, that's what makes me think it must have been a dream, sir, because it was the same as Mr. Manchester drinks in the house, India pale ale. I like it, but I can't afford to drink it."

"See, those bottles have crown caps, haven't they?"

"They have, sir," said Temple, "but this wasn't on."

"Mm!" said Knollis. "And you went to sleep as soon as you had disposed of the beer, and the bottle?"

"In my dream, sir; yes."

"Look, Temple," said Knollis, "would you have any objection to having your finger-prints taken?"

Temple looked surprised. "Why, no! I don't think so, sir."

"Then I'll have a man call round and take them. I think that will clear you entirely. By the way, you did not have other dreams, did you?"

"I can't remember them if I did, sir."

"No dreams about finding bloody axes and taking them to your dustbin?"

"Certainly none like that, sir."

"Mm!" said Knollis again. "Have you any idea whether your wife was out after tea on Tuesday? You'll understand that I'm trying to find out who put the axe in your dustbin."

Temple called his wife. "The Inspector wants to know if you went out after tea on Tuesday."

"Why, yes, sir. After I heard about poor Mr. Manchester I didn't feel too safe in the house, and I went up to my sister's for half an hour, or perhaps it would be an hour."

"At what time did you go, Mrs. Temple?"

"Round about seven o'clock, sir, as near as I can say," she replied.

"And stayed until about eight, say?" asked Knollis.

"About that, sir."

"Thank you both," said Knollis. "I think that will be about all for now, although I may have to call round again to-morrow."

"Matt's all right, sir!" Mrs. Temple asked anxiously.

Knollis patted her shoulder. "Matt is all right, Mrs. Temple."

He paused a minute, and then said: "Would you care to help me? Then, if anyone asks you the question that you have just asked me, pretend that things don't look too good for him. You understand?"

Temple shook his head, but his wife replied: "I think I do, Inspector, and I'll see as Matt does, too."

"Bravo," said Knollis.

He stood under the elms for some minutes after leaving the Temples, and his forehead was furrowed. It was evident that the axe had been parked between seven o'clock and eight, and that meant that it had been hidden from the time of the murder until after seven. The state of the axe when found suggested that it had been in the water-butt. . . .

Knollis strode down the drive, and pushed behind the bushes to where the butt stood. He ferreted about in the fallen leaves that bestrewed the ground, and gave a grunt which expressed satisfaction rather than surprise as he retrieved a length of thin and yet strong string. There was a running noose in one end. Knollis found a stone, and tightened the noose round it; then lowered the stone into the butt. When it reached the bottom he was left with about seven inches of the string in his hand.

"Now where do I fix this?" he murmured, and then answered his own question by wedging it between two of the staves of the somewhat worn butt.

"That," he said aloud, "is that! Now who put it here? Who was missing between seven o'clock and eight? Who, that is, apart from Temple."

And then he remembered something, and nodded his satisfaction. He had asked Brailsford for an interview on the Tuesday night, and Brailsford had sought him out after Sir Giles Tanroy left, or as he was leaving. Knollis could hear his queer, high-pitched voice again in his mind: *I want to go into town in half an hour or so, Inspector, so I thought I'd better call on you now.*

Knollis was grim-featured as he drew the string from the barrel. He loosened the stone and threw it away. He coiled the string, soaking wet as it was, and put it in his pocket. Then he strode down to the house, walked in, and sought out Freeman. "Will you please tell Mr. Brailsford that I would like to see him in the study—at once."

CHAPTER XIII
THE GUEST OF BAXMANHURST

DESMOND BRAILSFORD entered the room cautiously, closing the door softly behind him and advancing in a wary manner to the table behind which Knollis was seated.

"You wanted to speak to me?" he asked in his high-pitched voice.

"I want to ask you a question," Knollis replied. "You will remember that our first chat was on Tuesday evening, and you said you wanted to go into town. Did you go?"

Brailsford gave an uneasy laugh. "I didn't know that you had the right to pry into my private affairs, Inspector. Whether I did or did not is my own business, and nobody else's."

"I see," said Knollis. "In that case I will not detain you. Good evening, Mr. Brailsford!"

Brailsford ambled over to the door, and stood there with his hand on the knob. "Why should you want to know, anyway?" he asked.

Knollis shrugged. "Since you have no intention of answering the question, there is no point in continuing the conversation. Good evening, Mr. Brailsford!"

He bent his head over his notes and ignored Brailsford's presence. Brailsford shifted his weight from his left foot to his right, and relinquished the door-knob.

"If I thought that the information would help you over Fred's death I'd have no hesitation in telling you, but I can't see how it could help you."

Knollis made no answer, but scribbled busily in his notebook.

Brailsford edged back towards the table. "As a matter of fact, I did set off for town."

Knollis looked up. "Did you get there?"

"Er—no, I didn't!"

"The car pack up on you?" Knollis asked casually.

"I haven't a car. I don't like the things. No, I intended to go by bus, and I missed it by about two minutes," Brailsford replied.

Knollis grunted. "Hm! Where is the bus-stop?"

"About twenty yards beyond Gate Cottage."

"You waited for it at that point?"

Brailsford nodded. "About five to ten minutes. It's the usual country run—y'know, runs to time when it feels like it, and when the driver and conductor are feeling so disposed."

"Now we are getting somewhere!" Knollis exclaimed with deep satisfaction. "Did anyone pass you while you were waiting for the bus?"

Brailsford gave an audible sigh of relief. "So that's why you wanted to know where I was!"

"You have only yourself to blame if you deduced anything more in the nature of prying," Knollis replied dryly.

Brailsford coughed his embarrassment. "Well, perhaps I was a bit sharp on the uptake. Anyway, the gardener's wife was the only person I can remember seeing. She went past me and continued up the hill."

"At what time would that be?" asked Knollis.

"Oh, five to ten-past seven. I asked her about the bus, and she said it would have gone, so I came back here and packed up the idea for the night."

"I see," said Knollis. "Now tell me; surely it was an odd idea to want to go into town a mere hour or so after you had discovered your friend's body?"

Brailsford wriggled, and his left eye sought the ceiling. "To tell you the truth, I wanted to get away from the place. It was giving me the willies. I could have got a drink in the house, but I wanted to get out. I thought about dodging down to the local, and then realised the danger of that—being quizzed and all that. I don't like villagers!"

"You just wanted to get away," said Knollis flatly.

"Just that, Inspector."

"By the way," said Knollis, "I suppose you have seen the murder-weapon?"

"The fire-axe? Oh yes!" Brailsford replied easily.

"Where?" asked Knollis.

Brailsford's mouth twisted queerly. "Where? Why, the thing was always hanging about the place. Couldn't miss it. Black-handled thing."

Knollis looked down at the table, and then quickly fixed his eyes on Brailsford. "You doubtless saw it on its nails in the woodshed?"

"Ye-es, that would be it," Brailsford answered. "Yes, it would be in the woodshed."

Knollis's lips twitched. "But I thought you never went near the staff quarters? I mean, I thought it was one of those things which simply isn't done."

"We-ell," Brailsford replied hesitantly. "I don't call the gardener's shed part of the staff quarters. I often used to drop round there for a chat with Temple. I rather like the cuss."

"And you saw no one else but Mrs. Temple?" Knollis asked anxiously.

"Not that I can remember, Inspector!"

Knollis gave a perfect imitation of a sigh of satisfaction, and closed his notebook. "Thank you very much indeed, Mr. Brailsford. You have relieved my mind." He rose, and collected his hat. "I can give myself a rest at last."

Brailsford followed him to the front door. "You—er—any nearer the arrest of the culprit, Inspector?"

Knollis lowered one eyebrow. "I've never been nearer, Mr. Brailsford, not after so few days. Good night!"

Knollis went no farther than Gate Cottage, where he once more began asking questions.

"When you went out on Tuesday night, Mrs. Temple, did you see anyone against the bus-stop?"

She put a finger to her lips. "See now—oh yes, I saw Mr. Brailsford, the poor gentleman with the twisted face. He asked me if he had missed the bus. Well, it was ten-past seven when I left the house, and I was sure that he had, so I told him so."

"It was dark, of course, Mrs. Temple. You are sure that it was him?" Knollis said with deliberation.

"The bus-stop is under the lamp, Inspector, and he was standing about two yards away, so that the light fell full on his face. Oh, it was him all right!"

"So you would see that he was carrying a parcel, Mrs. Temple?"

"Aye," she said slowly, "he had a parcel! A brown-paper parcel—"

"Brown paper!" Knollis exclaimed involuntarily.

"Brown paper it was, sir."

"Oh!" said Knollis. "A round parcel, such as—say—a cake, or a hat, wrapped up?"

"Oh no, sir!" said Mrs. Temple. "It was flattish, and funny-shaped. Sort of square at one end and thin at the other."

"As if he had a tennis-racket wrapped up?"

"Aye, like that, only not so long. A brown paper parcel it was. I'm sure of that."

"Mm!" said Knollis, and turned to her husband. "Is Brailsford very friendly with you, Temple?"

Temple laughed shortly. "We don't like each other very much. He's tried interfering with my work a few times, and I've told him off. One master is enough for any man, I always says."

"How often has he visited you in the shed?"

"Never, not as I can remember," Temple replied. "I've seen him hanging about round it a few times, but that's different."

"Why would he be hanging round it?" asked Knollis. Temple stared open-mouthed at the question. "I don't know, sir, now I come to think about it."

Knollis returned to Baxmanhurst, and asked Freeman to take him to Dana Vaughan's room, and ask her if she could see him for a few minutes. She could see him, and Knollis was ushered into the feminine atmosphere of her room.

"More questions, Inspector?" she asked caustically, "or do you need my birth certificate this time?"

"All I need is your memory," Knollis replied cheerfully. "I'm hazy about certain periods of Manchester's life, and I have an idea that you may be able to de-fog me. You will understand that I do not wish to bother Mrs. Manchester."

She seated herself, and indicated a second chair. "What do you want to know, Inspector?"

"How long have you known Mrs. Manchester?"

"Mrs. Manchester! I thought you were interested in Fred. At all events, I have known her for several years."

"And how long have you known that she was the daughter of Marlin, the one-time hangman?" Knollis asked sharply.

Dana Vaughan gripped the edge of her chair, and took in a deep breath. "So you know . . . ! How did you find out? Does she know that you know?"

"It is my business to find out," Knollis replied. "Scotland Yard is mainly a well-organised bureau for finding out. The question is; how long have *you* known?"

She hesitated before answering. "A mere two years. She told me herself."

Knollis lifted an eyebrow. "Two years? I suggest that you have known it for over four years, Miss Vaughan."

She bridled at the suggestion, her chin going up sharply. "Two years only, Inspector! Mildred will corroborate that herself!"

"Four," Knollis repeated stolidly, "and perhaps a little longer than that."

Dana Vaughan became transformed from a woman to an actress. Her features took on an expression of lofty disdain, and her eyes blazed fiercely at Knollis. "You appear to have a bee in your bonnet," she said frigidly. "May I ask how you arrive at the four-year notion?"

"Simply," Knollis replied. "I am thinking of the theme of *The Hempen Rope*."

Her hand went to her throat in a protective gesture. "The—theme! I don't profess to understand, Inspector."

Knollis clasped his hands and leaned across the table. "It seems that I must refresh your memory, Miss Vaughan. The play deals with a society lady who marries beneath herself in the social sense. She is immediately faced with the jibes and cold shoulders of her previous friends, but rides out the storm on the satisfaction of her husband's love for her. She then discovers that he was at one time an assistant executioner in an American gaol. The rest of the play deals with her efforts to resolve the situation, and ends with her murdering the person who informed her of her husband's late profession. The working-out of the situation does not concern me in the least, but I do assert that the main theme is based on the life of Mildred Manchester, albeit the positions of the main characters are reversed."

Dana Vaughan slowly nodded. "There is a certain resemblance of situation," she admitted, "but then you must remember, Inspector, that the number of situations available to the dramatist and the writer is low—thirty-six to be exact, and not all of those are allowable or desirable as dramatic material. A mere handful are used over and over again. No dramatist can truthfully say that the theme of a play is original, because whether he is conscious of it or not he is working on ground already well covered by his predecessors."

"That much I understand," said Knollis, "but coincidence is one thing I do not believe in."

Dana Vaughan nodded again. "Coincidences, Inspector, although not allowable in drama, do happen in real life. Further to the argument, I must remind you that I am an actress, and that the play was written by Leslie Danvers!"

"And you are Leslie Danvers," said Knollis.

She tensed herself as Knollis shot the statement at her. "So you know that as well. . . ."

"I have already told you, Miss Vaughan, that the Yard has unique sources of information at its disposal, although no great brain-power is needed to get beneath the *nom de plume* of a playwright. I don't know why you wish to hide your identity as the author of the play from me, but I do assure you that I know a great deal about you, and also about Mrs. Manchester, and Mr. Brailsford."

"Brailsford," she said slowly. "You know plenty about him? Then you have the advantage of me, Inspector. The man puzzles me . . ."

"I am sure that he does," Knollis said cynically, "but for the moment we are discussing your knowledge of Mrs. Manchester's parentage. I suppose you will admit now that you knew Mrs. Manchester's secret many years ago?"

"Ye-es," she answered. "There would appear to be no point in denying it, would there? I was told by Desmond Brailsford."

"How long ago, Miss Vaughan?"

"Oh, about four and a half years ago. I was taking a Mediterranean cruise, and Brailsford forced his company on me. He tried to impress me by pointing out various well-known, and not so well-known, personages who were on board. Among them was Mildred—she was single then, and calling herself Martin. He told me who she was. He said that he had visited some house where she had been engaged as governess-companion—although how he had discovered her secret I can't say."

"Manchester was on the same boat?" asked Knollis.

"Oh yes, Freddy was there, throwing his money about and trying his damnedest to push into the various sets which wanted none of him. He had tacked himself securely on to Mildred long before we made the home port."

"And your interest in Mildred Marlin?"

Dana Vaughan shrugged her shoulders. "I may as well tell the whole of the truth now that I have started. I had written two plays as Leslie Danvers, and they had been well received. I wondered if there was anything in Milly's personality, plus her past, which might provide dramatic material. That is the way of it, Inspector; we live on the blood and tears of the people who pay to see us."

"You engaged her friendship?" Knollis suggested.

"Yes—and I am frank about it now. The friendship endured beyond the period of the cruise, and I began to see her as she really was, a tragic figure. Someone has said that tragedy is not what people do, but what happens to them, and it seemed to me that life had made a great deal happen to Mildred. She had never had a chance. From the point of view of a reader or a play-goer she was a sympathetic character, and as we play on sympathy and empathy—feeling for and feeling with a character—I went ahead with *The Hempen Rope*. She had not told me her secret, and I was satisfied that I was betraying no confidences. All I knew of her came from outside. Well, I wrote the play, and it went into production. It was well received, and I played in it for three and a half years. Milly told me her story, and the thing began to work on my nerves. I began to feel that I had in reality betrayed a confidence, and rationalised my conduct. It was impossible for me to break my contract, and so I feigned a nervous breakdown and slipped out by the back way as it were."

"And now," Knollis nodded, "you are supposed to be convalescing at Baxmanhurst. What is your real reason for coming here?"

Dana Vaughan lifted her eyes and gave Knollis a direct glance. "You really want to know, Inspector?"

"I asked you," he stated bluntly.

"I am watching over her, protecting her."

"From whom?"

"Both Fred and Desmond."

Knollis gave a deep sigh. "Please continue, Miss Vaughan."

She took a deep breath, and rushed the words as she answered: "Desmond Brailsford is blackmailing her—and I can't prove that statement!"

"Explain your reason," said Knollis. "Perhaps I can help you to sort out your suspicions."

"I—I can't explain myself," she replied lamely. "Up to the time of Fred's death on Tuesday there was a peculiar atmosphere in this house. It was a house of undercurrents—oh, I know all this will sound silly to a man of the world like yourself who deals only in hard facts, but I am susceptible to atmosphere, and I know that something evil was at work. I know it! If I name both Fred and Desmond as the authors of it I am merely guessing—or using a woman's intuition. Please don't laugh at me, Inspector!" she pleaded.

"You hinted that Brailsford was blackmailing his—his hostess," said Knollis, and bit his tongue for the slip it nearly caused him to make. "Have you any facts whatsoever to substantiate your suspicions? I am in no way ridiculing your intuitions, but a charge of extortion must be based, obviously, on some fact, no matter how trivial."

Dana Vaughan jumped up from her chair and paced the room, her hands clasped before her. "I have a variety of reasons for reaching my conclusions, Inspector. For some reason or other, Fred would not allow her to go into town, even with myself or himself as escort. At least once a week she would hand me a cheque in the privacy of her room and ask me to cash it for her. It was always made payable to me, and the sums ranged from twenty-five to fifty pounds. I would return from town with the notes, hand them to her, and that was that as far as I was concerned. She never spent a penny herself, for Freddy paid all household bills by cheque. Her dressmaker, manicurist, coiffeur—they all came from town to Baxmanhurst, and Freddy again paid by cheque. I suspected that the money was going to Desmond, but could not prove it until a fortnight ago, when I made a small dot with a pencil point on each of the notes I drew from the bank. Later that same day I asked Desmond if he could give me three pound notes for six ten-shilling ones, giving as my reason that they were bulging my purse. He obliged me. Two of them were marked with a pencil dot. Wait a minute—"

She went to the dressing-table and returned with her handbag. She took her purse from it, and from the purse produced a handful of pound notes, the top two of which she detached and handed to Knollis.

"The dots are in the top right-hand corner, Inspector. As far as I am concerned, those two notes prove conclusively that Milly is paying Desmond for—what? Perhaps you can suggest a reason, Inspector?"

Knollis smiled dryly, and shook his head. "I haven't a notion. This is a brand-new development as far as I am concerned. Perhaps you have a suggestion, Miss Vaughan?"

"Well," she replied, at last coming to a halt before him, "I can only suggest that he is holding the secret of her parentage over her head, and threatening to expose it if she does not pay up. The exposure would make her position untenable in this district."

"Miss Vaughan," said Knollis; "in your opinion, did Fred Manchester know that his wife was Marlin's daughter?"

"I don't know," she said with hesitation. "It would explain his refusal to let her go out, wouldn't it? If he did know, he wouldn't want her to be recognised."

"That was running through my own mind," said Knollis. "Now can you suggest any reason why he should have been, well, murdered? It is a horrible word, but the correct one."

Dana Vaughan covered her eyes with her hands. "It is awful! I think you must excuse me now, Inspector."

"Certainly," said Knollis, rising. "I would like to ask you one question before I leave you . . ."

She uncovered her eyes, and stared somewhat wildly, perhaps fearfully at him.

"Why did you go down to the Green Alley on Tuesday evening?"

"Must I answer that?" she asked in a low voice.

"Either now or later, Miss Vaughan. Either now or at the eventual court proceedings—and I am a discreet man!" said Knollis.

"We-ell, Freeman told me that Sir Giles was there."

"Yes, Miss Vaughan?" Knollis said gently.

"He had gone when I reached the alley, but I hung around for a few minutes, and then walked into the hurst, hoping to see him. I did not, so I returned to the house, and to my room."

"Ah!" said Knollis. "So you would see the axe?"

"Yes," she replied. "It was leaning against the wall of the annexe, close by the doorway."

"And the newspaper? You saw that?"

She nodded. "It was pushed behind the spout that runs down the wall."

Knollis coughed discreetly. "Miss Vaughan, may I suggest that Sir Giles is your second reason for visiting Baxmanhurst?"

She looked him full in the face for a second, and then lowered her gaze to the floor. "Yes, Inspector, you may, but I am afraid that Giles is not aware of it. I'm afraid he sees in me a woman some years older than himself—which I am not, although my experience may be greater."

She fought for a short minute to control her features, and then an expression of intense hate lighted them. "Giles doesn't see me," she whispered, "and meanwhile I have to endure the persistent attentions of Desmond—the swine! I can't get away from him because I must be near Giles. It's hell! Hell, I tell you! And one day I'll do something to him!"

"Similar to what was done to Fred Manchester," Knollis said with a nod.

Dana Vaughan blinked. "To Fred Manchester? I didn't kill him, Inspector—but I think I know who did! And if I could prove it . . ."

"You think that Brailsford did it, don't you?" said Knollis.

Dana Vaughan's hands fell to her sides, and she sank into a chair. "I can't prove it," she said simply.

CHAPTER XIV
THE TACTICS OF KNOLLIS

ELLIS WAS SEATED at the breakfast-table when Knollis entered the dining-room at the Crown on the following morning. He looked up and smiled a good morning.

"Travelled all night?" Knollis asked as he joined him at table.

Ellis shook his head. "Landed at one this morning, but decided not to wake you."

"For which relief, much thanks," said Knollis. "What kind of luck did you have, if any?"

"Quite fair, but nothing startling," Ellis replied. "Want to hear it now?"

"I think not. We are due to confer with Colonel Mowbray at nine o'clock, and you may as well tell it then and save yourself the agonies of a second recital. This porridge is quite good, isn't it?"

"It is for peace-time," said Ellis. They both propped up their morning papers and disappeared behind them.

The nine-o'clock conference resolved into a three-sided discussion, although the Chief Constable, Colonel Mowbray, was desperately anxious for Knollis to say that he was within sight of the end of the case. Knollis refused to commit himself. "The case is ended when we have arrested our man, and have enough evidence to satisfy the Director of Public Prosecutions. We haven't reached that point yet."

"But you must have some idea," protested the Chief Constable.

"Maybe," Knollis replied, "but ideas unsupported by facts have never been legal tender in the police world. Anyway, sir, I think we should hear the results of Ellis's trip to London."

The Chief Constable shrugged, and grumbled. "Oh well, if you wish it that way!"

"Let's have it, Ellis," said Knollis.

Ellis laid a pack of large envelopes on the table.

"I took your cigarette case—which I will return—and had photographs taken of Brailsford's prints. He is not known at the Yard, but I brought the photos along in case. They are in the envelope marked *A*. While this was being done, I went and sought out Miss Vaughan's doctor. He was a bit starchy at first, but eventually consented to come clean with the main details of her illness. He says that she was suffering from overwork and nerve strain. Her main symptoms were occasional lapses of memory, and a tendency to talk to herself when she thought she was alone—a matter he learned from her maid. She further complained that she was having a succession of nightmares, which appeared to consist of distorted and garbled versions of the play she was in, and which, she told him, were horribly real and not at all like a play. I asked him what she meant by that, and he said that according to her description it was as if the murder was taking place in real life, and not on a stage. There were none of the footlights or other impedimenta of the theatre. He says that her condition was alarming, and he prescribed a bromide and a complete absence from the stage for a period of not less than six months."

"Interesting so far," commented Knollis.

"I asked him about the alleged attack on the maid," continued Ellis, "and he said there was ample evidence that it had, in fact, taken place. La Vaughan herself telephoned him in the middle of the night. When he got to her flat he found the maid in a collapsed condition, and bearing marks on her throat which indicated that someone had tried to strangle her. La Vaughan admitted that she was responsible. Her story was that she had suffered a particularly gruesome nightmare, and awoke to find herself trying to snuff the maid. It was then that he ordered the complete rest."

"And the maid?" asked Colonel Mowbray.

"I dug her up after a fair amount of trouble—and help," said Ellis. "She is now employed by Greta Fairchild, who has taken La Vaughan's part in the play. She was very reluctant to talk, but I managed to persuade her that I was acting on Vaughan's behalf, or at any rate in her interests. . . ."

Knollis smothered a smile.

". . . and she came clean. Vaughan had tried to strangle her in the middle of the night, and it was her struggles that had roused Vaughan from her trance, sleep, or what have you. Vaughan was horribly shocked by what had happened, and rang for the doctor. The maid was fond of Vaughan, and consented to keep it quiet because she loved her—after Vaughan had promised her twenty quid, paid for a holiday, and promised to find her a new employer."

"Darn queer story," said the Chief Constable.

"It now gets queerer," said Ellis. "I went along to see Miss Fairchild, and a fair child she is. I wouldn't mind taking her out to dinner."

Colonel Mowbray chuckled. "You did say dinner?"

"I said dinner, sir," Ellis replied innocently. "I went about the interview in a roundabout way, and found out what I wanted to know. The sum total of her story is this. A week before the strangling took place, La Vaughan asked Fairchild how she felt about stepping into the part. Fairchild was her understudy and wanted nothing better. She says that she was overjoyed. She jumped at the opportunity—and then Vaughan said there was a condition; she must take Flint, the maid, into her employ. Fairchild hesitated over this, and then realised that she would be able to afford it on the increased salary."

"Sounds like a spot of premeditation," said the Chief Constable as he breathed on his monocle and fished a silk handkerchief from his pocket.

"There is one other factor," said Ellis, "to be taken into consideration. Vaughan offered her the use of the flat for six months. A week later, the strangling takes place, the doctor orders the complete rest, Vaughan offers her the job with Fairchild and Vaughan packed to come to Baxmanhurst."

Knollis nodded. "It all fits in very nicely. Vaughan has admitted that she faked the illness to come to Baxmanhurst. She couldn't break her contract any other way without it being detrimental to her career. Her avowed reason for coming to Baxmanhurst is that she wanted to protect Mildred from Desmond Brailsford and Manchester."

The Chief Constable smiled for the first time during the interview. "That wraps that part of the case up very nicely. You've done a good job of work, Ellis. Now, Knollis, you left instructions last night for several jobs, and the results were on my desk this morning. There was, as you suspected, a minute trace of chloral hydrate in the wrapped bottle you sent in, and two sets of prints, imperfect ones, but still prints."

He threw a set of photographs across the table.

"Here are Temple's prints, taken last night. He has definitely handled the bottle. I'm now wondering if the other set may have something about them akin to Brailsford's, in Ellis's photos?"

"So am I," said Knollis grimly.

Ellis laid the photographs on the table, and the three men bent over them, comparing characteristics. Knollis rose first, clicked his tongue, and said: "We'll require a much more exact test, but if the second set from the bottle don't match Brailsford's prints taken from my cigarette case, then I'll eat my hat. So Brailsford actually did take the bottle to Temple, and Temple was not dreaming. He apparently gave it a quick rinse out afterwards, and that would be while Mrs. Redson and Freeman were upstairs, but he didn't make a good enough job of it. How about the sample of earth, sir?" Colonel Mowbray fished among the litter of papers on his desk, and triumphantly produced a laboratory report. "Here! Read it for yourself!"

Knollis read it slowly and carefully, and the cloud of doubt lifted from his features. "Chloral hydrate was present in a small degree, eh? Well, that ties up Master Brailsford with the doping, but I still can't regard him as a suspect for the killing."

"Difficult," said the Chief Constable. "And yet the report you sent in last night states that you are satisfied that he was responsible for removing the axe. That makes him an accessory both before and after the fact!"

"Ye-es," Knollis said hesitantly. "I haven't quite tied him up over the axe business, but I think I see a way of doing it. I'd like you to 'phone him, sir, and ask him to run over and have a chat with you this morning. Ellis and myself will search his room while you are keeping him busy."

"Search his room for what, Knollis?"

"A sheet of brown paper, and perhaps a pair of water-stained trousers. You see, while I am satisfied that he hid the axe in the water-butt, I have to produce more evidence. Now I can't see him getting that axe out in the darkness without splashing his clothes. The water is dirty, greenish stuff, and should have produced a fairish stain. I can't imagine Brailsford being so stupid as to try to dispose of the suit, or have it cleaned. I think he will keep it out of sight for a little while, and hope to have it cleaned later."

"And the sheet of brown paper?" asked the Colonel.

"He wrapped the axe in that after wrapping it in news-paper. He wouldn't mind dumping the newspaper, but the brown paper may have had a name and address written on it."

"I see," the Chief Constable said slowly. He picked up the telephone. "I'll get him now."

When he replaced the handset he said: "He'll be here at eleven o'clock. What the devil am I going to talk to him about?"

"Dana Vaughan," Knollis replied quickly. "Tell him that I was reluctant to question him about her at the house, and we thought it more tactful to ask him down here. Give him the impression that we have Vaughan under suspicion, and generally lull him into a feeling of security."

"Cunning," Colonel Mowbray said shortly.

"Now I want to ring Johnson, at Frampton," said Knollis. "There is a job for him this morning."

"Knollis speaking," he said when the connection was made. "I'd like your help. Desmond Brailsford is coming to the Guildhall this morning to be interviewed by Colonel Mowbray. Can you make it convenient to be around and see if you identify him as Daniel Marlin? Can do? Fine! Thanks a lot. I'll investigate your murder some day."

The Chief Constable grinned, and suddenly became grave again. "I thought you said that you had no one under suspicion?"

"You asked me," said Knollis in reply, "if I was in sight of the end of the case yet. I'm not! There is a great deal to be done before I can lay my hand on Brailsford's shoulder. For one thing, I haven't a clue to his motive, and I must know that before making an arrest."

"Lack of dough," Ellis interrupted.

"Meaning what?" asked Knollis.

"I caused an enquiry to be made into Brailsford's occupation and general condition while I was in town," Ellis explained. "Brailsford is the junior partner in a very small publishing firm which isn't doing too well, owing to lack of capital. He isn't very stable personally, either. He's lost a lot to bookies during the past season."

"Any women in his life?" asked Knollis.

"Yes, in the singular. He has a bird tucked away in a love-nest in Shepherd's Bush, but according to my information she isn't a chiselling type, and is waiting patiently until he can get a divorce and marry her."

"Then he's married!" exclaimed Colonel Mowbray.

"No, sir, he isn't," Ellis replied. "There's no trace of it at Somerset House, anyway. No, that is just the yarn he has spun to excuse himself from marrying her. He seems to be a one-woman dog, and there is nothing against his moral character otherwise."

"Pity!" remarked the Colonel. "That sort of fellow usually has two or three of 'em, and it always helps. Great pity! However . . ."

He looked sharply at Knollis. "What about La Vaughan, as Ellis calls her?"

Knollis looked worried. "I'm not at all sure, sir. She has provided information which indicates blackmailing on Brailsford's part, and has also hinted that she is interested in Sir Giles. I think I'll call on him on my way to Baxmanhurst—and we may as well get moving now. There is nothing more to be done at this end as yet. The rest is going to be patience and perseverance."

Sir Giles was on the point of leaving Knightswood for the site of his intended flying-club when they arrived, but he jumped happily from his car and showed no annoyance at being delayed in his plans.

"Something bestirring?" he asked as he joined them on the gravel drive.

"Nothing at all," Knollis said with a fair show of glumness. "By the way, do you happen to be interested in Miss Vaughan, by any chance?"

Sir Giles eyed Knollis gleefully, his head askew. "As an amateur criminologist I deduce that the remark is by no means by the way, and that you have called specifically to ask if I am gone on her. The answer is in the negative—and why the hell do you want to know?"

"I—er—merely wondered," Knollis said lamely.

"During the short time I have known you, Inspector Knollis," said Sir Giles, "I have learned that when you are merely wondering you generally have a first-class idea floating round your mind. Won't you be frank? Why did you ask me?"

"Er—well," hesitated Knollis, "in case you haven't noticed it, Miss Vaughan seems to be very interested in you, and I merely wondered if your interest could be mutual."

Sir Giles gaped. "Dana, interested in me? Don't be absurd, man!"

"I'm not being absurd," replied Knollis. "I do assure you that the lady is very interested."

Sir Giles threw his cigarette away and stood gaping at Knollis. "Well, I'll be blowed! And yet I suppose I could do a lot worse. She's good-looking, talented, and knows how many beans make four. Yes, it's quite an idea—but I'll stick to my aircraft, thank ye. I can make a kite go which way I want it to go by a slight pressure of my hands, and a sideways kick of my foot. You can't do that with a woman, not in the best circles, that is."

"How old is she?" asked Knollis.

"Oh, level thirty, I should say. Milly's only about thirty-five, you know. She probably looks older as a result of all her troubled life, and living with Freddy. He'd age anybody."

"And you are definitely not interested in Miss Vaughan?" Knollis insisted, as if he was not yet sure.

"Definitely not, Inspector!"

"In which case we will leave you. Lovely morning, isn't it? Now what time is it? Five to eleven, so we'd better be moving. Good morning, Sir Giles!"

"Hey! Give me the wire when you make the arrest!" Sir Giles called after them. "I've never seen it done!"

"You've had that!" Ellis called over his shoulder.

On arriving at Baxmanhurst, Knollis sought out Freeman, and asked her if Brailsford was out.

"He is, sir. He asked Smithy to take him into town on business. He had to be there at eleven. There was a telephone call for him earlier in the morning."

"And Mrs. Manchester?"

"She is keeping to her room, sir, because she isn't feeling very well. A nasty rash has come on her hands, and she's worried about it."

"Thank you," said Knollis. "Now I wonder if you can remember which suit Mr. Brailsford was wearing on Tuesday evening?"

"Easily, sir," Freeman replied, "because I had his lounge suit to press. He only has two suits with him, so he would be wearing his ginger plus-four suit."

"Good enough," said Knollis. "Where does he keep it—by the way, he's not wearing it this morning, is he?"

"No, sir, he's gone out in the lounge suit. He keeps them in the wardrobe, of course."

She looked at Knollis as if she could not understand why he had asked such an obvious question.

Knollis thanked her, and set off upstairs with Ellis. In Brailsford's room, they stood for a moment and took stock of it, and then Knollis went to the wardrobe and opened the door.

"The jacket is here, but where are the trousers? Get cracking, Ellis, and search the whole room."

Ellis eventually found the trousers in the bottom drawer of the dressing-table, buried under Brailsford's shirts and collars.

"There are stains," he called across the room; "greenish ones, too. You hit the nail on the head, sir!"

Knollis got to work on them with his magnifying-glass, and finally folded it away. He gave a smile of satisfaction. "I don't think I'll be setting the lab people on a fool's errand if I get them to analyse those stains. See that a sample of water is taken from the butt for comparison tests. And now for the brown paper, if it still exists."

It was found in a hat box in the adjoining box-room.

Knollis had no doubts that it had been wrapped round the axe. The folds all indicated that it had been made into a trian-

148 | FRANCIS VIVIAN

gular parcel, and to aid the impression was a small hole such as might have been made by the spiked end of the implement.

"And now what?" asked Ellis.

Knollis parked himself on a chair and balanced his chin on his hands. "Exactly! Now what! I can satisfactorily prove that he put the doped beer in Temple's way, and I can satisfactorily prove that he removed the axe after the murder—and what else have I got? Nothing."

"Sweet Fanny Adams," said Ellis.

"You see," said Knollis, although it was only too evident that he was talking to himself: "you see, Ellis, Dana Vaughan suggests that Brailsford is drawing money from Mildred—but that doesn't tie-up with the notion that Brailsford killed Manchester. There is also the point that Vaughan suggests that Mildred was afraid of Manchester knowing how much she was spending. Now did Manchester know that Brailsford was Mildred's brother? Did he know that she was Marlin's daughter? Does Vaughan know that Brailsford is Daniel Marlin? These are the questions to be answered: Who killed the budgie? Who killed the cat? And, finally, who killed Manchester? That reduces the problem to its simplest terms."

"A pretty string of questions," Ellis remarked. "Who benefits by Manchester's death, apart from the whole world of suffering mankind?"

"Mildred, directly," said Knollis, "but I am more concerned with the question of who benefits indirectly. Is it possible for either Vaughan or Brailsford to be in a position to tap Mildred's bank balance now that Fred is dead? I'm hanged if I can see any motive other than a monetary one. Oh, damn it; let's get back to town. I've reached that muddled stage where I can't see the wood for trees. We'll call and see the Colonel, and then disport ourselves in a local pub until lunch-time. Perhaps the fog will clear then. Bring those pants and the paper for the lab."

Ellis drove back to town, dropped Knollis at the Guildhall, and went on to the Home Office laboratory.

Knollis satisfied himself that Brailsford was no longer in the building, and went up to the Chief Constable's room to face a contented man.

"Johnson recognised him, Knollis," he said happily. "Says he would recognise him anywhere, although he has aged since their last meeting. As for Brailsford, well, I got him talking, and he opened out beautifully. Told me all I wanted to know."

Knollis was dubious, and showed it by his expression, so that the Chief Constable removed his monocle, polished it, replaced it, and shook his head. "Don't be so suspicious, Knollis! I may not be a Yard man, but I'm not entirely lacking in intelligence, y'know!"

Knollis took a seat and planted his palms firmly on his knees. "What did he tell you?"

"All about Vaughan. Says he is sorry for Mrs. Manchester, too. She has some secret, he told me, that is giving her a great deal of worry. That will be the secret of her parentage, of course. He implies that Vaughan is aware of it, and is pumping the cash out of her regularly.

"It seems that there have been rows in the house over the amount of money spent by Mildred. Manchester was suspicious of her, and challenged her. She told him that she was helping a poor relative—"

"That may be true," Knollis said grimly. "However, please continue, sir."

"Brailsford did not say so outright, but he gave me the impression that he suspects Vaughan of doin' in Manchester." He shook his head. "Most convincing fellow! He almost had me believing him at one time. By the way, what did you find?"

"Everything I looked for," Knollis replied. "His trousers were hidden away, and are stained. I also found the sheet of paper, and the folds in it substantiate Mrs. Temple's story of him carrying a triangular parcel. Things don't look too rosy for Mr. Brailsford at the moment."

"Then pull him in!" the Chief Constable exclaimed. "Why potter about with him like this? He's done it, hasn't he?"

Knollis did not answer.

"Well, hasn't he?" repeated the Chief Constable.

"On the face of it, yes," Knollis replied slowly.

"Then why on earth—"

Knollis rose, and slapped his hat against his leg. "I can't prove it, and I can't trace any motive to him."

The Chief Constable sucked a tooth, and then looked hard at Knollis. "You mean that you are stuck?"

"Temporarily, yes," Knollis admitted. "I've slipped somewhere, and I don't know where it is."

Colonel Mowbray left his chair and came round the table. "But look! What are you going to do about it! You must do something! I mean, we can't let the case go into the unsolved file. What are you going to do?"

Knollis walked to the door. "I'm going to lunch, sir."

"And after lunch?"

Knollis clicked his tongue. "Is there a good news theatre in Trentingham?"

"News theatre?" the Chief Constable gasped.

Knollis nodded. "One with a couple of Donald Duck's in the programme."

"This—this is a murder investigation, Knollis!"

"Yes, I know," replied Knollis, "and Donald is very funny. I always find him most refreshing."

CHAPTER XV
THE VIRTUES OF HERR GLASER

AT THREE-THIRTY that afternoon Knollis emerged from the news theatre with a smile lurking on his lips, and a brighter gleam in his eyes. He had long since learned that true mental relaxation was not to be found in idleness, but in a change of subject, and he no longer felt jaded. With a springy step he returned to the Guildhall, collected his car, and drove to Baxmanhurst. Here he asked to see Mrs. Manchester, for the second time only since her husband had been so violently butchered. She received him in the sitting-room, and Knollis lost very little time in exchanging courtesies, although he did comment on her bandaged hand.

"I don't know what is the trouble with it," she said wearily. "My finger-tips are sore, and Denstone does not seem to know what has caused it—but I don't suppose you have called to discuss my health."

"No," said Knollis, "my errand is nothing so pleasant."

He looked at her carefully. Sir Giles was right; she looked considerably older than her thirty-five years. He would have placed her age another ten years higher.

"I have tried to avoid bothering you," he said, "but the investigation has reached a stage where a great degree of frankness is necessary on your part if we are to find your husband's murderer."

She gazed down at her hands, folded in her lap.

"If I can help . . ." she murmured weakly.

"You are the daughter of Marlin, I believe?" Knollis said.

"Yes," she said without looking up. "I suppose it was natural and inevitable that you should find out."

"It was," Knollis agreed. "Did your husband know that?"

"Yes, he did."

"How long had he known?" asked Knollis.

"Merely a few months. Brailsford told him—although how he knew I cannot imagine," Mrs. Manchester replied.

Knollis nodded to himself. It was to be a game, apparently. Well, he was quite capable of playing it. He would suppress his knowledge of Desmond Brailsford's true identity.

"The morning that you discovered the cat in the cactus house; why did you go there that morning?"

"To look round, of course, Inspector."

"You made a purpose journey, Mrs. Manchester?"

"Ye-es," she answered hesitantly.

"Your husband asked you to do so?"

She looked up then. "How did you know that?"

"I didn't," Knollis replied frankly. "It is a surmise—but he did ask you to take a look in the cactus house!"

"Yes," she admitted. "One of the cacti had flowered, and he was anxious for me to see it before it faded away. Some of them only flower for a few hours, you know," she added listlessly.

Knollis beat a tattoo on his knee with his finger-tips. "Mrs. Manchester!"

"Yes, Inspector?"

"You know that your husband killed both the cat and the budgerigar? You are aware of that, aren't you?"

Mildred Manchester nodded. "Yes, I knew that on Tuesday morning. Yes, it was Fred."

"You were afraid for your own life, were you not?" Knollis next asked.

Her hands tightened on each other, and she looked up again and stared dully at him. "How do you know all these things?" she asked wonderingly.

"You forced your husband into asking for a police investigation so that there would be policemen around and he would not dare to attempt your life?"

"Yes. That is the truth, Inspector."

Knollis gave a deep sigh. "Suppose you tell me the whole story. It will save me a lot of work, and yourself a great deal of trouble and worry."

"Inspector," she said, "I will tell you what I know."

"You told me during our first interview that you were perfectly happy with your husband, Mrs. Manchester."

"I was trying to keep up appearances, Inspector," she said with a wan smile. "And now—well, I don't care. Fred and I were happy at first, although at the best our marriage was no more than a marriage of convenience. Fred wanted my social contacts; I wanted his money—and security. All my life I seem to have been wandering from place to place, seeking a haven.

"I left home when I was fifteen. I discovered the nature of my father's trade, and I fled from it. I changed my name to Martin, studied in my spare time, and fitted myself to become a governess. I obtained positions, but they never lasted long. Someone would find out who I was, and shudder at the thought of their children being in the care of a hangman's daughter.

"After this had happened half a dozen times I grew weary of it all. I wanted a rest, and time to think. I had saved a little money and so I went on a cruise, hoping that some solution would present itself before I got home again. Fred was on the same boat, and he made up to me. I was not quite so balanced in those days, and I wanted to impress him, so I talked about Lady This and Lord That and the Honourable So-and-So. He talked about his money. Before we left the boat he had proposed to me—and it was the most cold-blooded proposition imaginable. I was to help him to become a socialite, and he was to give me a home, and money, and a name. I accepted, because I thought that once we were married I would find some means of keeping my part of the bargain."

"And you did not?" Knollis interrupted.

"I did not, Inspector. We were married, and Fred eventually bought Baxmanhurst. We were living in London then, and he did not tell me where the house was that he had bought, not until he brought me to it. I scented danger as soon as we neared the district, because, as you may know, I was born in a hamlet not many miles from here. I tried to get him to sell, but I had no valid reason which I could use to persuade him, and I dare not tell the truth, and so I had to lie low and pretend to be an ailing woman.

"While on the cruise I had made the acquaintance of Dana Vaughan, and a very pleasant woman she seemed. We promised to meet again, but did not do so for a long time afterwards, when Fred took me to London and we saw her playing in *The Hempen Rope*. The theme of the play was so obviously based on my own early life that I had Fred make enquiries about Leslie Danvers, and then learned that 'he' was Dana.

"In some way she had learned my secret. I was so afraid of her going any further with it that I resumed our friendship in the hope of enlisting her sympathy, which I am pleased to say that I did. Dana is now a firm friend, and my secret is safe with her."

"So that it was definitely Brailsford who told your husband, Mrs. Manchester?" said Knollis.

"It could have been no one else." She nodded. "He knew it, and he played on it. From time to time he would 'borrow' money from me, money which I knew I would never see again. At last I refused to lend him any more, and Fred's attitude towards me changed from that day. I taxed Desmond with his betrayal, and he just grinned at me and said he had no qualms; a wife had no right to have secrets from her husband. He added that quite a lot of our friends would probably be interested as well—and borrowed fifty pounds on the strength of it. I can't prove it, but I think that he was playing the same game on Fred. I'm afraid that Desmond is a cad."

"I see," said Knollis quietly. "Tell me, Mrs. Manchester, did your secret ever become the subject of an open quarrel with your husband?"

"Yes, it did, Inspector—a few weeks ago. He said he had learned who I was, and ironically thanked me for my promise to make him well known. There was nothing I could say to excuse myself, so I let him rave on for about ten minutes. He finally reached the pitch of his rage, and struck me across the mouth. I neither cried out nor tried to protect myself, for I knew that I was in the wrong. The sins of the fathers . . ."

"And now? What do you intend to do?" asked Knollis.

"I think I shall sell Baxmanhurst back to Sir Giles Tanroy, and then go abroad and see if it is possible to start again. Perhaps Kenya, or New Zealand. I don't know. I don't know what I shall do!"

"Who killed your husband, Mrs. Manchester?" asked Knollis quietly.

"One or the other of them, and I don't know which," she replied. "Either Dana or Desmond."

"Why should Desmond kill him? What motive has he?"

"A woman is easier to blackmail than a man, and with Fred out of the way—you see?"

"If Dana did it, then she did it for me. She is a true friend. *You know* that it is one of them, so please do not think that I am being faithless to a friend, Inspector! Dana would give her life for me—if only to atone for writing that play."

"I think I should tell you something," said Knollis. "The medical experts are of the opinion that no woman could have swung the axe with such violence."

Her hands fell apart, and she looked up with an expression of intense relief. "Oh! Then I am glad—glad for Dana! She knows that I believe she did it, and now I can tell her—"

"Nothing!" Knollis interjected. "You will not repeat a word of this interview to anyone."

"Oh!" she said in a crestfallen manner. "And yet I see your point. Very well, Inspector, I will keep my silence."

Knollis excused himself, and went for a stroll in the hurst. Donald Duck had revived his brain, and it was now working overtime. His main difficulty was to keep track of the thoughts that arose in his consciousness. He made a page of notes, and then strode back to the house, once more seeking out Freeman.

"This conversation is to be regarded as confidential. You are not to mention it even to Smith. Understand?"

Freeman smiled. "I know how to hold my tongue, sir."

"There is a question I want to ask you. Miss Dana had been ill before she came to Baxmanhurst, hadn't she?"

"Oh yes, sir!"

"Is she still taking medicine?"

"I don't think so, sir, although she brought several boxes and bottles with her. She put them in the box-room soon after she arrived."

"The box-room. Where is it?"

"Next to Mr. Brailsford's room, sir."

"Locked?" asked Knollis.

"No, sir, I've never known it to be locked."

Knollis handed her a much-folded ten-shilling note. "Put that towards your trouseau, and don't talk!" Freeman smiled. "Thank you, sir. I promise I won't say a word to a soul, not even to Smithy. You go straight up the stairs, and the box-room is facing you, with Mr. Brailsford's on the right."

Knollis drove furiously back to Trentingham. Leaving the car at the kerb, he charged into the headquarters and went straight to the official technical library, and there he banged on the table for the librarian. The constable in charge ambled through the doorway, changing his pace considerably as he recognised his client.

"I want Dixon, Mann and Brend on *Forensic Medicine and Toxicology*, and Glaser's *Poison*," said Knollis, "and I'm in a hurry."

The constable supplied the volumes and slammed them on the table. "Paper and pencil, sir?"

"Please," said Knollis.

He pulled up a chair, and seated himself. "While I'm doing this, ring through and ask for the name of the London doctor who attended Miss Dana Vaughan. Sergeant Ellis's report."

Knollis opened Glaser's book first. In the chapter headed 'Soporifics' he found the reference to chloral hydrate. The first paragraph was mainly historical, dealing with its discovery, and stating that it is "no harmless sleeping draught," but at the time of its discovery there was little to replace it. Knollis read on:

This is a colourless crystalline substance easily soluble in water and alcohol and causing inflammation when laid on the skin. Small doses are insufficient, but two—or at the most three—grams are sufficient to calm even very violent excitement and procure sleep. More, however, must not be given, otherwise the patient relapses into unconsciousness, and the heart and respiratory organs are paralysed. . . .

He read on to the end of the passage, and then returned to the beginning and made a note of the fact that: *Many pharmacologists strongly disapprove of this medicament and Lewin calls it "the most dangerous of all soporifics which ought to have been discarded long ago."*

An idea was beginning to dawn in his mind when the constable interrupted to say that he had found the name of the doctor.

"Then look him up in the medical directory and see when he was born," said Knollis. "See, where was I? Oh yes, I'd better have a look at Dixon, Mann and Brend."

These two gentlemen were far more technical than their European colleague, and he had to work his way through toxic and non-toxic doses, temperatures, and a catalogue of chloral poisoning cases.

He shut the book and pushed it away, scratching his head. "There was something else," he muttered.

"You put me off. Now what the devil was it? I suppose it will come back to me. Got that date yet?"

"Born eighteen-eighty-three, sir," said the constable proudly.

"That makes him sixty-two, according to my mental arithmetic. A member of the old school. It might be possible! Can you get Dr. Clitheroe on the telephone?"

"I can't get him on the telephone, sir," he replied. "But I happen to know that he's across at the dead-house. He was in here about ten minutes ago, consulting a few books."

"Then I'll go across," said Knollis.

He strode across the street to the mortuary, and found the doctor examining a suicide who had been brought in to keep Manchester's remains company.

"Clitheroe!" said Knollis anxiously. "Have you a minute to spare!"

The tall doctor glanced up. "Knollis excited, eh? Unusual, surely! What is wrong?"

"Look," said Knollis, "if you had a nerve case—amnesia, sleeplessness, sleep-walking, nightmares, and all that, would you prescribe chloral hydrate?"

The doctor laughed. "Not in these enlightened days. It's a bit tricky."

"Would any doctor?" persisted Knollis.

The doctor hesitated. "Well, yes, some of the old boys might yet if they are sufficiently conservative." And then he added: "Why?"

"See you later," Knollis replied.

He returned to the library, and once more took up Glaser's book on poison, meanwhile asking the constable to ring up Dr. Denstone at Bowland and ask him if he could see him straight away. "Tell him I'll be right over if he can," he said.

He pored over Glaser and groaned so loudly that the constable turned from the 'phone. "All right, sir?"

"In health, yes," Knollis returned, "but not in temper. It can't be, I tell you! It can't be!"

"Dr. Denstone will see you, sir," said the constable.

"Right," replied Knollis. "Now ring round and see if you can find Sergeant Ellis, and tell him I want him straightway."

The constable grimaced as Knollis looked away, and once more picked up the telephone.

Knollis read and reread the sections in both books which related to chloral hydrate, and was closing them when the constable informed him that Sergeant Ellis had left a message to say that he had gone over to Barston on a hunch.

"Where is Barston?" Knollis snapped.

"Near Frampton, sir."

"Is that the village or hamlet where Marlin used to live?"

"That's right, sir. He died there, too."

Knollis grabbed his hat. "I wonder what bee he's got in his bonnet this time!"

He drove to Bowland and rang Dr. Denstone's bell.

"You said you would call on me," said the doctor, ""and I was wondering when you would come. Have a drink?"

"I need one," said Knollis. "I'll take it neat."

The doctor busied himself with the decanter, and passed a glass of whisky to Knollis. "Your health, Inspector!"

"Your health!" said Knollis, and almost in the same breath said: "If you had a nerve case whose symptoms were insomnia, amnesia, nightmares, and sleep-walking, would you prescribe chloral hydrate?"

"Chloral hydrate!" repeated the doctor with upraised brows. "No, I don't think I should."

He then asked the inevitable: "Why?"

"Would any doctor prescribe it?" asked Knollis.

"Why, yes—but not me. Look, perhaps I can help you more if you explain what is behind your question."

"Well," Knollis explained. "I've been looking up the books on toxicology, and they seem to agree that chloral hydrate is an out-dated drug."

"I wouldn't say that," Dr. Denstone replied. "It is used, and some of the older members of the profession swear by it in preference to the newer drugs of that nature. But why do you ask?"

Knollis drained his glass. "Temple was doped. We agree on that?"

"Yes, we agree on that, Inspector."

"Where did the dope come from? You can't walk into a chemist's shop and buy knock-out drops as if they were aniseed balls!"

"Agreed again. What do you suggest?"

"Simply this," said Knollis, "that Miss Vaughan came down to Baxmanhurst as a near-wreck. You may not know all this, but she had suffered loss of memory, sleep-walking, and had also tried to strangle her maid during the course of a nightmare. Her doctor was a West End man, and he is sixty-two years of age. Now, taking all those facts into consideration, do you think it likely that he prescribed chloral hydrate?"

Dr. Denstone mused, and recharged the glasses.

"It comes within the bounds of possibility, but not within the bounds of probability. I'm fifty-eight myself, and almost a member of the same school, but I wouldn't use it. Tricky stuff. Look, I suggest that you get in touch with the fellow concerned. You will be certain then. As it is, you are only hoping that he prescribed it!"

"*Touché!*" said Knollis with a grin. "Perhaps you are right—but if he didn't, then where in the name of heaven did it come from?"

"That," said the doctor dryly, "is your job. I am not a detective."

Knollis returned to Baxmanhurst, and after making sure that the coast was clear he invaded the box-room. Here, in a small attaché case, he found several bottles, one of which was labelled C.H. and contained crystals. He tipped a few into his match-box and went back to Trentingham, where he sought out Dr. Clitheroe.

"Are these chloral crystals?" he demanded.

"I think so," said Dr. Clitheroe, "but I'd prefer the verdict of an analyst. I'll take them along if you like, and ring you later in the evening. That do?"

"Fine," said Knollis.

He wrote a long message to Scotland Yard, requesting that the doctor and Vaughan's maid should be re-interviewed with reference to the chloral, and handed it in to the teleprinter room.

CHAPTER XVI
THE STORIES OF THREE PEOPLE

ALTHOUGH KNOLLIS RELAXED physically for the next few hours, his brain was working at full pressure as he sat in the office allotted to him and watched the market-day throng in the Square below. There was a certain rhythm in the movement of the shoppers and stall-gazers which encouraged his thoughts to flow easily and smoothly. He was no psychologist in the academic sense, and therefore he was not interested in the whys and wherefores of the phenomenon. He was satisfied, and more than satisfied with the results. Ellis was away at Barston. Colonel Mowbray had slunk away for a surreptitious eighteen holes on the Trentingham links. The sergeants and the constables were engaged on their various routine tasks concerned with the case. The gentlemen of the Press were being dealt with by a diplomatic Inspector of police on the floor below. Knollis was alone, and consequently inclined to agree with the poet that God was in his heaven, and all was right with the world. He could now attempt to reconstruct the tragedy as he believed it had occurred, and strictly according to the evidence collected.

There were three people concerned, apart from the corpse—and even he had only been a corpse-elect when the affair opened. But when did it open? Perhaps back in those dim days when Marlin had been blown sky-high by a German mine, or perhaps it was one of our own. At any rate, he had been blown sky-high, and had descended with a torn face and a lacerated mind. That was the initial cause. As a result of that, Daniel had been born, and his wife had committed suicide. As a result of that, Marlin had turned hangman—and probably God alone was able to trace the peculiar twists and turns of thought that had taken him towards the noose and the trap and the other grim impedimenta of his new trade. As a result of that, Mildred and Daniel had left home; Mildred, it would seem, to attempt to better herself, and Daniel, it would seem, to live as easily and with as little work as possible.

Mildred. She had studied, and fitted herself for a post as governess, and there seemed to be little doubt but that she had equipped herself well, and had obtained the type of post she wanted—until the secret of her parentage leaked out, and then she passed on, a sort of female Wandering Jew, welcomed until the truth was known, and then turned from the door with threats and imprecations. As a result of that, she decided to seek security by some other method.

Knollis picked up his pencil and made a note: *How did Mildred Manchester get the idea of going on a cruise? Was it a planned attempt to find a wealthy husband? Having found a husband, she married him, and considered herself safe at last from the slings of outrageous fortune. Some people seem to be cursed to a life of trouble and unhappiness. Enter Dana Vaughan, with her play based on the basic facts of Mildred's life. This was a threat of exposure, when she would surely lose all that she had gained. She made a friend of Dana, and the bonds of friendship sealed the secret.*

Enter her own brother, with demands for money, and a threat of exposure if she did not pay. She paid, and kept on paying. One refusal, and Manchester was informed of her secret.

Knollis closed his eyes, so that only the murmuration of the human starlings reached his mind. Turn to Manchester. What was he? A journeyman who wanted to be a gentleman. And then an amateur gentleman with an acute feeling of inferiority. He discovered Mildred on the cruise, and her talk of society and high-life refired his ambitions. He married her, only to discover that he had married the daughter of an ex-hangman. Mortification and a dread of the truth being known.

Knollis opened his eyes and made a second note: *Find out from bank if Man. was paying to Brail.*

He returned to his reverie. There was Dana Vaughan, an actress almost at the height of her fame. She had written a play which had run for three and a half years, and bade fair to run another year. Conscience-smitten by her ruthless, or thoughtless, use of the facts of Mildred's life, she had effected her escape from the stage—for what purpose? She averred that it was to watch over Mildred. Such an action was quixotic, and particularly so in the case of a West End actress who had fought her way to the top. Her absence from the stage would damage her career, and her bank balance. What did she hope to get from it? It was incredible, in this materialistic age, that she should throw away her career in the name of friendship, no matter how sacred that name might appear to her.

Knollis wrote again: *Vaughan's sacrifice suspect. What is she after?*

He closed his eyes. Manchester meant to make his wife pay for her deceit and for the humiliation which she had brought upon him, not realising that he was only paying the price for his own hasty greed for social recognition. It was poetic justice. Nevertheless, he meant to make her pay. He broke the neck of the budgie, and tied a cord round it—the whole a fiendish reminder of her father's profession. Then he broke the neck of the cat, and again tied a cord round it. The third cord was found in his pocket after his death. For whom was that intended? For Mildred? Did Manchester mean to clear her completely out of his life? It hardly seemed possible. The killing of the cat and the bird revealed a certain subtlety in Manchester's thinking apparatus. Was there some third object of Mildred's affection which he could kill? Vaughan seemed to be the only possibility, for it was certain that she had no love for her brother. It might be Vaughan, for she had insinuated that Manchester had made advances and had been repulsed, and so it was quite on the cards that he had developed a two-fold hate for her, based on her refusal to fall in with his suggestions, and on Mildred's avowed affection for her. So Manchester might have planned the death of Vaughan, and was keeping the third cord in his pocket in readiness.

Knollis roused himself and made yet another note: *Ask Freeman if Man. emptied, his pockets each night.*

And then Knollis found himself faced with another possibility that sprang full-grown, Athena-like, into his mind. Had the murderer pushed the cord into his pocket? And a further note resulted from the thought: *Ask Mil. if she knew how much cord in workbox, and whether all had disappeared after death of budgie.*

His attempt at a continuation of the reverie was cancelled by the entrance of a sergeant from the C.I.D. of the Trentingham Borough Police. "I've some reports for you, sir."

Knollis looked round, and saw a fearsome sheaf of official-looking papers.

"Are you particularly busy, Sergeant?"

"Nothing on at the moment, sir, and not off duty for another two hours," he replied.

"Then make yourself comfortable in a chair and read the things out to me. I'll listen with my eyes closed."

"Very good, sir."

"And you can smoke," said Knollis. "Here, have one with me."

"Thank you, sir."

The sergeant watched Knollis light up, sit back, put his feet up on the radiator, and close his eyes. He then made for the swivel chair, and put his own regulation boots up on the table.

"Miss Dana Vaughan's doctor reports that at no time did he prescribe or authorise the taking of chloral hydrate. He regards it as a risky drug to administer and would as soon prescribe laudanum to a crying child. He is not aware, and has never been aware, that Miss Vaughan had any chloral hydrate in her possession, and had he been aware of her possession of such drug he would have demanded the handing-over of the said drug, or would have refused to continue treatment and would not have accepted any responsibility for her."

"That's fair enough," Knollis commented. "Let's have the next instalment."

"Dr. Clitheroe wishes to report that the crystals submitted to him by you have been declared by the Home Office analysts to be chloral hydrate. They have suffered somewhat owing to exposure to the atmosphere."

"Also fair comment," said Knollis.

"Statement made by Miss Peggy brackets Fifi brackets Coulson of Berkeley Mews and Streatham Hill, late maid to Miss Dana Vaughan and now maid to Miss Greta Fairchild, actress. Miss Vaughan used to suffer from first-night nerves and often took 'something' to quieten herself before going on the stage. She was in touch with somebody who on various occasions supplied her with veronal, barbitone, and what are commonly known as knock-out drops. These last were in a small glass bottle labelled *C.H.*, and were last seen by Coulson when Miss Vaughan was packing to leave London. She saw Miss Vaughan put them in her case. As Miss Vaughan was handing over her flat furnished to Miss Fairchild, Coulson thinks that she didn't want Miss Fairchild to discover her little weakness. Coulson says that as Miss Fairchild takes four fingers of neat Scotch before going on she can't see the difference."

Knollis chuckled.

"Anything else, Sergeant?"

"Well, sir, the sergeant who interviewed her seemed to have had ideas of his own—"

"What name?" asked Knollis.

"Sergeant Trotter, sir."

Knollis smiled. "Inspector Ronnie Drew's man! He does have ideas of his own, and very original ones. What did he discover?"

"Trotter asked Coulson about Miss Vaughan's correspondence, and learned that she had letters from two people at Baxmanhurst, a man and a woman both called Manchester."

"Yes?" Knollis asked anxiously as the sergeant paused.

"Coulson says that Vaughan—Miss Vaughan—destroyed the letters from Mrs. Manchester before she left the flat, but carefully tied up the others and put them in her case."

"Phew!" Knollis whistled. "Go on!"

"Sergeant Trotter persuaded the maid to admit that she had happened to see one or two when they were lying around, loose like,' and said they were 'hot stuff.'"

"So that's how the land lies," said Knollis slowly. "When I get back to town, Sergeant Trotter shall have as much beer as he can hold, and two ounces of that nasty shag tobacco that he smokes. This information is distinctly a break. Anything else?"

"Only that the letters were numbered as they were received, and there were thirty-two of them, tied into a bundle with blue ribbon. That's the lot, sir."

Knollis rose and took the reports from the sergeant. "You can depart now. Tell Sergeant Ellis where I am when he comes in, please."

He strolled back to the window and looked out over the crowded square. There might be a thousand people down there, ambling along between the lines of stalls, or gossiping to neighbours and friends they encountered. From this height they all looked pretty much alike. They were members of the human race—and yet, if the lives of each of them could be explored! That youngish woman with the green hat—was she married? Was she happily married? Was she married and having an *affaire* at the same time? Was she planning to murder her husband, or to do a Thompson-Bywater on him? It seemed silly to think such things about an innocent shopper, and yet, less than a week ago, any one of the protagonists of the Baxmanhurst tragedy might have been a member of this crowd and have looked just as innocent, just as casual, just as contented with life, and just as aimless as the rest of the human race, and yet a thought of murder had been lurking in that one mind. Perhaps at that time it had been unformed, a mere flash of energy in the convolutions in the brain, a spark that developed, grew into a lightning flash that burned away and destroyed all resistance, an irresistible force that had no memories of yesterday nor warnings of the morrow. The human mind was a delicate piece of apparatus, capable of withstanding a gigantic shock, and yet thrown off-balance and out of all normality of action by the thought of a split-second, or the impulse of a moment's duration.

Knollis shook himself. This was no time for philosophising on the frailty of the human being. His profession allowed no time for such mental meanderings. It was an objective profession, dealing with hard facts, times, places, and actions. Somewhere at Baxmanhurst was a murderer, a romantic-enough figure in the cold print of the daily newspaper, but in actuality a dangerous menace to the community. And he was paid to apprehend him. He was expected to track him, discover his motives, prove that he had the opportunity, satisfy a jury that he was capable of the crime, demonstrate that no other person could have committed the crime for which he would be tried—and then step aside and let a nation which professed the Christian faith turn a blind eye to it and put into execution a Mosaic law which demanded an eye for an eye and a tooth for a tooth in a spirit of elemental vengeance.

"The Englishman," he said aloud, "is a damned inconsistent fool!"

"Agreed!" said a voice from the doorway.

Knollis turned to see Ellis grinning at him.

"I often think that," said Ellis, "and to-day I've been convinced that Sir James Fell is the biggest fool of the whole bunch!"

"You do, eh?" Knollis asked interestedly.

"Next to coroners and local J.P.s."

"What hasn't he done this time, my Ellis?"

"It isn't this time. It was when Marlin fell down the cellar steps that he either ratted on his job or was purblind to Johnson's theories."

Knollis nodded. "Of course! You've been to Barston! What news on the Rialto, Antonio?"

Ellis brushed his moustache from his mouth. "I think I can call it news, sir. If I was a reporter I'd be rushing the yarn through to the Street and pinning a feather in my cap at the same time."

"That's one hand for the telephone and one for the feather," said Knollis. "Yes, it would be possible. But suppose, my friend, that you stop blathering and tell me the best or the worst."

"Well," said Ellis, grinning, "I saw your report of the visit to Frampton and Inspector Johnson, and I was pretty interested."

"Interested you may be," said Knollis, "but your best friend couldn't call you pretty. But proceed!"

"I was *very* interested," continued Ellis, "and as you weren't available for consultation I shot over to Frampton and had a chat with the Inspector. After telling me the yarn again he took me to Barston, and showed me the haunted cottage where Marlin lived and died. It hasn't been occupied since he snuffed it; nobody seems to fancy living with the ghost of a hangman. I can think of a gag there."

"If it has anything to do with the ghost being a noose-sance, I've heard it—thirty, years ago," said Knollis.

"Well, Inspector Johnson is well known in the village, so I asked him to oblige by waiting at the cottage, and I took a stroll down to the local. The rustics soon started quizzing me, and I let them. They gained the impression—somehow—that I was a writer gentleman looking for material on hangmen in general, and Marlin in particular. They were only too anxious to oblige me, although they were the thirstiest set of witnesses it has been my misfortune to encounter. Cost me fifteen bob, at a bob a pint! Anyway, the results were worth it."

"Then let's have them without further preamble," said Knollis, cocking a severe eye at his sergeant, while his lips belied the look.

"The main point is that Mildred and Daniel were along at Barston to see him the day that he died," Ellis said quite casually.

"They were!" Knollis exclaimed. "You have proof of that?"

"One of the villagers was on the same train from which Mildred and Daniel disembarked at Frampton. The bus service was not too good, and so they walked to Barston, with this johnny bringing up the rear. Their arrival in the village was witnessed by two old granfers who apparently spend their time cud-chewing on the bench outside the local.

"According to all the best rumours—and it is one of those places where everybody knows everybody's business but his own—a reconciliation scene took place in Marlin's shop, with everybody falling on everybody else's neck and promising to kill the fatted calf. Mildred then went to the cottage, sent the daft girl home for the day, and took over. She cooked a meal for the three. She also tucked into the washing. In the midst of this the clothes-line broke, and she sent Daniel, who had now arrived, to the ice-cream-paraffin-and-skipping-rope shop to buy a new one. The old boy went back to work after the meal, and Daniel repaired to the pub while his father repaired boots and his sister repaired the old boy's socks. On his return, he looked after the house while she shopped at the above-mentioned shop and provided a ton of provisions for the larder. They left Barston at three o'clock, and—according to village guesses—retrained at Frampton. Inspector Johnson did not know all this, and when I told him he said some very rude things about Sir James Fell."

"I can well imagine it," said Knollis, chewing the end of his pencil thoughtfully. "Well, we haven't a chance with that case now. We would have to prove that Daniel didn't retrain, or that he broke his journey in order to return surreptitiously to the village, and it happened seven years ago! We would also have to prove that he was away from his own home during the vital hours—and who the devil can remember what happened all that time ago? No, Ellis, I think we are beaten on the Marlin case unless we can force a confession, and I can't see Daniel doing any other than giving us a dirty smile. Still, if we get him for Manchester's death we can consider that Marlin is avenged. . . ."

"It's a pity we can't hang him twice," Ellis remarked, "because I'm in full agreement with Johnson that Marlin was murdered, and I'm satisfied that Daniel did it. If Johnson had been given the chance to investigate at the time I think he could have brought off a good catch."

"Well, we may only have to hang him once," said Knollis. "Now there is a job to be done at Baxmanhurst, and I think you'd better come with me."

"It's late," said Ellis.

"It's not too late," Knollis replied softly. "Get the car round, please."

Knollis came straight to the point as he faced Dana Vaughan in her room, and her attempt to play a part was wrecked from the outset.

"I am enquiring into the source of the drugs that you have in your possession, Miss Vaughan," said Knollis. "I refer, of course, to barbitone, veronal, and chloral hydrate. Would you care to explain why you have them, and where they were obtained?"

"I haven't—"she began, and then stopped as she saw the expression on Knollis's face.

"The box-room, Ellis," he said, and waited silently until Ellis returned with the bottles and placed them on the table.

. "Those are yours!" said Knollis.

Dana Vaughan nodded. "Yes, they were prescribed by my doctor when I began to fake my illness."

"They were not," corrected Knollis. "We have been in touch with your doctor, and have obtained a statement from him. At no time did he prescribe chloral hydrate, and it is with chloral hydrate that I am interested."

"I . . . I . . ." said Dana Vaughan.

"Yes?" Knollis prompted her.

"Oh, what's the use!" she exclaimed. "You'll find out if I do try to mislead you! I got the lot for Mildred. She wrote to me months ago, and said she was in a nervy state, and could not sleep. She had read of odd cases in the papers where actresses had been in possession of such drugs, and wanted me to get them for her because Denstone refused to give her a sedative. He said she needed a tonic. Well, I brought them down with me—and I shan't say where I got them! I told her to try and manage without, but that if her health did not improve I would let her have them. I parked them in the box-room, thinking she was not likely to find them there."

"And did she find them?" asked Knollis.

"I—I don't think so!"

"Did anyone else know of their presence?"

"I don't think so. I never told anyone else—but why do you want to know?"

"That," Knollis said solemnly, "is neither here nor there. I ask questions and do not answer them. Now tell me; were the bottles sealed while they were in your possession?"

She lowered her head. "They were all sealed with white wax, paraffin wax I believe it is."

She cast a glance towards the table. "The chloral one has been unsealed!"

"Exactly,'" replied Knollis. "That is why I am making enquiries about it. You insist that you never opened the bottle?"

"I'm prepared to go into the witness-box and swear to it, Inspector."

"Thank you," said Knollis. He collected the bottles, slipped them into his pocket, and beckoned Ellis to follow him downstairs.

He found Mrs. Redson in the staff sitting-room, and again went straight to his point.

"I am looking for the caps from the beer bottles, Mrs. Redson. Can you help me?"

She pulled her reading-glasses down her nose and looked over the top of them. "They mostly go in the dustbin, Inspector. They are thrown in the waste-bin under the sink, and Smithy empties it for me every night."

"Thanks," said Knollis.

He took Ellis out to the rear of the house and shone a torch while he tipped over the dustbin and fished among the refuse.

"This is a bright job, and no mistake!" Ellis exclaimed. "Still, the end must justify the dirty work!"

"Exactly," agreed Knollis. "We aren't playing at dustbin-emptiers for fun. What's that?"

He bent down and scraped amongst the rubbish.

"Four crown caps," said Ellis.

"Yes," said Knollis, "but look at this one. It has been in a fire. Very interesting indeed. Collect all the others, Ellis, and put them in the car. I'll keep this one in my pocket. See, our next call will be on the local doctor."

Dr. Denstone was not at home, but Knollis traced him to a club in Trentingham, and there cornered him.

"I don't like disturbing your leisure hours, but I'm in urgent need of information which you can supply."

"Chloral hydrate again?" the doctor asked with a smile.

"Not exactly," said Knollis. "I'm enquiring about Mrs. Manchester's health over the past year. Has she at any time during this period been under you for nerve trouble?"

"Yes, she has, Inspector. I hope you don't want to know anything more intimate about her!"

"I'm afraid that I do," said Knollis, "and I'd like you to relax your confidence as far as you possibly can, For instance, did she ever ask you for sedatives?"

The doctor hesitated. "Well, yes, she did!"

"And did you prescribe a tonic instead?"

"Yes, I did, Inspector."

"So that at no time has she ever had veronal, barbitone, or chloral hydrate on a prescription supplied by you?"

The doctor looked alarmed. "Good God, no! Why on earth do you ask?"

"Because she asked Miss Vaughan to obtain those three drugs for her. To the best of my knowledge and belief she has never taken any of them, but they are present in the house. Further to the point, I am now satisfied that Desmond Brailsford was responsible for doping Temple—from Miss Vaughan's store."

"Well, I'll be damned!" exclaimed the doctor.

"No, Brailsford will be damned—unless another idea floating round my mind comes to fruition."

The doctor scratched his head. "This is an astonishing development. Is there any other way in which I can help you?"

"Yes, and I rather think that you will jib at answering this question. Earlier in the case, when I was interviewing Mrs. Manchester, she was lauding her husband, and said that he would have made an excellent father if circumstances had not made it impossible for her to bear them for him. My question is simply this: Was there any physical reason why she could not bear children?" Dr. Denstone hesitated a moment, and then reluctantly answered: "A doctor is supposed to regard as sacred the affairs of his patient, you know!"

"I know," Knollis replied. "The Hippocratic oath is observed even when not sworn. *What things soever I shall hear in my practice . . .*"

The doctor shook his head sadly. "There are times when one wonders which is the right course to take." He squared his shoulders. "I believe I am doing right! I will answer your question, Inspector. There was no physical reason why Mrs. Manchester should not have borne children to her husband. She was physically healthy. Mentally, well, she was worried about something or other, and I am not a psychiatrist! I tried to send her to a specialist, but she would have none of it. She said it was a matter for a priest, and that she was haunted."

"Yes," said Knollis, "haunted by the ghost of a hangman."

CHAPTER XVII
THE ACUMEN OF
COLONEL MOWBRAY

KNOLLIS WAS AT Baxmanhurst very early the next morning, asking that Mrs. Manchester should be made aware of his presence and of his desire to talk with her. She was at breakfast, and made him wait, a fact which did not annoy Knollis in the least. He smiled at Freeman as she delivered Mrs. Manchester's message to the effect that she would be along presently, and he smiled at Ellis and pushed him gently towards the study door.

"We may as well have a smoke, Watson. The lady needs time to think. She may suspect my errand."

"I see," said Ellis, "she doesn't know that we know her brother, but she has to shield him all the same!"

"I wouldn't say that she is trying to shield him," Knollis said quietly. "Up to now she has done her best to push him into the ditch. Anyway, let us smoke and meditate, and await the good lady's pleasure. After all, we are only police officers, you know!"

"Going to say anything to her about the Barston affair?" asked Ellis.

"Who knows?" Knollis said mysteriously.

Ellis gave a deep sigh and resigned himself. When Knollis grew mysterious it was time to see a magistrate with regard to the swearing of a warrant. He wondered idly if Desmond Brailsford, *né* Daniel Marlin, was in the house, and, not so idly, if he would make a dash for it when he smelled danger.

His reflections were disturbed as the door opened, and Mrs. Manchester walked into the room. She walked to the table, and Ellis arose and gently closed the door behind her.

"You wished to speak to me, Inspector?" she said in a formal tone.

"It isn't anything important," Knollis replied casually. "I just want to check upon a few details. Do allow me to get you a chair."

"There is one here. There is no need for you to rise, Inspector. Now . . . ?"

"Earlier in the week," began Knollis, "you mentioned that you met your husband on a cruise. I wonder if you can tell me why you went on that cruise?"

Mildred Manchester stared at him. "For my health, and because I wanted a complete change and a rest. I told you that, Inspector."

"Yes, yes, so you did," said Knollis, making a pretence of examining his notes. "Perhaps it was Miss Vaughan who suggested that you should go?"

She shook her head. "I did not know her then."

"You went on the cruise without knowing a single person on board?" Knollis asked in an incredulous tone.

"Perhaps I could suggest that Mr. Brailsford put the idea into your head?"

"Mr. Brailsford?" she gasped.

Knollis looked at his notes. "I have good reason to· believe that you were acquainted with him before you booked for the cruise."

"Well, yes, I did know him slightly, and he may have mentioned it casually, but I am not conscious of the fact that he specifically suggested the cruise to me."

"But he could have done so?" Knollis persisted.

"He could have done so, but I don't say that he did," Mildred Manchester replied.

Knollis stared at his notes for a full minute, and then slowly raised his head. "Now that I am aware of your maiden name, Mrs. Manchester—"

"My God!" she interrupted. She covered her face with her hands. "Is this thing going to follow me right to the very edge of the grave?"

"Not necessarily," said Knollis. "We can be discreet, you know! The only reason I mentioned it is because I think the fact may have some bearing on your husband's death—indirectly, I should add."

Mildred Manchester's hands slowly fell from her face, and her wide eyes regarded him curiously.

"We have evidence," Knollis went on, "suggestive of the fact that Desmond Brailsford was aware of your secret and was blackmailing you—threatening to tell your husband unless you paid him certain sums of money. Can you deny or verify that surmise?"

She fidgeted with her hands. The first two fingers of her right hand were unbandaged, but inflamed, and she stroked them continually with her left hand.

"He—wasn't—blackmailing me," she said slowly. "I have lent him money from time to time."

"You admit that he knew your secret?"

"Yes, he knew my secret."

"And Miss Vaughan? She was also aware of it?"

"Yes," Mildred Manchester replied. "She knew, too. I told her myself, two years ago."

"And yet she knew of it four years ago!" said Knollis bluntly.

Mildred Manchester shook her head. "I—I don't think she did?"

"Then," asked Knollis, "where did she find the theme of her play, *The Hempen Rope*? She learned it on the cruise, Mrs. Manchester, and you must know that yourself!"

"I have wondered," she said.

"She was told by your friend, Brailsford," said Knollis. "I have it in her own signed statement."

Mildred Manchester straightened her back. Her eyes narrowed, and she gazed deeply into Knollis's eyes. "Desmond told her. . . . ! So that was it! It was Desmond!"

Knollis, satisfied with the interview so far, decided to change the subject.

"In a previous interview, Mrs. Manchester, you told me that you were unable to bear children for your husband. I realise that the subject is a very delicate one, but would you care to say why?"

She slumped again, and became a dismal figure. "Isn't that obvious, Inspector? You know my secret! How could I bear children for my husband? I, the daughter of a public hangman! The Fates themselves would have cursed it at its birth. No, let the Marlins die out!"

"The Marlins?" said Knollis softly. "So you had a sister, Mrs. Manchester?"

She shook her head coldly. "No, a brother, and he is best forgotten. A thing with a warped mind that should never have been born!"

"A brother," said Knollis. "Where is he now, Mrs. Manchester? Still in this country?"

"I have not set eyes on Daniel these past fifteen years—oh, quite fifteen years," she replied. "I have disowned him as my brother. If I saw him I should regard him as a stranger."

"I see," said Knollis, and returned to his notes.

"Is there anything else?" Mildred Manchester asked after an uncomfortable pause.

"The silk cords," said Knollis; "I would like to ask two questions regarding them. Did you, on discovering your dead budgerigar, immediately recognise the blue cord as being from your workbox?"

"Oh yes, immediately," she replied.

"Did you go to the box to verify that?"

She shook her head. "Not immediately, Inspector. I was terribly upset by the sight of its poor little body, and I rushed downstairs to find my husband and tell him."

"You found him?"

"He was still breakfasting. I had left him."

"What did he say when you informed him that the bird had been killed?" asked Knollis.

"He—he just laughed!"

"Mrs. Manchester," said Knollis; "we agreed the other day that your husband was responsible for the deaths of the bird and the cat. Now then; did your husband know that you were Marlin's daughter?"

She lowered her eyes. "He did—and I think that either Desmond or Dana told him."

"Then perhaps you will agree with me that his action in killing your pets was in the nature of a cruel joke, intended to hurt you for having dared to marry him?"

"Yes." Mildred Manchester nodded. "Yes, I do believe that myself."

"Now," said Knollis, "on your examination of the workbox, was all the embroidery silk missing, or merely the one strand which was found round the neck of the budgerigar?"

"It was all missing, Inspector—all the blue, that is."

"I see," said Knollis. "That is a most important point. It indicates that the killing of the cat was premeditated at the time of the death of the budgie."

Mildred Manchester inclined her head. "I see your argument, Inspector."

"You told me," said Knollis, "that when this case is cleared up you intend to sell Baxmanhurst back to Sir Giles Tanroy. Where in England do you intend to settle?"

"Probably somewhere on the south coast," she replied.

"I see," said Knollis again. "Well, I think that will be all, Mrs. Manchester, and thank you for bearing with these interminable questions. I regret that I have to embarrass you in such a manner. Ellis!"

Ellis slipped his notebook in his pocket and rose to open the door for her. She made a dignified exit.

"Now what," said Ellis as he closed the door.

"Get Freeman," Knollis said shortly.

Freeman was herself again now that the shadow had passed from her own and Smithy's lives, and if anything she was more perky than she had ever been—and that may have been due to her own sense of importance in the case. She flounced into the room, and made a mock curtsy to Knollis. "Here I am, sir!"

"Take a pew," said Knollis. "You understand that anything I may say to you is to be regarded as confidential until such time as you are examined in court?"

She pointed a finger at her own bosom. "Me, in court? Oh lord!"

Knollis smiled. "The chance of a lifetime. The reporters will all be making references to the pretty housemaid from Baxmanhurst who gave her evidence in such a lively manner and helped Scotland Yard so expertly!"

Freeman preened under the praise, and Ellis winked heartily at Knollis.

"You remember last Sunday morning, when Mrs. Manchester found the budgie dead in her room? Well, did you go upstairs to have a look at it?"

"Oh yes! Madame came screaming downstairs, and I rushed up to see what was wrong."

"So that you saw the blue cord round the bird's neck?"

Freeman nodded. "Oh yes, sir!"

"You recognised it?" asked Knollis.

"It was out of her workbox," said Freeman.

"You are sure of that?" Knollis said.

"Well, I looked in the box, and I'm certain that most of it had gone!" Freeman said indignantly.

"Ah . . . !" exclaimed Knollis with a deep sigh. "*Most* of it had gone! Not all?"

"No, sir."

Knollis looked at her keenly. "Your position being what it is—that is, I mean to say, that you are more or less responsible for the whole household's comfort—you—er—well, you get around the house pretty well; more than the average housemaid? Is that correct?"

"Why, yes, sir," she answered in a puzzled tone.

"Since last Sunday morning, have you seen any of that blue silk anywhere else but in Mrs. Manchester's workbox?"

Freeman stared. She hesitated. And then she licked her upper lip and nodded dumbly.

"You did!" said Knollis. "Where did you see it?"

"In—in Freddy's drawer when I was putting his clean shirts away. It was about so long," she explained, holding her hands perhaps eighteen inches apart.

"And after that, did you look in the workbox again?"

"I—yes, sir, I did! I was curious, and I—well—"

"Don't apologise," Knollis said curtly. "You are doing very well indeed, and helping me a lot. How much of the silk was left in the workbox when you looked?"

"None, sir. It had all gone."

Knollis went back to his notes. When he again looked up he asked: "You should be familiar with the habits of this household, Miss Freeman. I wonder if you can tell me whether Freddy emptied his pockets every night when he went to bed?"

"Oh yes, he did," she said quickly. "I have noticed that when I have taken the morning tea in. He used to pile everything on the dressing-table."

"Thank you," said Knollis. "Do you get many tips in this house?"

"Miss Dana gives me ten shillings a week, and Mr. Brailsford gives me an occasional pound."

"I see," said Knollis. "Did Mr. Brailsford seem to tip you regularly, or just when he felt like it?" Freeman considered. "It was generally when Miss Dana had been down to the bank. He told me that she cashed his cheques for him, because he didn't like going out a great deal, on account of his—you know! He told me that once when he'd been here for three week-ends and hadn't given me anything."

"Thanks," said Knollis. "That will be all—but wait a minute! Who cleans the ashes from the fireplaces?"

"Why, I do!" Freeman answered in a surprised tone. "Can you remember a crown cap being amongst the ashes at any time during the past week?"

Freeman's eyes brightened. "That was Tuesday, sir— Wednesday morning when I found the cap. I thought it was funny, and I went to the larder to count the bottles and I said to myself that somebody would catch it when Mrs. Redson found that an extra one had gone. You see, sir, she is a very close sort of woman, and she reckons so many bottles for so many days, and starts asking questions if her calculations go wrong."

"Now why should you think that way?" said Knollis. "Surely the guests aren't limited in a house like this?"

"It wasn't that, sir," said Freeman, struggling with her thoughts, "it was—well, Freddy was the only one in the house who drinks bottled beer, and it meant that someone had swiped one. Taken one, sir. I was going to ask Smithy if he had pulled a fast one on Mrs. Redson, although he doesn't like bottled stuff as a rule, and then it slipped my memory."

"Which grate was it in?" asked Knollis.

"The kitchen grate, sir."

"That will be all for now," said Knollis. "Thanks." As soon as Freeman was clear of the room, Knollis reached for his hat. "Come on, my Ellis! We have an interview or two in Trentingham—one of them a much-belated one to which I should have attended earlier in the case. And then I think we can see about a warrant."

Manchester's solicitor regarded them cynically as they trooped into his office. He was a lean man, with silvery hair and a long face, and long fingers which he insisted on cracking throughout the interview, to Knollis's intense annoyance.

"So you would like to know the minor bequests in Manchester's will? Colonel Mowbray was round an hour ago, and I gave him a copy of the will."

Knollis flashed a glance at Ellis. The Chief Constable was getting either impatient with them, or was fancying his own chances as a detective.

"Anyway," said the solicitor, "the will is several months old, and not particularly sensational. He leaves Mrs. Manchester an annuity of a thousand a year, and the interest from his holdings in Manchester Furnishings for the period of her lifetime. On Mrs. Manchester's decease the whole estate goes to two young nephews, aged twelve and fourteen respectively. Minor bequests? A thousand pounds to a Desmond Brailsford 'for friendship shown,' and a thousand to Miss Dana Vaughan, the actress—without comment."

"His personal estate?" asked Knollis.

"Also in trust for Mrs. Manchester during the period of her lifetime, and then to the nephews."

"Thanks," said Knollis. "Sorry to have troubled you."

He next went to the bank. The bank manager scrutinised his credentials closely, and then laid before him the information that he needed.

"You ask," he said, "if many payments have been made to a Mr. Desmond Brailsford. You will see that he has been in receipt of fifty pounds a month from Manchester. He—Manchester—was somewhat profligate with his money, as witness the five thousand pounds he put into Miss Vaughan's account. He said it was there for her to draw on should she need extra backing for her play. By the way, Colonel Mowbray collected these details a short time ago."

Knollis controlled himself with difficulty. "I am merely making a routine check," he said soberly.

Outside in the street he gave vent to an oath.

"What the devil is the old so-and-so playing at? I'm supposed to be investigating the case, and he's playing behind my back! Probably trying to scoop me! Well, I'll show him—I think."

Ellis nodded glumly.

"Not a promising state of affairs, is it? By the way, what do you think of Freeman's evidence?"

"Well," Knollis said slowly, "it all points to one probability; that Manchester was planning a third death. Now who was it to be? It looks as if both Vaughan and Brailsford were milking his bank balance. You know, Ellis, I'm not too happy about this case! Oh well, let's go to the Guildhall and see what old Mowbray has to say for himself."

"There's a point that's worrying me," said Ellis. "You say that Vaughan and Brailsford were blackmailing him. If they were, then why did Manchester include them in his bequests?"

Knollis had the car door in his hand. The hand fell to his side, and he turned to face Ellis, biting his lip.

"That's a point," he said quietly. "Thanks, Ellis, I hadn't seen it. Now why . . . ? It's queer, and yet I think I see a glimmering of light. Come on! We'll get to the Guildhall."

The Chief Constable was busily engaged with a deskful of papers when they walked in on him. He rescrewed his monocle into his eye, and looked up with an air of triumph. "We'll go along to Baxmanhurst and pick him up in a few minutes, Knollis. I think I've got the case buttoned up this time. In fact I'm sure I have."

"Pleased to hear it," said Knollis. He pulled a chair towards the desk, and seated himself. "Perhaps you would explain it all to me," he added in a humble voice.

The Chief Constable smiled broadly. "The whole point is that you missed the chief clue! Sorry to say it, but I suppose it is because you are at it all the time and get jaded. I'm a fresh mind coming to the case. Further to the point, I have perhaps an advantage over you, inasmuch as I can see the thing from a psychological angle."

"Very interesting," Knollis murmured politely.

"I suppose I can assume that your statements—those taken from the various witnesses—are verbatim ones?" Knollis turned to Ellis, slowly lowering the eyelid farthest from the Colonel. "Your statements were taken verbatim, Sergeant Ellis?"

"Verbatim, sir," said Ellis. "Word for word, comma for comma, and period for full stop."

"Sergeant Ellis prides himself on his accuracy, sir," Knollis informed the Chief Constable.

"Good enough," said Colonel Mowbray. "Now I'll go over the case very slowly, so that you can follow my reasoning."

"Thank you, sir. I'm much obliged," said Knollis. The Chief Constable lit a cigarette and watched the smoke through his monocle as it curled and twisted to the ceiling, and then swung into a horizontal path and disappeared through the ventilator.

"It has been Brailsford all along. I suppose you are in no doubt about his having killed his father?"

"There is a suspicion," said Knollis, "but certainly no proof. However, please do continue, sir. I am most interested."

"Brailsford killed his father," Colonel Mowbray said in a dogmatic voice, "and then he arranged for his sister to go on the cruise so that she could meet Manchester—who had money which he needed."

"We have no proof of that," said Knollis, "but I agree with the proposition."

"Brailsford," went on the Chief Constable stubbornly, "arranged for them to meet, and probably spoke deep into Manchester's ear about Mildred's social connections—which were mostly fanciful. Manchester marries her, and Brailsford then proceeds to chisel his sister for money. Now Manchester is giving his wife an allowance which he considers sufficient for all her purposes, and when Desmond has reached the point in his demands where his sister can no longer provide he turns to Manchester and reveals the secret of his sister's parentage—still suppressing the fact that he is her brother. He tells Manchester—probably—that he knows someone who is going to give the game away and who can only be kept quiet by money. Manchester proceeds to pay up, and Desmond pockets the money."

The Chief Constable paused for breath, but the light in his eye was no less triumphant. Knollis was regarding him with genuine astonishment.

"Now suppose," went on the Chief Constable, "that Manchester was considering divorce proceedings."

"But he wasn't—as far as we know," Knollis protested.

"But he was!" exclaimed the Chief Constable. "I got that from his solicitor!"

Knollis rose from his seat, a dangerous look in his, eyes. "You mean to tell me, sir, that you have withheld that information from me!"

Colonel Mowbray wriggled uncomfortably. "Well, I only got the information a few minutes ago. I didn't know where you were, so I couldn't very well get in touch with you—now could I?"

"Well," said Knollis, somewhat mollified, "I suppose you are right there, sir. I'm investigating the case, when all is said and done, and—oh, the information in no way affects my view of the case, so why worry?"

"It only provides the motive," said the Chief Constable shortly.

"I don't see that it does, if you'll allow me to differ from you, sir," said Knollis.

"You fell down on the main clue," the Chief Constable said defiantly. "I'll prove it to you."

"I wish you would," Knollis said softly.

"Manchester was not aiming at divorce, but an annulment of the marriage. His story was that his wife had revealed her parentage on the day of the marriage, and that consequently the marriage had never been consummated.

"Now! He tells Brailsford this, not knowing that he is her brother, and Brailsford can see his money-for-nothing going down the drain, and so he plans to kill him before the proceedings are instituted. He drugs Temple, locks him in the woodshed, plants the axe handy, and awaits his chance. He knows that Tanroy is coming to see Manchester, and knows quite well that a row is quite likely, so that the quarrel will be the cause of the crime. Tanroy obligingly clears off early, and Desmond slips downstairs and kills him. Now, what do you think to that, Knollis?"

"I don't like it," Knollis said flatly.

"How do you regard it, Sergeant Ellis?" asked the Chief Constable.

Ellis grimaced. "It stinks to high heaven, sir—begging your pardon."

"What the hell's wrong with it?" the Chief Constable demanded.

"The main point is that Desmond Brailsford was in his room, and heard a woman talking below his window," Knollis pointed out.

Colonel Mowbray smiled. "Yes, that is where you fell down! You misinterpreted Brailsford's statement. As a result of seeing the truth, I've sworn a warrant against Brailsford, and we're now going out to Baxmanhurst to execute it."

Knollis shook his head sadly. "I do hope you know what you're doing, sir! It will cause an awful scandal if you are on the wrong person."

"I hope you aren't doubting my intelligence, Knollis! I'm not generally regarded as being a moron."

He rose, and collected a handful of papers, among which was the warrant for Brailsford's arrest. "Well, let's get going!" he said impatiently.

"Before we go, sir," said Knollis, "would you mind explaining where I slipped up so badly? I hate to be left in ignorance of my own ignorance."

The Chief Constable turned back to the desk and took up a single sheet of paper.

"Here is an extract from Brailsford's statement. *Somebody was talking under my window about the time that Fred was killed . . . one was definitely Fred's. The other sounded like a woman's voice.*"

"Well?" said Knollis.

"Nowhere, at no time, in his statements, does Brailsford say that he was in his bedroom! He says there were people talking under his window. Well—he was one of them. Can't you hear his queer high-pitched feminine voice? The voice that *sounded* like a woman's? It was his own!"

The Chief Constable laughed. "He twisted you, my friend, and you fell for it. It was Brailsford himself who was talking to Fred—as he killed him!"

Knollis's jaw dropped. "My God!" he exclaimed.

CHAPTER XVIII
THE THREEFOLD CORD

COLONEL MOWBRAY stalked into Baxmanhurst as if he owned it. As soon as he reached the study he rang for Freeman and ordered her to produce Desmond Brailsford without delay.

Knollis dallied in the hall until the Colonel was safely out of earshot, when he rang through to Knightswood and asked Sir Giles Tanroy to oblige him by attending him at Baxmanhurst. "You'll probably have a wish granted," he added. "Colonel Mowbray is rampant with a warrant."

He signalled to Ellis, and they joined the Chief Constable in the study.

Desmond Brailsford came round the door furtively, his left eye cocked to the ceiling, and his right one looking ahead. His mouth was twisted so wryly that it was impossible to tell whether it was the normal leer of his unfortunate deformity or whether he was looking cynical.

The Chief Constable stepped forward, one hand extended ready to lay on Brailsford's shoulder. "Daniel Marlin."

Brailsford smiled. "So you know me, eh? Not that it matters a jot, although I've almost forgotten what the name sounds like."

"I am placing you under arrest," began the Chief Constable, but Knollis interposed.

"I wouldn't, if I were you, sir! You are making a horrible mistake, which may prove expensive!"

Brailsford took a step backward. "You mean that you are charging me with killing Fred Manchester! Some detective you are—or are you making sure that you have a culprit? I've heard about the police before. Well, arrest me if you wish. Stick me up at the Assizes, and I'll make you look the biggest damned fool in England. Come on, Colonel! Arrest me—and break yourself!"

"You can't bluff me!" the Chief Constable shouted. "I know you for what you are! And threatening to break me, eh?"

"He's right, you know," Knollis said sadly. He shrugged his shoulders. "Still, if you insist on going ahead you had better warn him that he is not obliged to say anything in answer to the charge unless he wishes to do so, but whatever he does say will be taken down in writing and may be used in evidence. We must observe judges' rules, no matter what kind of a mess you make."

He turned to Brailsford. "I advise you not to talk until you have seen a solicitor."

Brailsford nodded his thanks. "Decent of you, Inspector. Let him go ahead. I'll sue the Crown for wrongful arrest. I am completely innocent. As for talking, I'm prepared to talk as hard as you like. Now, Colonel Mowbray, on what stupid grounds do you base your charge."

The Chief Constable's monocle was hanging loose on its black ribbon, swinging violently as he waved his arms. "I'll tell you! You were responsible for doping Temple on Tuesday last, so that he lay in a drunken stupor for nine hours, his whereabouts unknown, and so that he lay under suspicion for killing his employer."

Brailsford laughed loudly. "Me? Doped him? Don't talk so dam silly! How the hell could I dope him?"

"You supplied him with a bottle of beer!"

"Beer is pretty poor stuff these days," sneered Brailsford, "but I don't think it would put a cat to sleep. Anyway, I did give him a bottle if that is of any interest to you. Milly gave it to me, and asked me to take it out to the poor hound. Fred had been tearing strips off him that morning, and she wanted to make it up to him. The beer was a sort of gesture of sympathy—or a consolation prize. Call it which you like."

"Was Temple conscious?" Knollis asked quietly.

"So-so," Brailsford replied. "I stood the bottle beside him— he was lying on some sacks—and left him to it. Milly had taken the top off, all ready for him."

"You are sure that your sister gave it to you?" said Knollis.

"Why shouldn't I be?" Brailsford demanded. "I don't go poking about round the staff quarters, and I've told you that about a dozen times up to now. I just wouldn't dare to invade Mrs. Redson's quarters for a bottle of beer, and anyway, what the hell are bells, and servants for?"

"Logical enough," Knollis agreed. "Now answer this for me: Why did you persuade your sister to go on the cruise in the course of which she met Manchester?"

"To meet Manchester," said Brailsford. "I've no hesitation in answering that. Milly wanted money and a spot of peace and security. Freddy wanted a social position, so I planned to bring them together. Unfortunately, it didn't work out properly."

"Why did you take the name of Desmond Brailsford?" demanded the Chief Constable. "Was that the work of an honest man?"

"It was the work of a sensible one," Brailsford replied. "Would you keep your own name if your old man was a public hangman? Have some damned sense! The old boy had caused us enough humiliation as it was, without asking for more. Look at my face! I owe that to him—the swine!"

"I know the story," Knollis said softly. "Now I want to ask you one more question. You have twice told me that you heard a woman's voice under your window about the time that Manchester was killed. Did you recognise that voice?"

Brailsford shook his head. "I did not, and that is the truth, Inspector. I can guess at the owner, but I'd rather not, thank you. The voices were mere murmurs to me. One was deep and rumbling, and I'll lay all I possess that it was Fred's. The other was high-pitched and feminine—and that is as far as I am going."

"Did you hear the blow?" asked Knollis. "As you have been cautioned, you are not obliged to answer this or any other question. I think I should warn you, too, that you will be charged as an accessory after the fact, because I can prove that you disposed of the axe after Manchester's death."

Brailsford nodded gloomily. "Yes, I did that, and I'll take what's coming for it. I wanted to delay the investigation until I had some idea of who was responsible. I bunged the thing in the water-butt, and rescued it later in the evening. You will remember me saying that I wanted to go into town? Well, I had an idea for slinging it in the reservoir on the Trentingham road. I missed the bus, and was stuck at the bus-stop with a bloody axe under my arm. I had to get rid of it somehow. I saw Mrs. Temple trot up the village, so I crept round the back of the cottage and parked it in the dustbin, minus the outside wrapper. It wasn't a brilliant notion, but I was getting a bit windy. I mean, it wouldn't have looked too good if one of your bobbies had challenged me to unwrap the parcel. By the way, Inspector, you can keep the sheet of brown paper, but I would like my pants back when you've done with 'em!"

Knollis grinned at him. "In due course."

"Now," said Brailsford, "you asked me if I heard the blow. I did—and that is obvious, isn't it? I tried to look out of the window, but as you know from your own tests, it was not possible. So I hopped off downstairs, taking the back stairs for the quickest. I don't know why I made the next move, but I doubled back through the hall and put my head round the door of the sitting-room to ask Milly if she had heard anything unusual. She was knitting or mending quite happily, and shook her head, so I nipped through the annexe and found Fred. . . ."

"The man you saw going round the house was a figment of your imagination?" Knollis suggested.

"I'm afraid it was," said Brailsford.

"You went to Miss Vaughan's room, and reminded her that she probably would not want to be under suspicion. You regarded her as the possible killer?"

"You've got me there all right," replied Brailsford. "Milly was quite happy in the sitting-room, whereas Dana was just entering her room and closing the door as I started up the stairs. I reckoned that she must be responsible."

"There is a point which you may not care to clear up for us," said Knollis, "and you are not obliged to make any statement on it. I refer to the financial assistance accorded to you from time to time by Manchester."

"Well," said Brailsford, scratching his ear and leering, "he did lend me money from time to time, as you say. He had discovered who Milly was, and was scared stiff of the fact getting out. He seemed to think that I was capable of showing him up as the husband of a hangman's daughter, and he tried to keep in with me. Of course, I would never have given my own sister away!"

"Of course not!" said Knollis.

"Fred was handing out money left and right, and I didn't see why I should refuse fifty quid now and then. He'd got more money than I had, and wasn't working for it!"

There was a tap on the door, and Freeman appeared.

"Sir Giles Tanroy, sir."

"Come in," said Knollis. "Freeman! Will you please ask Mrs. Manchester and Miss Vaughan to oblige me by stepping this way? Now, Sir Giles, I would like to ask you a question. Mrs. Manchester has told me that on Tuesday evening she suggested that you go and have a look at the cactus house in order to satisfy yourself that her husband had not ruined it even though he had chopped down the vines."

Sir Giles nodded. "That is true."

"And yet you told me that you went out for a quiet read, to pass the time until Manchester returned from Trentingham."

"Well, both yarns are true in a way," Sir Giles answered. "I think she was bored with my presence, and wanted to get rid of me. She suggested that I should go to the cactus house, but I don't think she could have expected me to stay for long, because she knows that I have strong feelings about those vines. You see, Inspector, we Tanroys have always grown dam' fine grapes, and they have always been reserved for the local hospital. Vines, in case you don't know it, take some rearing, and I regarded Manchester's action as selfish, and about as sacrilegious as if he had ploughed up the lawns and planted cabbages. At the best, he was a lout and a vandal."

Mildred Manchester and Dana Vaughan entered the room at that moment, and Sir Giles subsided. Dana Vaughan planted herself straightly against the wall, and waited. Mildred Manchester walked dreamily to the one arm-chair and carried on with the knitting which she had brought with her, apparently uninterested in the meeting.

"For the clarification of what follows, Mrs. Manchester," Knollis explained, "I should tell you that I am aware that Desmond Brailsford is your brother."

"Oh, how interesting," she murmured, without raising her eyes from her knitting.

"Now, Brailsford," said Knollis, "your father died on the fourteenth of September, nineteen-thirty-eight?"

"I believe that is the date," Brailsford said with a slight inclination of his head.

"Neither your sister nor yourself attended his funeral?"

"Not on your life," Brailsford replied. "For my own part I had seen enough of him up to the time I left home."

"Yet you both called on him the day that he died!"

Brailsford blinked. Mildred did not move a muscle.

Brailsford shrugged. "It was Milly's idea, not mine. She said that we ought to let bygones be bygones, and give the old man a spot of peace before he died."

"*Before* he died?" Knollis asked significantly.

"Well, he was getting on, you know! And I never heard of him being in possession of any elixir of life! I mean, he couldn't live for ever, could he? Anyway, I let Milly overrule me, and we went over for the day, although I spent most of it in the local."

"You returned to London together?"

"No," said Brailsford, "I went on to London, but Milly broke her journey at Trentingham to spend the night with some old friends."

"Can you prove that you went to London?"

Brailsford shifted uncomfortably. "Well, have a heart! It's about seven years ago—although I dare say that if I plough through my diaries I can find out what I did that night."

"And you, Mrs. Manchester," Knollis said softly; "can you prove that you spent the night with friends in Trentingham? Who were they? Where can they be found?"

She looked up with eyes so vacant that they startled Knollis for a second. "They are dead. Everyone is dead. I am dead. Dead people are happy."

She looked down at her knitting.

"You knew that your husband was instituting proceedings for the annulment of your marriage, Mrs. Manchester?"

She was counting stitches in a low voice. She paused to nod, and then continued her counting.

"Fred was a beast to her!" Dana Vaughan burst out. "He killed her two pets—a mean and petty device to remind her that her father was—was what he was! He was always reminding her. He was smooth and sleek, and utterly cruel! He would sit at table and tell crude jokes about hanging. Oh, I could have killed him myself!"

"Why did he give you five thousand pounds?" Knollis enquired, fixing her with eyes that were mere slits. The attention of all in the room was drawn to Mildred Manchester. Her eyes were wide; her face expressionless. She dropped her hands into her lap, straightened herself in the chair, and said: "You, too, Dana!"

"You were fine friends," said Knollis, regarding Dana Vaughan and Brailsford with contempt. "You, Brailsford, sold her secret to her husband when you could get no more from her—or not enough from her, for you were still taking her allowance. And then you blackmailed her husband! Oh yes, you didn't call it that, but it amounted to the same thing. You, Vaughan; you learned her secret, and exploited it on the stage. Then you learned from Brailsford how easy it was to chisel Manchester."

Dana Vaughan put her hands over her face. "I didn't blackmail him! Desmond told him, on the night of their wedding. Fred came to me to ask me if it was the truth. He forced the truth from me. I couldn't say more than the truth, could I? Fred said he would never forget me for saving him from the humiliation of bringing into the world a son whose mother was the daughter of a—a hangman. But it wasn't me! It was Desmond! And then Fred put five thousand pounds into my bank—in gratitude he said—and I didn't know until it was too late!"

"And included you in his will!" said Knollis.

"I didn't know that! I swear I didn't!"

"Of course you didn't!" said Knollis. "That is why you threw up your career on the West End stage! You were altruistic all the way through. You wanted nothing better than to be by Mildred Manchester's side. Gratitude!"

Mildred Manchester began to rock to and fro in her chair, softly crooning to herself. Knollis gave a gasp of dismay.

The Chief Constable, who had been restlessly changing his weight from one foot to the other, suddenly tapped Knollis on the arm. "Look here, Knollis! It looks as if my ideas have gone badly astray, but who the devil did kill Manchester? Heh?"

Knollis glanced across the room at Sir Giles. "What was that about the threefold cord, Sir Giles?"

"*And if a man prevail against him that is alone, two shall withstand him; and a threefold cord is not easily broken,*" he quoted in a firm and resonant voice.

"There is your answer, sir," said Knollis. "Mrs. Manchester was only up against her brother at first, and he prevailed. Then Vaughan entered the fray, and the two withstood her. With the entrance of her husband she was up against a trio that could not be broken: a brother who sold her, a friend who betrayed her, and a husband who despised her. It was a Gordian knot that could not be untied, and so she cut it—with an axe."

"Mildred Manchester killed her husband!" the Chief Constable exclaimed.

"Wasn't it obvious?" Knollis challenged him.

"And I thought it was Dana," Brailsford murmured. "She killed her husband," said Knollis. "She also killed her father!"

"What!" Brailsford screamed in his high-pitched voice. "Killed my father?"

Knollis looked at Mildred Manchester, now smiling placidly. There was no comprehension in her eyes of the scene that was being played out before them.

"You did kill your father, Mrs. Manchester?" Knollis murmured in a soothing voice.

"I pulled the rope. The door went bang! He fell at my feet. And then I said to him: *That was more than a six-foot drop, you silly old man!*"

She smiled, and closed her eyes.

"Good lord!" said Colonel Mowbray, fidgeting with his monocle.

"Last Tuesday," said Knollis, "she planned everything perfectly, and luck was on her side. She had witnessed the bawling-out that her husband gave Temple, and she saw Temple go to the inn for his usual after-row bout of drunkenness. She knew that her husband had an appointment with Sir Giles for five o'clock, and she wangled—I suspect—her husband into going to the Guildhall for the same time."

"That is correct," Dana Vaughan said in a low voice. "She told Fred that if he didn't go and see what the police were doing she would go down herself, and he didn't want her to go to town in case she was recognised."

"Thank you," said Knollis. "When Sir Giles arrived she encouraged him to go out to the Green Alley, probably realising that he would not stay there. You see, Sir Giles and Temple were to be used to confuse the issue. She had arranged everything. There was a bottle of chloral in the box-room. She removed the cap from the bottle and poured some of it into the beer. She got some of it on her fingers, and that caused the inflammation—unless I have misread Glaser. She then asked her brother to deliver the bottle to Temple because she wanted to do a little to make up for her husband's temper."

He glanced at Brailsford. "Correct?"

Brailsford nodded gloomily.

"By these devices," Knollis continued, "she thrust suspicion on Sir Giles, Temple, and her brother. She had placed the axe in readiness, and now waited until her husband came home. It is not too much to assume that she had circumspectly watched Sir Giles, and saw him leave *via* the hurst. It was the hour after tea, and again we need no stretch of the imagination to conclude that she knew where everybody in the house would be at that hour—the hour, I repeat, after tea. Vaughan and Brailsford were in their rooms. Mrs. Redson was upstairs. So was Freeman. Smithy was outside the house. Right! She told her husband that Sir Giles was waiting in the Green Alley. He went out to see him, and she followed. We may never know what she said to him—"

Mildred Manchester was sitting like a waxen figure, pale and immovable, but from her lips came her own story, in an uncanny monotone:

"I had saved my strength. I smote him like unto the philistines, and he fell dead at my feet. I dropped the axe and went back to my knitting. . . ."

"So you are right," sighed Colonel Mowbray, "but how the devil you arrived at the solution is beyond me!"

Knollis explained. "When I considered that Manchester had left all his money in trust to her, and that after her death it was to go to his nephews on the male side of the family, I was puzzled—until Sir Giles told me that she was Marlin's daughter. It was clear then, for she told me that she was unable to bear children for him. He wanted sons—the old urge to perpetuate his name—and as he could not have them he did the next best thing—financed his brother's sons so that at least one Manchester might have a chance to achieve fame, the fame that he so badly wanted himself.

"Again, the significance behind the cords became obvious when I learned that she was Marlin's daughter. Manchester's killing of her pets was a cruel method of taunting her, and of warning her that she was to be the next. I am certain that he was going to kill her, and that the third cord found in his pocket was intended for her neck. His will, conveniently worded, gave the impression that he was fond of her and had made provision in case he died first—but it also provided for the state of affairs which would exist when she was dead." Mildred Manchester's monotonous voice came coldly from the waxen figure now merely propped in the chair by its back and arms.

"I found the cord in his drawer. I knew it was meant for me. I sent him out to the Green Alley, where it was quiet and peaceful. I followed him. I told him what I knew. I upbraided him for destroying the vines as he intended to destroy me. Then I struck him, and he fell. He looked smug even as he lay dying, and I kicked him in the face. I had the cord in my hand, and I pushed it into his pocket and went back to my knitting. Madame Defarge always knitted at the foot of the guillotine. For years in my imagination I had watched my father hanging men, and each time he did so I knitted, knitted, knitted—like Defarge. . . ."

"How the devil did you get on this thing in the first place?" muttered Colonel Mowbray to Knollis.

"Fred Manchester supplied the clue," said Knollis, wiping a weary hand across his brow. "He told me that his wife called him Humpty."

"I still don't understand!" exclaimed the Colonel. "Mrs. Manchester does. She could see the future. She will explain— if she is capable of telling you." Mildred Manchester smiled happily from her chair. Her thin right hand, the fingers still slightly inflamed, rose from her lap to beat out the time as she softly chanted:

"Humpty Dumpty sat on a wall.
Humpty Dumpty had a great fall.
All the King's horses.
And all the King's men,
Couldn't put Humpty together again!"

The song ended with an eldritch shriek of laughter that echoed round the room and brought a cold shiver to Knollis's heart.

"They couldn't put Humpty together again, together again, together again. He had a great fall, a very great fall. . . ."

"For God's sake somebody *do* something," muttered the Chief Constable.

"It's too late," whispered Knollis.

Mildred Manchester slumped in the chair, a gibbering wreck, and the foaming saliva dripped from her shapeless lips.

THE END

Printed in Great Britain
by Amazon